Checking Out

Meryem El Mehdati studied Translation and Interpretation. She has been a private tutor, secretary, shop assistant, nanny, assistant director and internal comms specialist. She has contributed to *Vogue*, *SModa*, *La Provincia*, *El Salto* and *Igluu Magazine*. *Checking Out* is her first novel.

Julia Sanches has translated close to thirty books from Spanish, Portuguese, and Catalan into English, including works by Geovani Martins, Andrea Abreu, and Eva Baltasar. Born in São Paulo, Brazil, she currently lives in Providence, Rhode Island.

CHECKING OUT

Meryem El Mehdati

Translated by Julia Sanches

Sceptre

First published in Great Britain in 2025 by Sceptre
An imprint of Hodder & Stoughton Limited
An Hachette UK company

The authorised representative in the EEA is Hachette Ireland, 8 Castlecourt Centre,
Dublin 15, D15 XTP3, Ireland (email: info@hbgi.ie)

1

Copyright © Meryem El Mehdati 2022

This edition is published by arrangement with Blackie Books S.L.U. c/o Aevitas
Creative Management UK Ltd

English language translation © 2025 Julia Sanches

A CIP catalogue record for this title is available from the British Library

Hardback ISBN 9781399734011
Trade Paperback ISBN 9781399734028
ebook ISBN 9781399734042

Typeset in Sabon MT by Manipal Technologies Limited.

Printed and bound in Great Britain by Clays Ltd, Elcograf S.p.A.

Hodder & Stoughton policy is to use papers that are natural, renewable
and recyclable products and made from wood grown in sustainable forests.
The logging and manufacturing processes are expected to conform
to the environmental regulations of the country of origin.

Hodder & Stoughton Limited
Carmelite House
50 Victoria Embankment
London EC4Y 0DZ

www.sceptrebooks.co.uk

To my mother, my mother, my mother, and to my father.
To my siblings.
To my pana, my best friend, Jorge de Cascante, for everything.

PART ONE

intern.meryem.elmehdati@supersaurio.com

I

November 2016

Nobody asked if I wanted to be born. If they had, I would've said no. Thanks, so kind of you to ask, it sounds like an interesting opportunity and all, but the answer is no. Mute, block, swipe left. Life is complicated. We have to be careful, we're really fragile creatures. One day you fit snugly in your father's arms, the next you're twenty-five and sobbing quietly in the back of the bus – where only tourists and the popular high-school kids sit – because you've just been through the fifth stage of the recruiting process for a measly internship. You leave the interview exhausted, with body aches, joint pain, convinced you're worthless. They asked what animal you identified with, and you said ants because they can't do a lot on their own, but in a team, they're unstoppable. The only reason you didn't throw up a little in your mouth is that you're dead inside, you feel nothing, you're a total fraud. The whole thing lasts over a month: they promise to call soon with their decision. You pay for the bus. You spent €7.55 getting there, now it's another €7.55 to get home. It's kind of wild that people in the Canary Islands aren't setting dumpsters on fire, that there aren't police vans chasing students and journalists down streets or firing rubber bullets. Do we have to threaten to secede from the rest of Spain for people to remember we exist? Time passes. No one calls.

I am not a chill person, a calm sea, a gently flowing river. I have . . . a certain rage. An anger. Don't sweat it, though. Everything's fine. Look at me. Check out this toothy smile. My childhood was happy – zero trauma, nothing to mark me forever. It's important to be nice, especially if you're a girl. Meanwhile, your outrage beats darkly in your chest – boom boom boom, it isn't sexy. Be nice, be nice, be nice. My boot's on your neck, but be nice. I'm twisting your arm and if I keep twisting it's going to snap in two, but be nice. Don't be mad. Why're you mad? Smile.

That joke of an interview costs you €15.10. You sob on the bus, and your mascara runs. You try blowing your nose without calling attention to yourself, but you're making a scene. You're wearing this beautiful silk blouse that your mom lent you because you don't own grown-up clothes. You're a clown who self-expresses through aesthetic choices that rarely hit the mark, the kind of person who thinks to herself: *They're interested in my skills, not my looks.* Inside you, there are two wolves. One of them howls at you to keep your chin up, you're young, a capable human with a piece of paper that proves you studied hard. The other one bares its teeth and says, I told you so, I told you a million times, you should've gone to medical school.

The point is you're born, you grow up, then you die. Maybe you procreate, maybe you don't. I don't think I will. When I tell my parents this, they look shocked and blurt out, as one: 'Astaghfirullah, don't say that.' Our daughter and her little quirks, they think. Even though I'm not being totally serious, the angels hear me, and there's no place for sarcasm or humor in this sort of pronouncement. Is it really the end of the world if I don't have kids? No procreating for me: once I'm gone, there will be nothing. My mind changes like the weather. My work colleagues claim I'll see things differently when I'm older, that all of a sudden I'll want to push out three little rugrats with a guy who talks shit about me with his coworkers over coffee.

At some point I got this idea stuck in my chest: I'm not at all what I thought I'd grow up to be. I was convinced I would . . . succeed. That I'd become a financially independent adult who argues with her friends over who gets to pay for lunch, just like my parents. One of my girlfriends is dating this guy who's always tagging along with us and dropping bombs like: 'Your problem is you did everything you were supposed to . . . like sheep . . . And now you have to face reality.' When he says this kind of thing, I try not to look at him because I'm scared he'll read my mind, which is thinking that he's such a massive douche he's going bald at twenty-seven. If he's so clever, if he saw it coming, then how come he's as broke as the rest of us?

My biggest flaw is that I'm a smarty pants with a motor mouth. I say things like 'dichotomy,' 'performative,' 'ad hominem fallacy,' 'Manichaeism,' and 'Sontag.' I push my glasses up my nose and wear blazers. But it's all an act. I fact-check things on Google a zillion times before opening my mouth on the off-chance someone notices I'm human and make mistakes. Because of this, because I'm a know-it-all, I underestimated the intensity of the reality check. I was too busy thinking I'd hacked the system. I'd done everything I was supposed to, and I'd done it well. When you're a kid and an adult singles you out, crouches down to eye-level, and asks, 'So, what do you want to be when you grow up?' what they actually want to know is how you're going to

5

make a living. They couldn't give less of a shit what you want. A bummer, I know, but it's the truth.

From the moment you're born, your days revolve around choices your parents make for you, at least in the beginning. Regular daycare or bilingual daycare? Public, private, or charter school? Lycée Français or the neighborhood high school? Ballet classes, Mandarin classes, English tutors. It's all geared toward opening doors in your future. You must be well educated, though no one knows to what end. Because my family was poor, the decision was basically made for us: public primary school, high school, and college. Get good grades, win scholarships, make us proud. I'm not sure it's kosher to use the word 'poor' anymore; these days people prefer 'working class.' You can work all you like, but chances are you'll never stop being poor. Funny, isn't it?

Your degree and many of your personal choices become the butt of jokes over family dinner. What future is there in Art History? Come on, you're smart, you studied abroad, explain it to your Khalti Salma. You're not studying Art History, but that doesn't matter. None of the things you enjoy come with job security and buckets of money. How do philosophers pay their bills? And journalists? With the truth? Give me a break . . . Eventually, you'll tell yourself you should've gone into engineering; I mean, you had the grades. The world always needs engineers. What good is a humanities major? You don't even like children. Do you really want to waste thirty-five years of your life teaching the verb *to be* to a class of forty-plus kids? Not unless your dream is to have your face splashed across the crime pages of *Canarias7*. Many years ago, your parents left behind their home (Morocco), their families, and everything they knew, and made sacrifices so they could give you what they'd never had. They dreamed of a future where you were a doctor or an engineer or, worst-case scenario, a lawyer. Now you're going to keep a straight face and tell them you're thinking of studying languages? Come on, mi niña.

You're a burden on your family, because time is running out, because you're part of the most educated generation in history, the worst paid, the most overcaffeinated, the most insecure, the most depressed, the one with the most hang-ups.

If you're lucky, you'll get an internship somewhere. An internship that makes you weep with joy, like an idiot, on the balcony of your house. It'll be totally unrelated to what you studied, but at least, for a few months, you'll be employed. You will become The Intern. This is how you survive the dread and routine that stretches like a piece of chewing gum between the floor and your shoe: by clamping your mouth shut every morning and dressing up as the kind of person everyone hopes you will be. You enter the building. You only get to be yourself again once you're back home, far from the fluorescent lights, the click-clack of designer shoes, and the reek of your coworkers' delusions of grandeur. You will not take over the company that employs you. You're smart enough to remind yourself of this every so often, except for when you forget. Before you know it, the scent of coffee and the rattling of the photocopier dulls your senses, and you morph into a robot. There will be times when all you'll want is to leave because you can't take it anymore. You want your mommy. You google how to get yourself fired and, when nothing useful turns up, you close your eyes for a minute and bury your face in your hands. If you killed yourself right then and there, you think, if you threw your-self off the roof or hanged yourself from your purse strap in one of the bathroom stalls – what would happen? Would

7

they investigate your death? Would they try to figure out what made you do it? Would they nose around your search history? You still don't have the three years of experience needed to get a job at another company. Is heaven taken by force or by consent? Try working at an office with people twice your age and see if you still feel the same. I for one don't know where heaven is anymore, or hell.

In the end, you will stay and you will keep getting older. Daydreaming about your own death will become something of a hobby, a happy place you can go to when the conversation is too suffocating to be navigated with a healthy, conscious mind. This is my secret. This is why I haven't offed myself yet in some melodramatic way. I owe today's look to Zara: white poplin shirt, black skinny jeans, oxfords, frizzy hair (courtesy of the humidity), dark undereye circles, dumbstruck expression, two blue checkmarks. What my outfit says about me: *I am young but serious, dynamic and also versatile.* Location: a chair across from a mahogany desk in my supervisor's glass office.

'Okay now, where was I? Oh, yes. On a scale of one to ten, how would you rate your experience at Supersaurio these past few months?'

He reads the question out from a piece of paper. If only God, in his infinite wisdom and mercy, could pluck me out of here and take me with him. The summer I turned nine (I'm a Cancer, which means I am loyal, sensitive, headstrong, and also a bearer of grudges) I spent three months throwing eggs at the rooftop terrace of my grandma's neighbor's house in Casablanca. Every afternoon I'd buy a carton of eggs, climb up to the roof, peer over the wall, and lob eggs at everything in sight: plants, hanging clothes, her grandkids' abandoned toys. I'd heard the neighbor insult my grandmother, and it was seared into my brain. You may call me Batman. Do I regret what I did? No. My experience at Supersaurio these last few months? A punishment for past crimes, no doubt. When I feel I can't draw out the silence any longer, I say:

'I think I've learned a lot these past few months, especially considering how little I knew when I arrived . . . I knew practically nothing about the kinds of things I do now, but I've taken it as a challenge. I always refer back to the list of goals we made when I first started.'

Between us, I'd rate my experience at Supersaurio as a −1, but every month I take home €500 in welfare-slash-grant money, so I smile and sit down, and pray from the bottom of my heart that they don't fire any more questions at me. Even though my day-to-day here is not unlike that of a prisoner in Guantanamo, I will stick it out to the very end. I will be whoever my boss wants me to be for however long and in whatever manner he so desires. Synergy? I seek it out, I create it. Calls? I plan them. Holistic strategies for creating strategic frameworks? I pull them out of my ass.

'Again, on a scale of one to ten, how would you rate your relationship with other colleagues in your department?'

'I can honestly say I've felt really supported by everyone. They're so patient with all my questions and concerns. My experience here wouldn't have been the same without their help.'

'And how are things with Yolanda? Have you been able to clear the air?'

Supersaurio S.L. is the largest supermarket chain in the Canary Islands. The company mascot is a blue, ten-foot-tall dinosaur in a white bowtie and yellow cape. (Those are the colors of the Canary Islands' flag, in case you missed the reference.) If it was up to me, I'd stick a Canarian mastiff on either side, really drive the point home.

But whatever. Supersaurio has 211 stores across the archipelago. Fifty-seven are in Gran Canaria. Of those fifty-seven, three are two- to three-story hypermarkets. There's one in Las Palmas, another in Telde, and another in Arguineguín. All three have underground parking lots, cafeterias, and playgrounds. All three smell the same. Twenty out of these fifty-seven establishments are Supersaurio Expresses. I memorized this information and regurgitated it during my first interview, right before I told them that if I could be any animal, it would be an ant. Most of these supermarkets are in the southern part of the island, where tourists will happily pay two Euros for a thawed, re-heated loaf of bread. I live in Puerto Rico, a town in the south of Gran Canaria, where there are two Supersaurio Expresses and also a regular Supersaurio, even though fewer than five thousand people live there. One is in the old shopping mall, and the other is on the beach. We also have two McDonald's, for good measure. I don't think my boss knows this. I suspect I am the first and only person from Puerto Rico he's ever met. The other Supersaurios are all regular, one-story establishments. A few days ago, I heard in a meeting that another shopping mall is being built in Puerto Rico and that Supersaurio is in talks with them about opening a supermarket in that one too. I don't know what will happen with the two Supersaurio Expresses we already have. Maybe they'll close. The giant dinosaur over the entryway will have to retrain, take a couple of vocational courses, find something outside his skill set. Maybe he'll serve drinks at a chiringuito on the beach and comfort himself by saying: 'At least I have a job.'

Every morning, I stare up at the colorful lights of the eight-story building where I work. The first three floors are taken up by the hypermarket, the largest Hipersaurio on the island. The rest are corporate offices. It's the kind of lightshow you'd expect to see at an amusement park or a Bershka, not at a supermarket. First they glow green, then purple, then red, then blue, then yellow. At night, they're the only thing you can see from the street. Sometimes I'll pop in my headphones, crank the music all the way up and pretend I'm at a club. The elevator to the offices is the one on the right, across from the newsstand. It's happened more than once that I've had to hide behind a shelf to avoid riding up with one of my coworkers. On the ground floor are the cash registers, the produce department, the gourmet section, the bakery, and a very large café. With the loyalty card, you can win points that get you discounts at gas stations. Plus, you can sip on free coffee from the vending machine while you do your shopping.

'Oh yes, absolutely.' I smile. 'Though I don't think there was any tension between us . . . We just have our differences.'

We have our differences, alright. I'm a human being. She . . . I'm not sure what she is. My boss, Ferrán-Matiqui-you-can-call-me-Ferrán-or-Matiqui-whatever-works-for-you, looks down at his hands and sighs. The poor thing is struggling.

'I was worried you two wouldn't be a good fit.'

More than once I've dreamed of fitting my hands around her neck. Waltzing into her office, taking a swing at her, and winning. Dismissal without notice and a probable assault charge – I googled it. I am an informed person. If I really hurt her, I might have to pay victim compensation. It's not worth the trouble.

'I think we've both made an effort to understand each other.'

We're like night and day.

'Glad to hear it. I won't take up any more of your time. I just wanted to check in, see how things are going. Is there anything I can do for you?'

Hire me full-time? Fire Yolanda?

'No. I'm good, thanks.'

He smiles, and I smile back. I'm a mirror, a black hole, it depends on the weather. I'd rather throw myself in front of a moving car than make peace with Yolanda, clear the air. I was born in the nineties and came of age in the noughties. I've survived all kinds of terrible things: low-cut jeans, Kate Winslet being coded as fat, ultra-thin brows. I will survive this too.

2

November 2016

I write in the Three Chicklets WhatsApp group:

[16:12] Me: Guyyyyyys, I'm hiding in the bathroom laughing my ass off because apparently it's Yolanda's birthday?????? AND I HAVE TO BUY HER FLOWERS FROM THE WHOLE TEAM LOL!

[16:13] Teresa: OMG lolololol noooooooo

[16:14] Teresa: buy her super pretty flowers that smell like shit

[16:15] Me: Hahahahahaha, I'm gonna faint from trying not to laugh, like . . . Oof. I can't.

[16:16] Carmen: or like one of those funeral wreaths, then you can say 'they reminded me of you' lol

[16:16] Carmen: and you give them to her with the cellophane on, all kkkhhh kkkhhh

[16:16] Me: LOL, 'they reminded me of you telling me every day that you're throwing a birthday party and everyone's invited . . . except me . . .' hahahahaha. Fucking loser.

[16:17] Me: Fos, I can't believe the shit I put up with for money.

3

November 2016

'So your name doesn't mean anything?'

He seems legit upset. I shrug.

'No, sorry. Nothing.'

There are four people on the Supersaurio Supermarkets S.L. Compliance team. Ferrán Matiqui is the team leader, director, and company VP – he's been here eight years. Everyone calls him Matiqui, except Yolanda, who for some reason only uses his first name. Then there's Víctor Márquez and Pedro Otero, forty-one- and forty-three-year-old *enfants terribles* and Matiqui's seconds-in-command. The few interactions I've had with them have left me completely drained. They ask the most basic questions. At first I thought it was that they wanted to get to know me, but now I suspect they just enjoy getting into arguments that feel like they'll go on forever until the other side finally gives up and admits the two of them are right. People avoid them in the hallways, though they don't seem to realize this. They're attached at the hip and finish each other's sentences. Their vibe is way off. When I can't steer clear of them, I give them a blank look and pretend not to understand what they're

14

saying. They and Matiqui are all mainlanders. Then there's Yolanda. I'm not sure what her job is because I never see her do anything. I think she's been here since the corporate offices first opened, like some kind of totem.

Víctor shakes his head.

'I thought your names always meant something, like . . . deep or whatever. I had this friend in college called Badr. Great dude. His name meant . . .'

Your names, he says. The dickwad. I smile.

'Something to do with the moon, I think. That's why I thought your name would mean something.'

Badr means *full moon.*

'Well, now I'm second-guessing myself,' I lie. 'I'll ask my parents tonight. I could be wrong.'

'Yeah, totally, ask them. Like, it must have *some* meaning, right? Badr did drink booze, though.'

He looks like he's about to elbow me playfully. For a second, I wish someone would flay me alive.

'Well, you know,' I pretend-laugh. 'I don't have to jump off a bridge just because all my friends do.'

I didn't want to come here. One of the most annoying things about corporate jobs is the concept of 'after-work.' It makes zero sense. You work upwards of nine hours in an office only to leave said office for a cocktail bar to get a drink . . . with the same people you worked with all day. Supposedly to help you 'unwind,' even though most of the conversations end up being about work. I check my phone, it's 7:50 p.m. Earlier that day, Matiqui forwarded me an email from Yolanda with a note: 'I think Yolanda forgot to CC you, but I'd appreciate it if you came along.' He and I both knew Yolanda hadn't forgotten to CC anyone, but I was just a lowly intern. My feelings didn't matter, let alone my opinions, so I decided

15

to go. If Matiqui asked me to throw myself off a bridge, I would. The end.

It isn't too bad at first. I try to keep an open mind, take initiative, be a doer and not a downer. I talk to some people, some other people, everybody. The Compliance girl. Whenever anyone brings me a beer or offers me a G&T, I say thank you and turn it down. I don't drink, sorry. Afraid I don't drink. Thanks so much, but I don't drink. Every time, I get the same kind of response. What do you mean you don't drink? Why? Go on, just the one. Don't worry, it's only beer. Not even one? Come on. Tired of being assertive, I start accepting whatever people bring me and either abandoning the drink or dumping it somewhere: the toilet, an umbrella stand, pots with fake plants by the back entrance.

On my seventh trip outside, someone clears their throat behind me. I don't move from where I'm crouched. My bottle of beer hovers mid-pour.

'Hello?'

I turn around very, very slowly, trying to draw out that fraction of a second for as long as humanly possible. Then I get up. His face looks familiar, but I can't remember his name. He stares at me in silence, like an idiot. I say nothing.

'Are you okay?'

He aspirates his *esses*, but he isn't from here.

'I don't drink,' I reply.

'You don't?'

'I don't.'

He laughs.

'Alright.'

'And ugh, people . . . people keep bringing me beers, cocktails—'

'And you don't drink.'

'Not a drop.'

'Not even beer?'

'Why does everyone always say that when you tell them you don't drink? "Not even beer?" It doesn't make sense.'

He thinks for a moment.

'Surprise, I guess. A beer is nothing.' He reaches into his pocket. 'But you're right, it doesn't make sense.'

'What if I had a drinking problem,' I go on, 'and everyone in there is all why don't you drink ehh why don't you drink go on have a drink a beer at least.'

'You seem annoyed.'

'I am.'

'So that's why you're poisoning the plants?'

'The plants? They're fake.'

'They're fake?'

'They're fake,' I echo, exasperated.

He laughs again.

'Pretty tacky, huh?'

I hear myself being honest for the first time since I started working with these people.

'Yeah, pretty tacky.'

He pulls out a pack of cigarettes.

'They throw after-work drinks for business execs who take home minimum €100,000 a year, then deck the place out in fake trees.'

I raise my eyebrows. €100,000. My internship pays €500 a month.

'A second ago, you didn't know they were fake.'

'But I do now. I don't know if you've heard, but information is power.'

Yes, and *France is bacon*, I think.

'What?' he asks.

I look at him.

'What?' I reply. I don't know what he's referring to.

'You said something.'

'No, I didn't.'

'Ah, I thought I heard you say something. Never mind. Got a light?'

'Sorry, I don't smoke.'

He straightens up and looks at me.

'You don't drink, you don't smoke. You must hate these things.'

I shrug.

'The food's alright,' I say, watching him slide the pack of cigarettes back in his pocket. He holds out his hand.

'I'm Omar. I work in Quality Control.'

'Meryem. Compliance.' I squeeze his hand firmly, as hard as I can. I'm a serious person, a good person, the kind who would never give someone a weak handshake.

'So you work with Yolanda and Matiqui.'

'And Víctor and Otero.'

I think he's laughing. He tries to cover it up with a cough.

'The look on your face when you said, "Víctor and Otero." Like a dog on a speedboat.' Seeing my shock, he quickly adds, 'Don't worry, I think they're morons too. Always bugging people when they should be doing their jobs.'

'I don't know them very well.'

'I'm only saying this because I like you,' he adds. 'Even though you crushed my hand.'

'Sorry. It's just that . . . this is all so weird to me,' I say, gesturing at us. 'You're the first person who hasn't talked to me like I'm some kind of lost cause. I bet there's a camera hidden behind the trashcans, trying to catch me in a lie.'

'Like in *Undercover Boss*?'

'You don't look like a boss.'

He gives a faint smile.

'Well, the disguise is supposed to be good enough that no one recognizes me. Wig, narco look, the whole nine yards.'

Since 2009, Supersaurio has been owned by four people: the Bethencourt siblings, Alma and Jacinto, and the Santana-Moreno brothers, Andrés and Adolfo. They bought the chain from a group of banks. According to what I read one morning while organizing some of Yolanda's prehistoric files, in 1966, Saurus Supermarkets was sold to Premium Ventures, a partnership that included Timanfaya Bank, who renamed it Little Saurus. Sometime later, the Norwegian multinational, Autek International, bought it and changed the name to Little Saurus S.L. In 2001, Autek experienced huge losses and sold out to Kilgres Partners, a British venture capital fund. By then the supermarket chain was already €503 million in debt, so the group of banks assumed control. Which brings us to today. I'd compiled this information and summarized it in a chart that took up half a sheet of A4 paper. Matiqui replied to my email with a terse *Nice work, M*. I don't know if he was being serious or ironic. Yolanda's files were so dusty they triggered my allergies, and I had to take an antihistamine on the bus ride home. I sneezed for an hour and thirteen minutes.

'To be fair, you do look like a narco right now. You could easily be the head of the Cali cartel.'

He laughs again. He throws his head back and cackles. It makes me laugh.

'Listen, don't be so direct with the people in there. They won't take it as well as me.'

I push my glasses up the bridge of my nose.

'Don't worry about me,' I say. 'I never say what I really think.'

4

November 2016

My name is Meryem. That's two syllables. Mer-yem. The *y* should sound like a *j*, but most of the time I'm Mereym. Or Mereyn. I've also been called Meyren, Mérien, Meriem, Meyrem, Myrene, Meyreme, Miriam, Marian, Mariane, Meyremem. I have a folder on my cell phone with over a hundred screengrabs of all the variations, reformulations, adaptations, and interpretations that have sprung from my name. It's a constant source of surprise. I'm Steven Spielberg, forever moved to tears. A rose by any other name, yada yada, I know. We study Shakespeare in Canarian public schools too. When you're called what I am, when your name is unusual, weird, I've-never-heard-a-name-like-that-before, where-did-you-say-it's-from, you quickly learn an important lesson: never, ever look annoyed that the person you're talking to can't handle a two-syllable word. I was born, grew up, and now I've spent weeks of my life with someone calling me 'Meyrme' in work emails, and I think to myself, *Is it really so hard to copy and paste six puny letters?* I take that thought, bottle it up, swallow it. I don't die, I just get more and more pissed off. I'm Canarian: Not only do

20

I have the sexiest accent in all of Spain according to multiple surveys, but I am also highly resilient.

My ninth-grade math teacher, Doña Mercedes, used to call me Mary Jane. The first time she did this, I looked at her, she looked at me, we looked at each other, and I corrected her. For the next nine months of my life, I was called Mary Jane in her class (some of the kids in school used to shout PETER PARKER right after my name I think about them sometimes I hope they're well one of them is a taxi driver now one day I got in a taxi without checking and then when I looked up I saw it was him and he recognized me and I wanted to get out but we were already moving it was too late I nearly threw up in the backseat of the taxi cab and when I got out he said something I didn't understand and I ran away as fast as I could; a few days later he found me on Facebook and wrote me a four-paragraph-long DM apologizing for how he'd treated me 'when we were kids' and I went to his profile and blocked him I hope he dies and that the last thing he sees is my face flashing before his eyes). I wasn't going to get Doña Mercedes to crack, but she certainly got me to. In the end I gave up, disbanded, turned in my weapons. I don't object to anything anymore.

Miriam, Meriam. No matter the name, it rolls right off me. Sometimes I'm called It'll-be-faster-if-I-just-give-you-my-ID-card. I've realized I have nothing to gain by resisting. When I'm not Myenere or Meriané, I'm: Uy-that-name-isn't-from-here or Huh-you-look-Canarian or That's-such-a-pretty-name-I've-never-heard-it-before-where-are-you-from? It doesn't matter that I'm used to the string of questions, twenty-five years of explanations, it changes nothing. Just because I know the conversation by heart doesn't mean the endless interrogations don't weigh on my shoulders, and I don't feel any less powerless. 'I'm from here, from the island,' I usually say, to which they usually reply, 'Sure, but where exactly?' I daydream about turning around and answering: 'What the fuck do you care where I'm from *exactly*, you dickbag, what do you actually want to know, spit it out already,' but if I did then the person I'm talking to would get offended because they're not doing anything wrong, they're just wondering, they're curious. *L'esprit de l'escalier* except I'm at the bottom of the staircase screaming that I've had it up to here with being patient and friendly and smiling and turning the other cheek all the time there's no cheek left here have this one slap it instead if you want. 'From Morocco,' I say finally, even if it's a lie, because I was born here raised here educated here lived here my whole life. *Right here.*

Which is why I don't get angry with the mailman when he asks me the same thing today. I answer all his questions with a smile. I'm the most gracious person in the world, calm, easygoing, charming. I read out my national ID number and none of my features move when he asks for my foreign ID number instead because how could I possibly be Spanish with a name like Meryem, Myren, Mereyenen, I'm not always so sure. Plus, my surnames are so long and strange, so not-from-here. What's that there on my national ID card? KINGDOM OF SPAIN, in block letters. Am I the only one who sees it? I'd like to shove it in his face and say here, take it, enjoy. I sign where he tells me to and take Matiqui's package. There isn't so much as a quiver in my voice. I'm so proud of myself, but oh do I hate him, oh do I despise him, with his blue vest and yellow cap and stupid digital whatchamacallit. Time passes, and I find it harder and harder to put my finger on what exactly incenses me: whether it's the knowledge that no matter how long I live in this place, some people will never believe I'm from here, or the fact that I am not and never will be from there.

5

November 2016

I have this theory about short people. Sometimes I'm like one of those racists who thinks they're being less racist by calling somebody 'tan.' I say, 'that non-tall person.' It just slips out. There are two categories of short people: the nice ones and the raging assholes. The evilest person I've ever met is shorter than me. Her name is Yolanda. When we're together in the elevator, or in the office, I gaze down at her and try to guess what she's thinking, what she dreams about at night. It's impossible not to stare at the top of her head from my vantage point, at the black, wavy hair she almost always wears in a super-tight bun. I wonder if all that tension gives her migraines. That would explain why she's so toxic and hostile. Franco was five foot four. Does she know that? Maybe not. Maybe she has no idea Margaret Thatcher was five foot five or that Benito Mussolini was barely five foot seven. Winston Churchill? Five foot six.

When Yolanda and I cross paths in the hallway, there are days when she says hi and days when she doesn't. I try to picture her life outside work. Does she move her hands the same way? Say the same things? Does she have friends?

I'm aware there are two versions of me that swap places depending on where I am and who I'm with. Sometimes I'm not totally sure which one I'm being: the person I fold away, tinker with, and modify every day before coming into work, or myself. I wonder if she feels the same, if she dislikes me as much as I've begun to dislike her. I wonder what she sees when she looks at me. On the more difficult days, I ask myself why she treats me the way she does, with such glaring cruelty. I've never been mean to her. The opposite, actually. I take a step back and see our interactions from the outside; there's just no way people aren't catching the tone she uses on me, like every bad thing that ever happens is my fault. In the dead hours after lunch, when there's barely a sound in the office, I mentally draw her a house in the south of the island. I sketch an electric-yellow sun in a corner, a house with tall white walls, and a red-tile roof under a blue sky. She is a black shadow lurking in the background. That's what she feels like to me: a dark burst of rain over my head that soaks me to the bone in an imaginary micro-climate where clouds do not exist.

She took out a mortgage so she could buy the house I'm drawing for her. I make it up as I go along because I have no idea where she lives or what her house looks like. The place doesn't have a garden, but it does have a pool. A semi-detached building in a housing development where you can't hear any children because most of the neighbors are tourists who vacation on the island between October and May. Their skin is burned, and they wear their bathing suits up to their pits so they won't spill out of them in the street. Sometimes they get on the bus looking like that and sit beside to you, their arm against your arm, their knee against your knee, the scent of after-sun lotion clinging to your nose. When I'm very tired and there aren't any free seats I stick my belly out as far as I can and pretend to be pregnant so a guiri will give me theirs. I place my hand on my gut and stare them down until one of them has the decency to get up. I think of it as a form of peaceful protest. Gran Canaria is a graveyard of drunk elephants of British, German, Swedish, and Norwegian extraction, and I am sick of them, each and every one. Of course, nobody screams at *them* to go back where they came from. They're white.

In the house I am picturing for Yolanda, there are no pets, no children, only silence and the dust she cleans every day with the precision of a Swiss clock. Every now and then she sits next to me at a meeting I'm only invited to so I can take minutes, and I have to fight the urge to prod her in the face with my finger. To check if she's made of flesh and blood or if she's made of rubber. To check if she's human or something else entirely. We are Palestine and Israel. One of us has her own office on a separate floor. The other sits in an open-plan cubicle that any random passerby could easily invade. Always on the alert, waiting to see if she comes downstairs and imposes a brand-new sanction or boycott, or else reduces me to rubble in a matter of seconds. Take these five hundred files, then scan and shred them. I need it done by EOD today. Jesus, are you still doing that? Drop it. I need you to run an errand on the other end of the island, take these with you. How have you not finished the first assignment I gave you? It's not like I've interrupted you fifty-nine times in one day to run a bunch of stupid errands.

Sitting at my desk, where everyone can see me, I paint her a daily routine that is bright orange and dark blue, a borderline personality. Gentle on some days, cruel on others. You're all invited to my birthday party, she says. We're going to celebrate in style. The woman has forty-six bullet holes in the heart. *Yesterday, my partner and I went to a tasting with the catering company*, she announces in a studied performance intended solely to unsettle me, exclude me, and make it absolutely clear that I am not and never will be one of them. Sitting in the bathroom where I sometimes hide to cry – almost always because of her – I go round and round in my head, tuku tuku, wondering what would happen if one day I decided that enough was enough, if I turned around very slowly, looked her in the eyes, and asked her what her problem was, out loud, right in front of everyone. I don't do it, of course, I haven't lost the plot quite yet. It's still there.

6

December 2016

Here's the thing: my first day at Supersaurio, Matiqui was on vacation. *I am away from my desk with little to no access to email. For any urgent matters, please contact my colleagues Pedro Otero (pedro.otero@supersaurio.com) or Víctor Márquez (victor.marquez@supersaurio.com).* I only met him a few days into my internship. He shook my hand, introduced me to Víctor and Otero, and treated me to coffee. What this means is that Yolanda was the person who showed me around when I first set foot in the Supersaurio headquarters. I gave it my all. I wanted her to like me, wanted her to think I was great. I showed her that I was dynamic, active, pro-active even. I thought: *She's the only woman in my department. I can learn a lot from her.* I told myself: *The corporate world is super competitive. The fact that she's been here this long must mean something.* She showed me my cubicle and her office, then explained a grand total of two things: where to find the kitchen and the location of the photocopier. I pointed at a paperweight with a UD Las Palmas soccer club logo and asked: 'UD fan?' She looked me up and down, decided then and there that she would not make my life easy, and neglected to answer the question. When I die I will see her face and hear her voice as she says: 'Okay, Miriam. Chop chop. Follow me. I haven't got all day.' I followed her, of course I did. What other choice was there?

7

December 2016

I'm late I'm late I'm late. It's so hot I can't tell if I'm sweating, if I just got my period, or if I'm in the throes of early menopause. A fine dusting of Sahara desert sand coats everything, even the sky, which isn't blue but orange. When I run, I feel the sand get in my eyes and throat and sear me as if I were drinking lava. The blank looks on the tourists' faces keep my spirits up. Didn't they want a beach to go to in winter? Well, here it fucking is. In ads for sanitary pads, women stare into the camera, smile, and make ridiculous assertions like ISN'T IT WONDERFUL TO BE A WOMAN. Except they never explain what's so wonderful about it. Is it buying sixteen sanitary pads for €3.64? Is it that the sanitary pads in question are thin and wingless? Or is it that they're extra-large, winged, and super-absorbent, so that all you have to do is slap them on your panties to go back to business as usual, as if nothing has changed? In ads for sanitary pads, the women put on big smiles and do things that make you question whether the person who created, thought up, brainstormed – or whatever, I don't know how this stuff works – the ad in front of you has ever had a period in their life. What kind of person does backflips when something inside their body is coming loose, breaking apart, slipping, tearing through everything in its path just because she failed to get pregnant? I'm late, and by the time I find Carmen and Teresa in the usual back corner of our usual bar, I decide I'm allowed a bit of melodrama, some theatrics.

'Sorry, everyone,' I say when I get to their table. 'My day got totally insane because that bitch Yol—'

I point to Teresa.

'You cut your hair.'

'Yeah. Sit down, we're discussing every mistake I've made in the last ten years of my life.'

I stare at her.

'But yesterday . . . your hair . . . was down to your ass?'

'Apparently it's the end of a cycle,' Carmen explains.

'You don't think it looks good? I might go blonde.'

Teresa lifts her sunglasses to her forehead, then slides them back like a hairbrush. Her hair is barely chin-length now. She looks amazing.

'You look amazing,' Carmen and I say at the same time. I leave my backpack on the floor by the chair and sit down.

'Thanks, guys.'

'It's just a big change,' I say. 'I'm sorry I'm late. I feel like I missed a major announcement or something.'

'The deal is that yesterday, as I was drifting off to sleep, I had this epiphany: I'm always falling for guys who meet the loves of their lives right after dumping me.' She glances down at her phone, locks it, leaves it on the table. 'I just can't catch a break. Then these jerks go and thank me for teaching them how to be "good" boyfriends.'

As a teenager, I had girlfriends I liked and girlfriends I didn't like. I can't tell you exactly why I didn't like them, just that I felt uncomfortable in their company. The dynamic between us was dark, constantly shifting: one false step, and you were out. Some days we were BFFs; others, we hated each other's guts. I was introverted, ambitious, a wise-ass. Nothing mattered, everything was dumb. Having a social life as a teenager was more about survival than anything else, at least to me; there was nothing worse than not being part of the group. The price of independence was too steep (the jokes, the pointing, the defenselessness), and I wasn't ready to pay it. Besides, the conditions that had led to our friendship – age, location, social class – were all outside our control. It didn't matter what I did, I always felt out of place. My classmates were into things I couldn't get myself to care about. All my efforts to fake it or else force myself to like those things just made me hate them even more. For years, I thought I was the problem and carefully squished all the parts that didn't fit into tiny little piles that I flattened down, hid away, and collected inside me. I'd go to the mall and wander around with no clear goal beyond not saying no to an invitation because I was scared of never being invited to anything again. I took quizzes in magazines like *Bravo* and *Superpop* during recess and tried to work out if I was a perfect match for Zac Efron. I decided which of the girls in my grade were sluts or not according to criteria as bizarre as 'does she wear eyeliner?' or 'are her hips too thick?'

Then I discovered the internet. One day I typed 'theories about Sirius Black's death' into the Google search bar and pressed Enter. It was 2004, and we didn't have internet at home. Whenever I needed to write a paper for school, I'd spend entire afternoons holed up in the only internet café in Puerto Rico, which was in the mall. There were all kinds of theories about Sirius Black's death, but most people were over it and had moved on to writing their own

31

takes on what had happened in the Department of Mysteries. Sirius Black wasn't dead, he was just in a different dimension, another astral plane, in limbo or a coma . . . Harry needed to save him. I came across a website called Harrylatino and opened an account there. At first I mainly read other people's stories, but eventually I began writing my own. I published my first piece of fanfic at the age of thirteen. The premise was: Lily Evans and James Potter go on a first date. I got five comments. I wasn't any good, neither were the stories I wrote, but it was fun. With time, I improved and swapped Harrylatino for Fanfiction.net, the Premier League of fanfiction. Nearly every piece I read had been written by girls a lot older than me and way more talented; I learned loads from them. Fanfiction became something of a safety valve, a gateway to people in other parts of the world who were obsessed with the same kinds of things as I was. Maybe I wasn't actually that weird or abnormal or incapable of fitting in. Maybe my issue was that Puerto Rico, Mogán, was too small and had almost nothing to offer in exchange for stifling me. By the age of sixteen I was writing about *The X-Files*, *House*, *Skins*, *Bleach*, *Harry Potter*, *Twilight*, *A Song of Ice and Fire*, *One Piece*, *Dragonlance* . . . I met Teresa and Carmen when I was fifteen because they used to leave comments on my *Twilight* fanfic. Every now and then I like to remind them that they were my first groupies.

'So then you cut off all your hair.'

'It's like when Veronica was having a really shitty time and decided to shave her head so she could be reborn as a whole new person.'

'I don't know any Verónicas,' I say.

'Veronica Mars. "Lock by lock, she is reborn."'

My face is still blank.

'Huh?'

'I'm quoting you,' she grumbles. 'Literally.'

Carmen laughs.

'Fuck, I can't remember writing that, like ever.' I pull my cell phone out of my back pocket and google my fanfic username. 'Published: 2006. Wow, I feel old.'

'Anyway, the point is I've been reborn.'

Carmen and I look at each other and have the decency to say nothing.

'Hey, so, are you ever going to update "Map of the problematique"?'

'Map of the problematique' is a piece of fanfic I've been writing for about a year. I posted the last update the week before my internship at Supersaurio started. I don't have time to write fanfiction anymore, only to photocopy documents, read reports, and recycle Power-Point presentations.

'I wish I could. The only fanfic I write these days is about my coworkers. It all sucks. Anyway, Teresa, how do you even know your exes are meeting the loves of their lives after dumping you?'

'Because a few weeks later, I see them posting these cryptic pics that aren't actually cryptic at all, with stupid captions like, "The best medicine," or "Big little changes," and the pic is like this mirror selfie where all you see is two people's shirts.'

Those kinds of photos are in my top three favorite categories of Instagram pics, followed by the ones of a woman looking back while holding the hand of a person outside the frame and by pictures of feet half buried in the sand with the caption 'Sucks to be me.'

'But you're okay?' I ask.

'Yeah, totally. I mean, I think so.'

'Yesterday I burst into tears as I was leaving yoga,' Carmen said. 'I took one step out of the studio and started, like, softly weeping.'

'Oh, no.'

'Oh, yes. I don't even know why. It's not as if anything's wrong. Mercedes is fine, I'm fine, Dana's fine . . .'

'Maybe it's the stress, from deadlines or something,' I say and put my phone down on the table. Carmen is an illustrator. She never turns down commissions from major brands or companies, so she always has a string of projects that are all needed by yesterday. 'When I'm stressed or nervous, anything makes me cry. The other day I was hanging out minding my own business when all of a sudden, I thought: "Chias, Mery, it's been three years since you kissed a man."'

The two of them laugh.

'Three years?'

'A bit over three years, but yeah. Anyway, I started freaking out, so I downloaded Tinder and spent half an hour like, pim pam, swipe left, swipe left, swipe left. Then I got depressed and deleted the app again.'

I believe in the mythical click. You meet someone. You look at them. They look at you. And things just click. You say: 'Mundo,' and he smiles and adds, 'Na tu ral,' like in the radio ad. Tinder is a drag. The men on it are generally boring, and the ones who aren't are scary. Jose, 33. 'We'll tell our kids we met at a museum.' Pedro, 29. 'Crossfit, beer, *Fight Club*.' Matías, 31. 'Jazz, Crossfit, sunsets.' They're all basically the same person. Sure, I get that human beings copy each other so they don't come off as complete psychos – given that having a personality is usually considered a crime, especially when you're a woman. Looking for love is so cringe and panic-inducing. You're never fully yourself and you tell white lies because you want the other person to choose you, to swipe right.

When you read, 'Jazz, Crossfit, and sunsets,' you understand that what this guy is conveying is that he is just like everyone else, that there's no originality or imagination to be found there. Nothing. Swipe left, but the next dude is over thirty and balding and puts zero effort into his selfies. You've got nothing against bald guys. They're just not your type right now. You're twenty-five, still superficial. The next dude's pic is of his naked torso. He self-defines as 'dominant' and is seeking a submissive. Then comes a guy who only posts pictures of him surrounded by small African children. You delete the app. You don't believe in love. The worst part is that Tinder makes me feel super vulnerable in a way I can't quite put my finger on. When you don't immediately reply to a guy's message the second you get it, he asks you why the fuck you bothered matching with him, slut. You're not even that pretty. He's sick of divas. It's the gratuitous hostility you find frightening: *hey gorgeous* and *fuck you, bitch* are two sides of the same coin you toss in the air and wait to see what happens. At least the Joker is a wacko for a reason.

'I'm done trying,' Teresa says. 'I'm ready to join a convent.'

'Sister Teresa.'

'It has a nice ring to it.'

'Sister Meryem?'

Teresa cracks up.

'Sister Carmen?'

'Okay, we get it, we have very nun-like names.'

'Especially Meryem.'

'Meryem basically translates as Maria. Read a book. Educate yourselves.'

Despite everything, I do believe in love. I always sigh at the end of *Pride and Prejudice* (the 2005 adaptation) when I watch it for the zillionth time. What woman doesn't want a condescending man who doesn't appreciate her at first but then falls at her feet the minute he realizes she hates him twice as hard? Textbook enemies turned friends turned lovers. Maybe my problem is that I grew up reading fanfic instead of Miller or Bukowski.

8

December 2016

I open the fridge in my kitchen and pull out a container of maakouda, zaalok, and breaded chicken cutlet that my dad made last night. The best of both worlds – and people say we don't assimilate. I double-check the contents of my backpack before leaving: work laptop, check; water bottle, check; phone charger and headphones, check; wallet, check; scarf and cardigan because the air conditioner in the office is set to −4° Celsius, check; the desire to spend the next six hours of my life being bullied by Yolanda, whoopsie, missed that one. My parents are nearly done praying in the living room. I hope they finish before I have to leave. 'Did you pray for me?' I ask, and my mother says: 'We pray for you and your siblings every day.' I take the 91 bus at 6:45 a.m. The driver and I are on first-name terms. I don't tell my parents that every morning, when my alarm rings, I get the urge to quit my internship. That I feel like the ice has cracked beneath my feet and I've plummeted into freezing water without knowing how to swim. I walk from my house to the bus stop feeling spongy on the inside and very loved, like someone enveloped me in bubble wrap. I try to be strong and hang in there, like them.

9

December 2016

There are several people at the Supersaurio Supermarkets S.L. headquarters who believe they will take over the company. They come in all shapes and sizes: tall, short, fat, skinny, blond, brunet, white, Black. Even shaved and bald. (I've got nothing against bald people. They don't scare me, I swear!) Our HR department has a list of nationalities that it trots out at every opportunity, as if each new hire were a Pokémon Go match and the company's goal were to collect one from every single country on Earth. We have employees from Spain, the United Kingdom, Mexico, Venezuela, Colombia, Cameroon, even France. Everyone's given a chance, there is no discrimination. Though most employees from the countries mentioned above are stock clerks. Or cashiers.

Three out of five Supersaurio employees are the sons and daughters of workers who busted their asses so their offspring could study engineering or, as a last resort, law or economics. (This is not hard data; I just made it up.) They look at you askance for wearing a T-shirt to work. Yesterday, they were the future. Today, they are dinosaurs with perfectly knotted ties, freshly ironed shirts, and pants hemmed just below the ankles. They still wear wrist-watches. Now they've been made to compete with people ten to fifteen years their junior who know their way around every Office suite, speak three languages, have MBAs and MSs in data analytics or business assurance, and whisper 'OK boomer' behind their backs. Even so, I've noticed that both parties have a lot in common. They work overtime for no pay, take on duties outside their remit, and stretch their patience to the limit in pursuit of recognition that will never arrive. The main difference is that the people in the first group already have a mortgage, children, cars, and make more than €2,000 a month. The others . . . don't.

When I was seventeen I decided to study translation and interpretation because I was good at languages and didn't want to fall into the trap of going to journalism school just because I enjoyed writing. I don't want to talk about it. Usually, I just pretend it never happened and that translation was my vocation. My parents weren't upset. The opposite, actually. *Follow your dreams. Believe in yourself. We'll support you*: That's what they fed me. Did it do me any good? At least I'm not getting ready to sit a public examination for some random position. No one I know who studied under the Bologna Process has all their ducks in a row, as my friend Silvia likes to put it. I did undergrad, an MA, then another MA, then I worked as an au pair because I wasn't sure what to do with my life (get another MA?) – quack quack – then I came back and got an internship at the supermarket with the best prices on the archipelago.

The first time I set foot in the corporate offices of Super-saurio Supermarkets S.L., I had less than €100 in my bank account, no savings, and zero faith they would hire me. The career development center at Fundación Universitaria Las Palmas hadn't quite known what to make of me. 'You have a complicated profile,' said the person I met with. 'If only one of your languages was German . . .' Point-blank shot with silencer. This is how things work in the Canary Islands: if all else fails, if you're good for nothing, if you're confused and need some time to breathe, recalibrate, figure out next steps . . . you can always enter the service industry and make a pathetic living from tourism. You just need to speak English and German. If you have a basic grasp of Norwegian, hotels in the south of the island will literally sword fight each other for you. Why would anyone study French in the Canary Islands? If I were French, there's no way in hell I would come *here* on holiday. No, I'd go to one of the former colonies, like Algeria, Tunisia, Morocco, places where everyone speaks French because years and years of occupation have turned the colonizer's language into the cultured language of the colonized. My complicated profile and I decided to lower our standards and take what we were given, like a vacancy for INTERN – COMPLIANCE DEPARTMENT OF AN IMPORTANT CANARIAN COMPANY: PAID OPPORTUNITY.

For whatever reason, they hired me and not the other guy. My first month interning, I got to work every day convinced someone was going to point their finger at me and yell 'imposter!' I was young, dynamic, pro-active, and decisive. I could work independently or in a team. I was a quick study with a positive attitude. At least that's what I'd written in my CV; therefore, it was the Truth. I spoke three languages: Spanish, English, and French; I'd lived abroad and had done a truckload of internships. I knew my way around every Office suite and a lot of other programs too. All of what I've just said is true, by the way, just twisted and embellished to the point that every time I run through it in my head, it sounds pretty close to a lie. I'd tricked everyone and didn't deserve to be there. I didn't talk like them, or dress like them, and most of all, I'd never be able to think like them.

The point is I'm still here. I used to think the problem was other people. Now I know for sure that I'm the one who doesn't fit in. I don't invest my savings in company stock (or any other stock for that matter), I don't have a Google alert set for Supersaurio news, I don't take photos with my coworkers, and I always check 'Maybe' on Doodles about after-work activities. I have zero interest in getting a mortgage, I don't wear pencil skirts or pinstripe pants, the last thing I want is to look at pics or videos of people's children, and to be brutally honest, I don't think it's healthy to blur the line between coworkers and friends. I get to the office on time and leave on time, do my best to make sure nothing happens at work that puts a dent in my soul, cross one more day off my work calendar, walk out of there, and don't think about the place again until the next day.

I mull over this while sitting in the conference room on the eighth floor of Supersaurio Supermarkets S.L.'s corporate offices. Tucked away in the last row of chairs, phone in hand and hands in lap, I spy the head honchos in the first row: the president, the VPs, and the department managers. In the second row, on the far right, Marcial from Accounting is whispering something to Fernando, the office manager. Lucía 1 and Lucía 2 – they're both executive assistants (hilarious, I know) – are typing furiously on their phones. On the far right, Víctor and Otero get up from their seats and sit down again, over and over. I cross my legs and type in my phone: 'I'm going to save my future boyfriend in my contacts as MY SWEET, SICK NARCISSIST,' then publish the tweet.

Yolanda is late and walks in saying *sorry, excuse me, sorry*. The click-clack click-clack of her heels doesn't stop, not even when she walks past me while staring right through me. And there I am, still seated in the last row, ready to leave the second the meeting ends, while she, the most loyal worker the

41

company has ever known, heads straight to the first row. She sits to the left of Lucía 2, in the only empty seat, and for one second, for one tenth of a millisecond, I think to myself that I could've sat with them if I'd wanted. The IT team isn't part of the group, probably because they're nerds, nor are the temps or the interns. Lucía 1 and Lucía 2 went out of their way to let me know on my first week at Supersaurio that the company never hires interns. They told me this for my own good, because they didn't want me getting my hopes up. I thanked them with a faint smile and said: 'Don't worry, I'm not a hopeful person.' Now they give me the occasional side-eye.

When I turn around, I see Omar from Quality Control sitting a few seats away from me. He smiles. I smile. The head of HR, Macarena, finally arrives. She has extremely important news to share with us. She looks dead serious. Something about her expression tickles me. It's like she might throw up if she opens her mouth. I recognize it as the same expression I wear whenever I have to say something I don't know how to put into words. I pinch my thigh so I won't laugh. Omar raises his eyebrows. I raise mine back. I think of Pacho Herrera, from the show Narcos. Now I'm really worried I'm going to snicker. 'I'm sorry to be the one to break the news,' I hear Macarena say. 'I know there have been a lot of rumors about a workforce downsizing. There will not be mass layoffs, but we will be cutting back on our cashiers.' Everyone falls silent. There's nothing to fear. Someone in the first row giggles, maybe out of relief. The cashiers are part of a different species, the 'should've-gone-to-school' species. No one cares about them. I bite the inside of my cheek to keep myself from making a sound. The company will be installing self-checkout machines on the ground floor of the supermarket as a pilot program. They're overstaffed. It takes me a very, very long time to realize that while I observe them, there is always someone observing me.

10

December 2016

10:43 a.m. I ask the man behind the bar at Dinardi to pour the coffee in my thermos because it's eco-friendly and I'm woke and the man behind the bar says what do you mean fill your thermos that's a Starbucks flask it says so right there and the coffee is expensive and nothing like good real coffee I smile with no idea what to say because I do know a thing or two about coffee and I wouldn't drink the stuff he serves if he paid me but Matiqui loves it and Matiqui is my boss and if my boss says jump I'm like how high so then I ask the man behind the bar if he can (please) pour the coffee in my thermos and he says can's got nothing to do with it and the man behind the bar at Dinardi and I stare at each other and I know he's going to win but I don't lose hope so I say that what I really want is for him to pour his better-than-Starbucks coffee his good real coffee in the thermos and he tells me he can't refill my flask and instead pours my coffee into a paper cup and after swiping my boss's card sshhww sshhww I ask him why he couldn't pour the same coffee he'd poured into a paper cup into my thermos instead doesn't he realize that doing so generates less waste because you can get a thousand uses out of a thermos but only one use out of a paper cup and he explains that it's not advisable to fill the flask all the way because it affects the quality of the coffee and so the man behind the bar successfully gets me to stop trying for the nth time to explain that all I wanted was for him to pour the contents of the paper cup into the thermos instead so that we can save the planet because if there's one thing that will spare us from dehydrating and burning to death in the desert our planet is becoming it's rich people and corporations not draining all our resources as if they're the only people who exist on this earth and using a thermos once in a while instead of a paper cup to transport my boss's coffee to the office. The bad guys win again.

I I

December 2016

Matiqui calls a meeting to inform the team that none of our jobs are at risk, that supermarket personnel will be the ones to take the hit. Everyone knew it was coming, it was to be expected, a matter of time. The second the self-checkout machines roll through the door, the cashiers start going out the window. I keep my mouth shut. We're a good team, he tells us. Even the work I do as an intern is important; it seems I have an eye for detail. We've done a great job this year. There's no reason to be afraid, but we can't let our guard down at any moment. I look straight at Yolanda and she looks at me. Otero says: 'They can't fire us. We're fucking ace.' Víctor agrees: 'Results, results, results, at any cost. That's the secret.' Yolanda has been slowly but surely dumping every little thing she can't be bothered to do on my desk. Organizing the company's articles of incorporation in chronological order, for example, then scanning and shredding them. Keeping an up-to-date list of the managers of every Supersaurio branch and their teams. Reporting on the department's expenses. Budgeting for next year even if I myself will not be here next year. Taking minutes for every meeting Matiqui has with departments like Logistics, Corporate Communications, and Legal. Doing coffee runs. I am aware of the exact moment she realizes that everything she has devised as a form of torture is actually a double-edged sword: If I can do all this while making a fraction of what she does, then what exactly is she good for? I smile.

I 2

December 2016

I have this theory about love and hate. I mull it over while watching my cup of coffee spin in the microwave in the sixth-floor kitchen. The cup is bathed in a yellow glow, and I can't shake the feeling that we're one and the same: trapped in a very small space with a spotlight over our heads while several people stand in front of us with their arms crossed. Waiting. Sometimes I play this game with myself: if I make eye contact with my nemesis when she isn't addressing me, I lose. For a whole minute, I study the microwave door as if it were the most interesting thing I have ever seen in my life. If I say hello without looking at her, I lose. If I turn my head just slightly and give even the smallest indication that I know she's there and that I'm keenly aware of the fact that I am, once more, the only person she hasn't said hello to that morning, I lose. If I make it clear to her in any way that I know she knows what I'm thinking, I lose.

I am an ocean of calm. Unflappable.

So here's my theory: love and hate are the same thing. They do not complement each other. They are not two sides of the same coin. There is no thin, nebulous line separating the two. They're just the same thing in different states: one is liquid, the other solid. Love flows, hate clogs. They both generate cold and trigger heat, vertigo, the sweats, occasional bouts of nausea. They burn in your stomach and on the tips of your fingers. They make your skin tingle. Love and hate are intoxicating. They take hold of you, possess you, rob you of your self-control: you see yourself doing undeniably stupid shit you know you would never do under any other circumstance, like taking your already-hot cup of coffee out of the microwave, stirring the liquid with a spoon, and putting it back in for another minute just so you won't have to turn around and acknowledge the existence of a certain someone who has spent the last two minutes droning on and on about stock options.

When I graduated from college, I was sure I was leaving cliques behind me for good. Not only are they not behind me, but the people in them are my parents' age. Your sanity, or what little sanity you have left, reels for days, weeks, even months. You can neither help thinking nor stop thinking about the other person. The person you love. The person you hate. They're like a song you know by heart, an earworm that follows you wherever you go. The click-clack of her high heels, the way she dresses (today, head to toe in Burberry, knee-high stiletto boots, turtle-neck sweater, puffer vest: any second now, she's going to pull some carrots out of her pockets, cluck, and call us Rocinante), her tone. You memorize the melody, the lyrics. You can't get them out of your head, no matter how hard you try.

You don't realize at first. You think back, trying to pinpoint the exact moment it all started, to freeze it in time and examine it closely. You don't always succeed, though sometimes you catch a brief glimpse of it. The first time you saw her pull a face when someone asked for your opinion. A strange look in her eye. An offhand comment in the elevator that wasn't really offhand at all but meant to make you feel more and more insignificant for the next nine hours of your life. A report that took you several days to put together and that she copied and pasted into Word before passing it off as her own. All the little things she's done to make your life miserable and that have gotten you to question if you're crazy or if someone twenty years your senior is in fact actively trying to send you home in tears three out of five days of the working week.

Love and hate are overwhelming and shove aside half the stuff that used to fill up your days. You push away other people to make time for this thing that has you in its grip, this thing that's making you tremble. The only difference is that you're allowed to talk openly about loving someone but not about hating them. If I wanted, if the spirit moved me, I could give Yolanda a compliment. Except I'd rather be dragged all over the island by a horse-drawn cart than say a nice word about her. The thing is, no one would raise an eyebrow if I did. No one would look at me funny. And yet I will never be allowed to shout from the rooftops the laundry list of reasons that have led me to be standing here today, face glued to the microwave, because I refuse to give in again. No, when you hate someone, you have to play down the disgust you feel in their presence. You have to take it graciously and maturely, to hide your true feelings, pretend they don't exist. Who cares if they turn your stomach, if sometimes they make you see red, if they swell in your chest, get caught in your throat, fill your mouth with bile. Like love, hate is just there. You can't get rid of it. It won't leave.

If love brings out the best in people, then so does hate. Love makes you a better good guy. Hate makes you a better bad guy. All your senses hum, your eye for detail sharpens, your emotions flow – it's ecstasy. Thanks to this hate, I've discovered I have a flair for cruelty. My observations are more cutting now, my words weapons of mass destruction. Hate changes things, even when you don't want it to. There used to be something inside me that worked in a certain way but now doesn't. A time comes when you don't want to be the one sneaking onto the roof to finish your banana just to avoid yet another put-down. All the twisted parts of you throb beneath your skin, because you could talk back, but you don't. Time and again, you choose not to. You tell yourself there is a line you will not cross because that's not the kind of person you are. (Though you could be.)

Which is why I grab my now too-hot cup of coffee and pretend I'm reading an email as I walk out of the kitchen. The next time I'm there on my own, I take all Yolanda's favorite mugs and put them on the highest shelf I can reach. I have to get on my tiptoes, and it takes me ten minutes to arrange them in a way that no one else can spot them. Let her hunt around; I'd like to see her try and find them.

13

December 2016

Checkered shirt, jeans, Vans, phone in hand. You looked at me. I had on a brand-new shirt with a lowish cut. You slowed down until we were side by side, then said 'nice tits,' and smiled like we had a shared secret. I hope you have a stroke before you get wherever it is you're going. I hope a truck runs you over and you end up as a mushy splat at my feet. I'm never wearing this shirt again.

14

December 2016

The door beeps, then opens. My cubicle is right behind the front desk, so my back is to the rest of the office. The cubicle across from mine is always empty, but I'm too embarrassed to ask if I can switch, so I just put up with it. You have to use a fingerprint reader to access this floor. At first I thought it was cute, now I think it's a huge pain in the ass. A few years ago, the ex-husband of a woman from Accounting showed up at the offices and made a huge scene right where I'm sitting now. She wasn't answering his calls or opening the door when he went to the house they used to live in together, so he figured he'd come all the way here to scream at her and threaten her because apparently cutting him out of her life didn't send a strong enough message. He got in with one of her old key cards, and security had to drag him out by the arms. The receptionist was fired for leaving the front desk to make herself a cup of coffee and for not informing her superiors that one of their employees was in possession of two key cards. The woman in Accounting was also fired for not informing her superiors of her two key cards and consequently putting her colleagues in danger. Lucía 1 and Lucía 2's eyes were like saucers when they told me the story. They'd been scared for their lives. In all the years they'd worked at Supersaurio, they'd never seen anything like it. I nodded and said it must've been awful for them. What I didn't say is that the mirrors of fitting rooms in women's clothing and footwear departments have stickers on them with the numbers 016, the domestic violence hotline. I didn't say anything else. I pulled the cover off my pot of yogurt, threw it away, and went back to my desk.

It's Thursday. Matiqui has four back-to-back meetings and Yolanda's too busy to handle all her tasks, so she dumps them on me. I've been waiting around for an MRW delivery guy to bring an envelope containing a series of 'extremely important' documents – these are the exact words Yolanda used while explaining everything to me very slowly and very carefully, so I wouldn't miss a thing – that I am to take to Matiqui. I am also to make sure that Matiqui signs every page of a contract that will arrive in said envelope at some point between his back-to-back meetings, after which I am to look through the contract again and send it back to a man called Gerónimo V. Martínez del Pino Rieni. Every day, my friends do really interesting things with their lives, and I do this.

'Look who it is! The one and only Meryem from Compliance.'

'You know, a few days ago I attended this HR workshop,' I say to Omar as he walks into reception. 'About identifying abuse and harassment in the workplace, and what to do if or when a situation like that arises.'

'You don't say.' He takes a seat to my right. We're both facing the front desk. I glance at him out of the corner of my eye. He's all long legs and straight back. He sighs like he doesn't have an iota of energy left in his body. I smile while mentally going through every item on my to-do list.

'It was fascinating, actually. See, that tone you used just now when you said "Meryem from Compliance," could be construed as toxic or abusive.'

He laughs.

'Abusive? I'm just happy to see you is all. You're mistaking friendliness for bullying. What kind of department is this, anyway? Oh, look, here comes your boss.'

Our new receptionist is on the phone, listing off next week's fruit order: seventy bananas, fifty apples, eight bunches of grapes . . .

'What boss?' I ask, turning to him.

I lift very slightly off my seat so I can see who he means. He gently nods in Yolanda's direction. I frown. Today *my boss* has been immersed in a conversation about who knows what with some other person in the office. This is why she is too busy to deal with the veryimportant envelope containing the superimportant documents that need to be sent to the uberimportant gentleman.

'That woman is not my boss.'

The second time Omar and I talked, we were standing in line at the supermarket cafeteria. I didn't have exact change for lunch, so he jumped in and treated me. We're colleagues, he said. I nodded. Paragon of serenity that I am, I hated every single one of the words that unintentionally left my mouth for the duration of our five-minute conversation and spent the rest of the day beating myself up over them. The next morning, I scanned the massive reporting tree behind the receptionist's desk for his name, found his department, and looked up his office. Quality Assurance – Head. He really was a boss. I decided to avoid him from then on.

I gave him two two-Euro coins, the shiniest ones I had. It was a matter of pride: I hate owing money. Now we're square, I said. I probably managed to offend him in some way, but I don't have time to take into consideration how the men in my life feel. He lent me four Euros because I only had a ten-Euro note. I paid him back. As far as I was concerned, we were even.

Ever since, he's started coming up to me like this, with no *hellos* or *how's it goings*. Just him and his questions, remarks, or observations of the day. If I'm having coffee and he's in the room, he sits next to me. If he's having coffee and I'm in the room, I sit next to him so I won't seem antisocial. Sometimes he makes me laugh. Other times, he makes my head judder like a washing machine. My friend Carmen thinks he probably hates working here too. I disagree, he always seems like he's in his element. I can't bring myself to ask him because what if he tells everyone? I enjoy being drab and uncharismatic at work. It makes me feel safe.

'Well, she doesn't seem to know that.' He extends his arm, puts his fingers to his temple, shapes his hand into a gun, and pretends to shoot. '*Miriam*. You should file a complaint.'

'Torture.'

Convene dozens of people from various backgrounds and force them to spend several hours a day together in a closed environment. Assign each one a role according to their education, age, and experience. Arrange them into a hierarchy. Then lock the door and let the magic happen. The Stanford prison experiment has nothing on what actually happens in a regular office setting. Give any of these people power over the other employees, however inconsequential that power may be, and they will transform into cartoon villains from one day to the next. Their underlings will become the recipients of their frustrations and fears. They will ask twice as much of them as they ask of themselves. They will lash out at them when things don't go their way. They will no longer consider them their equals. Now give an ounce of power to the underlings and let them exert it over the others. Sit back and watch.

Every *Miriam* I get from Yolanda is a reminder of what I mean to her and how she sees me. The newbie, the intruder, the intern. At first I tried my best to convey to her that I had no ambitions in the company, so my presence should not be construed as a threat. In a way, I'm still doing exactly that: I take up the least amount of space possible, vanish the second she walks into a room, avoid her at all costs. No matter how far I retreat into the shadows, she always feels personally attacked by the tiniest, silliest things. She doesn't like the way I dress, the way I talk, the way I work. She flat-out doesn't like *me*.

'What kind of system rewards a person who can't grasp something as simple as a six-letter name?' I mutter under my breath, so low that for a second I'm not sure he can hear me. He laughs through his teeth, then looks me in the eyes for the first time.

'What a piece of work,' he says gleefully, like he thinks I'm really funny. 'I've gotten eighty-nine incident reports since yesterday. How many times do you think I can explain the same procedure for the same problem to the same person?'

'Without screaming?' I hold my chin between my fingers and pretend to think.

'Graciously, of course.'

'Ah, José Luis Rodríguez Zapatero. Best eyebrows in the democratic world.'

This time, he laughs through his nose. He gets up from his seat and comes up to me.

'My department is going out for drinks tonight,' he says. 'I have to be nice to my underlings. Because I'm a boss.'

'A cool boss.'

'Exactly, a very important person in this very important company. I think the other interns will be joining. If you're interested.'

'What other interns?'

'You know, the other interns.'

'What, they don't have names?'

The air thins out. I feel like an idiot.

'The last 91 bus to Puerto Rico leaves at 9:15,' I explain, 'and the last time I missed it I had to take the 01 . . .'

'And that's a bad thing?'

'The 01 to Puerto Rico?' I frown with disgust. 'If you're lucky enough to get to your destination in one piece, then you also get to empty the contents of your stomach the minute you step out the door. It's more than two hours on windy backroads.'

Omar gives a light nod. He's one of those people who smiles with his eyes; it's hard to hold his gaze. All I can do is give side-eye and frown. I can't help it: I'm Canarian.

'Every time you say Puerto Rico, I want to laugh. It doesn't make any sense at all, and at the same time . . . it does.'

15

December 2016

A thought I had one day on my parents' roof terrace in Puerto Rico: Puerto Rico is probably the best place in Spain and in the whole world. The sunniest corner of the island, it's shielded from the trade winds by mountain peaks. Calm waters, calm people, 25° Celsius year round. I'm offering up some hard data so you can see where I'm coming from. Once I was eating ice cream in the park, minding my own business, when a dirtyish-looking man came up to me and yelled HAND IT OVER. I was seven or eight years old and so scared I did exactly as he said. I didn't tell my parents because I was afraid they'd be mad at me for not sticking up for myself. Everyone in my family is charismatic, willful, tough, capable, and disciplined – God knows where I came from. I've been thinking about this man a lot, about whether he liked the ice cream that he stole from me in that old park in Puerto Rico I loved going to even though the swings were shit. I wonder if he's still alive. Puerto Rico toughens you up, either because of the khaltis in djellabas who know exactly who you went to nursery school with (even though you can't remember yourself) and the color of your first bowel movement, or because of all the times you waited for the bus to high school next to a guiri who was puking up his last meal. The reek followed you around all day, you wanted to die. What doesn't kill you makes you stronger or whatever.

A few years ago I broke up with a self-proclaimed sapiosexual. Actually, it would be more accurate to say he quiet-dumped me by wearing me down until I pulled the plug. He was attracted to people's brains, not their looks, which was very convenient since I hate my looks but have complete confidence in my gray matter. His worst flaw was his perfectionism and brutal honesty, he said. He lived with his parents and had lots of opinions about all the mistakes made by 'working-class' people like me. I wasn't radical enough. I had no vision. Sometimes I'd look at him and wonder, *What am I doing with a guy who pronounces chauvinist as chow-vuh-nuhst?* My problem with love is that I always end up with the same look on my face. Always. I cross my arms, tilt my head slightly to the right (I have a problem with my ears, so my balance isn't great) and stare at the person in front of me in silence. My friend Teresa calls it my 'judgy face.' He used to write blog posts, which I'm guessing were read by an audience of one: me. I haven't told anyone about the blogs. It's so cringe. I didn't die or anything when we broke up, but that's because no one dies from love. Or from whatever it is I felt for him. I don't think I've ever been in love; I've just settled. Is that weird? What a jerk, the sapiosexual. I used to proofread his work. I guess being from Puerto Rico means that, too. Not dying, despite everything.

16

December 2016

Sometimes the 91 bus takes a sharp turn at full speed right by that funny little hotel on the old highway near Playa de Balito and for a moment I shut my eyes and lean back so that I can't see where we might end up if the driver gets distracted for even a fraction of a second. It lasts less than the blink of an eye, the distance between Balito and Puerto Rico, but the way the bus snakes along the bluffs clangs inside your body, and it always feels like you're going to end up at the bottom of the ocean while your parents grieve your loss from the clifftops. Flower crowns, the best photo of you in a frame, RIP. 'Somos Costeros' by Los Sabandeños and Los Gofiones playing on the radio. I like Los Sabandeños in a non-ironic way. I can't remember a single street party where one of their songs wasn't play-ing. The first thing I did when I cashed my first paycheck was buy myself a celebratory cake and upgrade to Spotify Premium because I was sick to death of the fucking ads. When you're broke and in the red, everyone thinks they can walk all over you. The tourists love the view: the surf, the craggy, black rocks, the tour boats on the horizon – is that a dolphin? But I hate the idea of falling. It wouldn't be so outrageous to end up there, at the bottom of the ocean. Navigating the island's complicated geography at 50kmh can cause vertigo, especially when there's a pair of cyclist adrenaline junkies up ahead (also tourists). The bus driver drums his fingers on the steering wheel. All it would take for disaster to strike is a little bit more speed, a momentary distraction, a scare.

My hometown is a string of hotels crowding the mountain and winding toward infinity. Palm trees, beaches, 365 days a year of high temperatures in the shade, tourists swanning down the street basically naked. Three Chinese restaurants per resident. Spanish tapas bars that would make celebrity chef Alberto Chicote throw himself out a seventh-story window. More Irish pubs than Irish people. Two minigolf courses on the verge of bankruptcy. Rec centers that were last updated in 2001. A bus station. A post office. A single school. Three supermarkets, two of them express. I guess this must be what they come here for. To lose themselves on a cheap island where they can afford to live like kings, where everything is catered to them despite the adverse effects on full-time residents, where people are willing to plunder nature itself for the tourists' satisfaction. The beaches are receding, the mountains shrinking. We're eternally bent over, hands held out like nice, friendly beggars – do come again and don't forget to throw some coins at our feet. Why would a tourist need a primary care center when there's a Norwegian health clinic across from the bungalow they've rented for a song for both the fall and winter seasons? A Northern European retiree's fantasy is an ordinary person's nightmare.

17

December 2016

I'm standing in the kitchen at home when I notice a hole in the lower part of my T-shirt. I poke at it, suddenly a little embarrassed because I'd been running around work all day, oblivious to it. My internship at Supersaurio is both too short and too long. Every morning I question my self-worth and every afternoon I conclude that I'm totally useless and instantly get the urge to quit. I work from nine in the morning to three in the afternoon, but when I leave, it's always with this weird sense of guilt that dribbles lower and lower down my back every day. As I get my stuff together, my coworkers stare. Some of them say things like 'You're so lucky,' and I smile uncomfortably and reply, 'Yeah,' even though I don't know what luck has to do with it or what they can possibly be talking about other than the fact that I get to leave two hours before they do.

Six hours a day for five days a week equals thirty hours per week. In other words, 120 hours per month for which I receive a compensation of €500. I'm twenty-five years old, and I still live with my parents, I have no savings or anything of value that's *mine* – meaning acquired by me – nor any future plans beyond the next three or four months. With those €500, I can reload my monthly bus pass (€152 for fifty rides), pay my phone bill and Spotify subscription, and treat myself to something nice, like a book (a book!) or a new shirt because the ones I own aren't appropriate for work.

The rest I put away and promise not to touch unless I really, really need it, like when my internship ends and the company sends me packing, as has been the case with every single intern in the Logistics department, one after another. The first intern was totally useless, the second didn't speak English well enough, the third didn't thrive under pressure. They're on their fourth now. Every time I think about the woman who muttered 'You're so lucky,' next to the Céline handbag on her desk, I get cranky and red in the face. €1,988 of calfskin, and I'm the one who's lucky. Me, the intern who commutes three hours a day on public transit because she can't afford to live any nearer. Me, the intern with a hole in her Zara shirt who's been bouncing from meeting to meeting and errand to errand for the past several hours.

'What's wrong?'

My mother stops what she's doing – chopping almonds – and looks at me closely.

'Nothing, I was just thinking . . .' I prop my forearms on the kitchen island and lean forward. 'I don't know. I'm kind of overwhelmed.'

It takes me a second to finish the sentence because I can't remember how to say *overwhelmed*. I'm never fully aware what language I'm thinking in, whether Arabic or Spanish, though I do choose the language depending on the topic of conversation. The more technical and precise I want to be, the more Spanish I use, because as much as a concept may exist in my head in Arabic, words sometimes still fail me.

'Why? What happened?'

She wipes her hands on her apron and looks at me. Some time ago, I realized that one day my parents wouldn't be around to cook my favorite dishes anymore. That the special way they had of preparing food would die with them and I would die from the sadness. I wanted to teach my hypothetical children their recipes so they could taste the food of their grandparents, who cooked the way they did thanks to their parents, my grandparents. From then on, I decided to play closer attention to how they made briouat, chebakia, and rghaif, to write the recipes down in a notebook, but all I can think about today is that I have a hole in my shirt.

'There's this person at work who treats me . . . badly. I don't know. She gives me the silent treatment, excludes me. She avoids my eyes when she talks to me. It's like she goes out of her way to make me feel unwelcome or something. She went on vacation recently and brought back a present for Matiqui, one for Otero, one for Víctor, and she gave them their gifts right in front of me.'

She gestures at me to pass her the honey.

'. . . Okay.'

'I got nothing.'

I will not cry. I will not cry. I watch her carefully pouring honey into a bowl. My mother, like everyone in my family, wears glasses and has bad posture. She's a fantastic cook, the daughter of another fantastic cook, even though when people tell her this she quickly points out that anyone can make good food with a little effort. I disagree with her, but so does she.

'Has it been like this since the beginning? You never mentioned it.'

'"Can we have taktouka for dinner today? By the way, I'm being bullied by a forty-six-year-old woman at work, crazy, huh?" It doesn't exactly roll off the tongue.'

She wipes her hands on her apron again, then looks at me. She's wearing my 'serious face.'

'Is there anything else?'

'She copies my work and passes it off as her own. I mean, I don't really care about the copying, but then she takes the credit, and I don't know how to stand up for myself, how to say it's mine, I'm the one who did the actual work.'

'What do you mean? Come help me with this, please.'

'This' is chebakia. I shuffle to the sink, wash my hands, then stand beside her so I can dunk the fried dough in honey.

'So . . . Yeah. She stole my report and sent it to Matiqui, like she was the one who wrote it.'

It's been on my mind all week. Five days of wondering why I didn't bring it up at the time, why I let myself be pushed around by someone whose only recourse against me is to scowl and act like I'm thin air. I just sat there, stunned, and let her go over my head like a missile because it was all so shameless I couldn't even process it. I watched her steal from me and didn't breathe a word. After I got home that day, I shut myself in my bedroom and screamed into my pillow. When the anger subsided, I burst into tears.

'And you didn't say anything.'

'I mean, what was I supposed to do, Mom? Call her a fucking thief in front of everyone?'

'Language.'

'Sorry.'

If I was in therapy, I'd slump into my analyst's fancy chaise longue and ask them why I always feel the need to act like nothing that happens to me is a big deal. When something hurts, I downplay it so much that the person I'm venting to always winds up laughing at my predicaments, whatever they are. I minimize every success as much as humanly possible, pretend it was sheer luck, a fluke, that I tricked someone, or that I don't deserve it, that it must be a mistake. Some people assume I'm being humble or modest, but I'm not. People who are humble or modest accept the good things that happen to them. I obsess over them, torture myself. I never bask in the glow.

'I don't understand what her problem is,' I continue, placing one ribbon of dough after another on the tray. 'I've done nothing wrong. She's had it in for me since day one. If she walks into the kitchen when I'm there, she doesn't say hello. But if someone else walks in, her personality does a one-eighty. She smiles, says *hi, good morning, how are you*. When she comes down to my floor, she gives everyone two kisses hello except me. It's like I don't exist. I don't even want her stupid kisses, you know? It's just that it doesn't make sense.'

'She kisses everyone hello every day?' My mother frowns, stops, and looks at me. 'How old did you say she is?'

'Forty-six. The woman is forty-six, Mom.'

My lips quiver and I look away. I will not cry. I will not cry over this. But a tear slips out, followed by several more, and even though I wipe them away fast, my mother sees. I'm the eldest of three. I shouldn't be crying over something as small and insignificant as this. My mother wraps her arms around me and hugs me to her body.

'Meryem. While you're crying—' she says under her breath.

'. . . she's happily relaxing at home.'

The image of me crying while Yolanda watches the late night show, *Equipo de investigación*, in her pajamas makes me laugh.

'If you're not going to say anything, then you have to beat her at her own game.' As soon as the last chebakia is done, we'll sprinkle them with sesame seeds. I stare at her hands, at the way she dunks each ribbon.

66

'The game where she's a total hag?'

'No, the game where she believes you're stupid. So she thinks you're an idiot? Let her.'

I lick my fingers. Only then do I remember the hole in my shirt.

'But I'm already doing that. What next?'

I reach for a ribbon, and my mother slaps my hand away, then shakes her head.

'Next . . . One day, when she least expects it, you put her in her place.' My mother raises her eyebrows. 'I'm not so sure they won't keep you on when the internship ends. Just picture the look on her face when she finds out you've been hired.'

I don't get my hopes up, but I spend the next ten minutes picturing Yolanda's disgust.

18

December 2016

Growing up in Gran Canaria means: a little green here, a little green there, but mostly blues, yellows, browns, and rocks – rocks everywhere. Cliffs, mountains, buses. Mountain hotels, beach hotels. Hotels in the vast territory between what constitutes a mountain and what constitutes a beach, a reality shared by every island where tourists are king, where the land is poisoned and prostituted so much that people may actually believe that, in Gran Canaria, hotels grow out of the very earth and need to be sprinkled daily with a mix of salt water and Canarian banana subsidies (€1.69 per kilo).

When you're from Gran Canaria, specifically from the south of Gran Canaria, you become impervious to despair. A feral creature, your native tongue is cynicism. You're very hard to impress because by the age of six, you've already gotten used to seeing grown-ups sleep off their hangovers in pools of their own vomit right next to the bench where you wait for the school bus. Physically, you may be a child, but psychically, you've survived multiple wars. Growing up in Gran Canaria means watching the bus zoom past you and having the world come crashing down because this isn't

Madrid, where there's a metro every five minutes, no, in Gran Canaria, with any luck, there's a bus every hour. The route from Las Palmas (the one in Gran Canaria) to Puerto Rico (the one in Gran Canaria) is seventy-three kilometers one-way and seventy-three kilometers back, and if you work or go to school in the capital you have to take it from Monday to Friday. More than three excruciating hours. While C. Tangana cries in his limo, you cry in the front of the bus on a Sunday afternoon because a woman who reeks of thawing fish has decided that none of the other free seats will do: she simply must sit next to you and only you. Then you remember that you missed the last bus by one miserable minute and get cranky.

That's when it sinks in: being Canarian is more than just a demonym, it's a way of life. A philosophy. We don't get mad. We get stressed. And, above all, we don't judge other people. Even when you're twelve and put in a class with fourteen-year-old juvenile delinquents, or if you're fifteen and three of your classmates are pregnant. You spend the rest of the year living in genuine fear that you're going to hit them accidentally while playing dodgeball because there is nothing more Canarian than playing dodgeball in gym class – it doesn't matter if you're pregnant or an amputee. At fifteen, you just know, it's crystal clear: there's the SOUTH of the island, for tourists, and there's the south of the island, the one you're stuck with. The one of kids flipping their desks, of at least five cop cars parked outside the high school at any given time, of restraining orders, and of the weird guy playing with his dick by the basketball court. Your eyes have met more than once, and every time you've felt something inside you die. But you've survived multiple wars. Nothing can touch you. Nothing can knock you down.

69

Which is why when you miss the bus yet again by less than a minute, you don't fall apart, you don't complain, your expression does not change. You don't bat an eye. You sit on the usual bench, open your bag, and take out a book. Two hours later, when you finally make it home, you bury your head in your pillow and scream.

Fandom: Supersaurio (Las Palmas – District 2)
Characters: Ligia, Patricia, Federico, Kevin
Tags: TW Racism
Category: General
Words: 567

Sorry if I Offended Anyone

Ligia's coworkers had started judging her, and they wouldn't even give her a chance to explain herself. They whispered behind her back whenever she walked into the break room. The label: racist. Okay, so maybe Ligia had let slip: 'Check out Machu Pichu over there,' but it was just a joke. She didn't know who exactly had spilled the beans to the division head, but she'd get to the bottom of it eventually. And then . . .

'I know I shouldn't have said what I did, and I'm sorry if I offended anyone, but it was just a joke. Don't you think it's a bit much to call me racist?'

The problem, in Ligia's view, was that people couldn't say anything anymore. The littlest thing was considered offensive. Ligia had a sense of humor; her coworkers apparently did not. You couldn't make jokes about black people or Chinese people or fags without someone blowing a gasket.

In the front row, Kevin said:

'Saying sorry "if I offended anyone" isn't a real apology, Ligia.'

'Well, fine, then, I'm sorry. I'M SORRY. What do you want me to do, get on my knees?'

'Don't shout. You're always shouting.'

A fist slammed down, ending the conversation. The division head crossed her arms, livid.

'I don't want to hear another peep out of you. I have a million things to do today, but I can't because instead I have to be here, babysitting you. The next person to shout gets fired. This is a workplace, not a nursery.'

Ligia shrugged.

'It was just a comment,' she said.

'Not another word. Sit.'

Ligia frowned so deeply that her face puckered like a raisin. She opened her mouth, closed it, frowned some more, then sat back down on her plastic chair.

'We're going to watch a video sent down from higher up. Once it's over, we can talk. Once it's over, not while it's still playing. Understood?'

The thirteen other people in the room said: 'Yes, Patricia.'

'Good.'

Patricia turned around and switched on the TV mounted to the wall. Onscreen, a white hand and a black hand were clasped together. 'What is racism?' a voice asked. Saurito smiled at them from the foreground, cape billowing in the wind. A scorching-hot sun shone down on his head. 'My fellow Sauruses!' He reached out his tiny hands toward them. 'Today, I want to talk to you about racism.' The video lasted thirty-six minutes. Before saying goodbye, Saurito smiled. 'And remember, my fellow Sauruses! It doesn't matter where any of us are from, but where we're going. Together!'

'Okay, questions?' Patricia looked around at everyone.

Ligia raised her hand.

'Yes, Ligia.'

'Can black people be racist?'

'What? Of course a person who's Black can be racist. Do you need me to play the video again?'

'Why "a person who's black"? Is it racist to say "black people"?'

'I guess it depends how you say it, right?' asked someone in the back.

Patricia put the remote on the table, then turned to face everyone.

'Federico,' she called out, 'could you please share your thoughts on the matter?'

Two rows behind Ligia, Federico stood up. He swallowed.

'Uh, I don't know. I think it depends?'

'But you're black. Shouldn't you know?'

'LIGIA,' Patricia roared. 'That's it. We're watching the video again.'

'No, for the love of God,' someone complained.

'Quiet!' Patricia turned the screen on again.

19

December 2016

On the wall in front of my desk is an A3-sized calendar where I keep Matiqui's monthly schedule. There's a perfect red circle around the date of the company's Christmas dinner party: it's in fifteen days. My main responsibilities are answering the phone, writing down messages, forwarding and replying to emails, taking the minutes for meetings with people from England, France, and Germany (Supersaurio is expanding, Supersaurio is parting the waters of the Atlantic Ocean, Supersaurio is going to conquer the world), scanning documents, and making photocopies. These last two are Yolanda's favorite assignments. Every day, she asks me to make countless photocopies, hundreds of thousands of millions of photocopies that I arrange into stacks and which I've taught myself how to bind thanks to a YouTube tutorial from some Colombian guy. I owe the man my life. I hope God repays him in mountains of cash. With a pair of pliers, I cut and bend the wire for these books, both big and little, then hand them over to Yolanda as if I were placing my firstborn on an altar for her consumption. I get so bored making them that I daydream someone saddles me with their coffee-and-donut run, already losing my mind, desperate for an excuse to get out of that building, even if just for five minutes. I don't know what it says about corporate culture that our entire staff would rather drink coffee from the café across the street than from the company's own cafeteria.

Standing in the corner of the office with the photocopier and scanner, I conclude that I'm invisible. No one teaches me anything because everyone's too busy with their own work, so I fumble through on my own. But being invisible is only a punishment if you're stupid.

The excuse I plan on using to get out of the Christmas party is that I need to study. I've calculated the exact amount of advance warning I need to provide so no one gets upset. I even tried out my excuse on Otero, who swallowed it whole, though that's not saying much: if there's one thing Otero likes to do it's swallow. Swallow and give out unsolicited advice because, man, we're just doing everything wrong. Do you have any savings? Right, so, think about it. Time flies. You're not getting any younger, Meryem. No boyfriend? Well, I guess you could always be a single mom; things are different these days. The 2016 Christmas dinner isn't exactly a dinner so much as an informal cocktail hour. This clarification does not appear on the e-vite, but I find out anyway. When you're at the very bottom of the corporate ladder, people have a habit of behaving like you're not standing right next to them, poring over every word they say. In my time as Junior Document Manager – a title I give myself on days I'm feeling especially clever – I've heard all kinds of things coming out of all kinds of mouths, and I've taken note; I keep their remarks in mind and teach myself to never, under any circumstance, lower my guard, not for anyone.

When curiosity gets the better of me, I ask Omar:

'Why's everyone so mad about the Christmas party?'

He's wearing a plain white shirt, which is unusual for him, but I don't have time to get to the bottom of this deviation. If I had to define his style, it would be: votes for the liberal Citizens party and has a soft spot for bullfighting and the casual bump of cocaine. He's an attractive guy; it looks good on him.

'Mad how?'

'Like upset. I don't know. Mad.'

He shrugs and pulls on his cigarette. I hate tobacco – the smell, the smoke, the way it feels in my throat. I pretend not to watch him. Not because it annoys me but because I find it sexy, which makes me want to stick my head in a toilet bowl and flush until I come to my senses.

'I guess because they weren't invited or something,' he replies, and I still don't understand because we all got the e-vite, even the interns.

'But everyone got the same e-vite.'

There is a short pause while he half closes his eyes.

'What did you say?'

'What?' I ask. I don't know what's gotten into him.

I watch him push up his glasses and recognize the same nervous tic I have when I'm anxious and don't know how to hide it.

'I don't think we're talking about the same thing,' he sighs.

No shit, Sherlock.

'No shit, Sherlock. What are *you* talking about?'

Omar tells me that every now and then, some of the employees on the important floors (floors seven and eight) make plans to go to the movies together or get a drink, casual stuff. How stupid, I think. The best thing about being invisible, it occurs to me later, is that no one gets in your face about going out and doing things. 'Sorry,' he adds at the end, seeing as I belong to the group of people who are never invited, 'I'm not the one planning these hangouts . . . I feel bad, though. If it was up to me, I wouldn't go anywhere. I'd rather be home watching the cooking channel.' I don't laugh right then, but I do after, on my way downstairs.

Hours later, on Skype, he sends me a link to a shared folder all employees have access to. 'Check out CHRISTMAS PARTY 2015,' he writes. I discreetly turn my monitor to the side so that no one can see what I'm doing, though there's no point, really, given that I've got my back to the whole office and my screen is visible to anyone who walks past me. The first thought I have is: *Lookatthem!* and the second: *This can't be real.* Five hundred photos of last year's Christmas party. I soak up every detail – the tuxedos and dresses, the glitz and sparkle, the shoes, balloons and photocall – then close each file and leave everything as it was. It takes me days to process the information. From then on, whenever I see Nieves, the most widely hated person in the company, I can't help thinking: *The woman has a coat made out of some poor animal's fur, and she goes and pairs it with white satin elbow-length gloves and a mauve velvet floor-length dress.* I fear her. I respect her.

So it turns out that the reason my coworkers are mad about Christmas this year is that this time they're only getting a small, informal gathering. Compared to previous years, the Christmas hamper leaves a lot to be desired. The people want a good time, I hear. A cocktail party isn't the same as dinner, some employees point out. The dress code is business casual and for days I kill myself trying to work out what the organizers mean by that, because there's business casual per my Google results, and there's business casual per these people. My mind jumps to Nieves and her fur coat.

Meanwhile, during the fifteen-day run-up to the party, I try out various excuses I'd like to use on Matiqui. Eventually, I land on the most convincing one: I have to study for an exam. I say it in my head over and over and, as soon as I feel like I'm ready to lie without flinching, I head to his office. I practice my speech in the elevator mirror. Matiqui, who sees me and always remembers my name, floors me with a gunshot to the chest when he says, 'If you like, we can go to the cocktail party together tomorrow. How does that sound?' before I even get a chance to open my mouth. He starts with 'you're going to love it,' then switches to first gear, second, and finally third gear: 'Plus, it'll help you settle in!' I start morphing into a little field mouse, then attend the Christmas cocktail party in business casual: a new pair of jeans that I iron at home while feeling like an idiot, a white cotton shirt, and a fuchsia blazer, in honor of Nieves. I do my makeup in the office bathroom and then, as soon as I'm at the party, I settle in, because that's what I'm here to do, even though Matiqui is traveling – as usual – and can't make it, and even though most of the people at the party look like they want to be there as much as I do. The only difference is that those people loosen up after three or four drinks, and I don't drink.

About thirty minutes in, there's a little surprise: someone hired a band. The booze flows, the guests let loose, the band starts playing Maná's 'Clavado en un bar,' 'for the Romeos out there.' My colleagues' laughter envelops me, colorful lights dance over my head, and as I nibble on a square of red-pepper cheese, I experience a moment of weakness: I betray myself by relaxing. Leaning against the back wall, I think about how things could be a lot worse, I could've wound up at a toxic company where I'm terribly mistreated. Maybe I've been lucky. I should relax and revel

78

in the opportunity. At least they pay me, below minimum wage, sure, but it's enough to set some money aside. Maybe I've had a bad run these past few months. Maybe I haven't really known how to focus properly, how to put things in perspective and attach the right amount of importance (close to none) to the 'negative' side of things.

My soul shrivels, and I feel something akin to Peace only then I hear Marcial from Accounting tell his coworker Esteban, 'Let's get a photo with the interns.' Peace hardens into a pit in my stomach, which takes me to the Light, and I knock back the rest of my tonic. I stand there for a moment, suspended. Two things are happening to me right now: the first is that I'm looking at Marcial and Esteban and thinking that if there is a time when someone like me should take a stand and say something, that time is now; the second thing is that I want to go home and never see anyone ever again.

Not only do I keep quiet, but I also walk to the place where I've hung my jacket and purse and head downstairs without saying goodbye to anyone. Then I make a bee-line for the exit because if I stick around a minute longer I'm going to do something stupid like scream at Esteban that he is a vile, heinous pig. Except Omar and his light-colored eyes and broad back are smoking outside, and at the sight of me running away at full throttle, he asks, 'what's wrong?' and I bark back 'NOTHING' so loudly that I immediately regret it, retrace my steps until I'm standing beside him and say, 'Sorry,' then leave with no further explanation. Days later, Human Resources informs us that photos from the Christmas cocktail party have been uploaded to a folder called CHRISTMAS PARTY – 2016. I keep the picture of Marcial, Esteban, and the interns open on my computer for a whole twenty minutes.

20

February 2017

It's a short call. *Miriam,* she says, *can you come up a minute? Thanks.* Then she hangs up. I'm clenching the phone so tightly that my hand seizes up, and I need to open and close it several times before it goes back to its normal color. No, I can't come up a minute because I'm staring at a recurring nightmare of a spreadsheet while waiting to develop those advanced Excel skills that I claimed to already have during my interview. As if a piano had just landed on my head, I get up from my seat and drag myself to the bathroom. *Relax,* I think. *It's nothing,* I think. *She's probably just bored and wants to torture you a little.* Nothing new under the sun. At least once a week I take part in this ritual where even though I know I'm going to be sacrificed like a sheep on Eid, I march toward my fate like a moron. I've come to learn that there's no better strategy in the world than playing dumb. Not squirming or making a fuss but absorbing the blow as best you can and keeping it in a special compartment until the day it finally becomes too much. I wash my face, give myself a once-over in the mirror, and whisper, *It's nothing, it isn't anything, everything's going to be okay.*

80

'Finally,' she mutters when she sees me knocking on her door. She has a glass office. Zero privacy for her or anyone else.

I swallow the first comeback that pops into my head and wait at the door.

'Aren't you coming in?'

'You didn't tell me to.'

I would bet my life that deep inside, Yolanda is screaming about what a complete twat I am.

'*Come in*. Please.'

I feel like I have extra arms, hands, tiptoes. I wish I could vanish into thin air. That I could say: 'I'm done.' Or: 'Whatever, godo hediondo, you stupid mainlander.' Most of the people I work with aren't from the Canary Islands. Don't think about it too hard or your head will do a tumble turn. Are there no qualified candidates here or what? Whenever I think of quitting I picture myself looking not annihilated, destroyed, or desperate, but triumphant. I'm twenty-five years old. This can't be the end, only the beginning. Which is why I lace my fingers together and look at her expectantly. We stay like that for a while. I'm playing this new game with her: the first one to blink dies.

'What have you done to the shared folder? I can't find anything. Why did you move things around?'

Yolanda's office is a mosaic of all the stuff other people have decided they don't want anymore. There are folders dating to 2011, boxes sitting atop other boxes, massive ring binders with overstuffed plastic pockets. Her place is covered in sheets of paper. The two chairs on the other side of her desk are taken up by handbags, binders, a coat. My nerves have reached breaking point. I think of how awful it must be to give so much of yourself only to wind up like this.

81

'I had to reorganize the files because it was impossible to find anything. There's no software, no plans to buy one . . . so this was the only solution.' She's summoned me upstairs to tell her something she already knows.

'When exactly did I okay this? I've spent the last twenty minutes trying to find a receipt. We used to have a folder for receipts and now it's gone.'

My first weeks here, I devoted several days to unstapling and restapling three kilos of documents that Yolanda had misprinted. I stand there, stunned, opening and closing my mouth. The look on her face is like stainless steel.

'We used to have *one* receipts folder for *three* different companies. Now you just have to search by company.'

'Well, I don't know how you designed this, but you're going to have to change it back because I can't find anything.'

'I'd be more than happy to change it to whatever you feel is more convenient, if the system we have now isn't working for you. But you'll have to take it up with Matiqui first. He's the one who told me to do it this way.'

We both know Matiqui won't change a thing.

'I can't believe other people are okay with this. The system should cater to the needs of its users, not to something you learned how to do three days ago.'

'Right, except it's not something I learned three days ago. It's what Matiqui wants us to do from now on.'

'Are you sure he told you to do things this way? I can call him and double-check.'

My stomach is in knots, but I still smile.

'Go right ahead. Call him now, if you want. Listen, I don't know what I've done to upset you, but you clearly don't respect me enough to look at me when we're talking. Whatever it is, it feels personal.' I'm so tense, it feels like something inside me could give at any moment, carving me open right in front of her, like a canal. 'I'm fine with you not liking me, but I'm supposed to be learning from you. Do you have any specific criticisms about my work? I'm not really sure how to move forward.'

I know I've stumped her because she says nothing and instead gazes at me in silence, like she's only just realized I exist. Then she takes a deep breath, pushes her seat away from the desk, and clasps her hands together. Her voice quivers as she speaks. If she cries, I vow to throw myself belly-first off the roof.

'I don't not like you.'

'Okay.'

'And I don't have any problems with you either,' she adds, eyes boring into mine. What is poetry, you ask? Poetry is seeing a woman twenty years your senior back up with her emergency lights on because you've just blindsided her. And you did it without screaming. Without losing control. Without crying. 'But I would like you to check with me before you make any more changes,' she continues. 'Someone needs to know what you've done to the system after you leave.'

What part of 'Matiqui told me to do it this way' does she not understand?

'I'll be sure to write up a handbook with everything I've been doing to the system and to inform Matiqui about it as well. Did you find the receipt you were looking for or do you still need my help?'

IhateherIhateherIhateher.

2 1

March 2017

'You have the best thinking face.'

I lift my chin toward the sun and shut my eyes. It makes my skin tingle.

'Wait until you see my hate face,' I say. 'You're going to love that one.'

Omar had messaged me on Skype: 'Heading up for a smoke.' Since I didn't have anything better to do, I went with him. We're peering out at these platforms in the ocean, on the other side of Avenida Marítima, arms propped on the railing around the roof. The roof, around twenty square meters where you can cry in private in case there's already someone crying in the bathroom.

'What's it like?'

'My hate face?' I pull a blank expression. 'Like this.'

He laughs and shakes his head.

'You're something else. What are you thinking about anyway?'

How tired I am, I want to say. Yesterday I got in at eight in the morning and left at eight thirty at night, and I know it's not the norm, that this almost never happens, but just knowing that I'm expected to sit in my cubicle for twelve hours *sometimes* makes me want to scream until someone calls an ambulance. I got five hours of sleep last night. This is my third coffee. A vein in my temple has been throbbing since I read my first email this morning. But I don't tell him that. Omar likes to behave like he's not a boss but just another cog in a wheel that spins and spins before running me over. Sometimes I forget his title, but most of the time I don't. I wonder if he actually enjoys my company or if one day he's going to tell Matiqui about some of the stuff I've said to him, like 'it's a gross, insanely fucked-up, broken system, brother,' or my epic eye rolls. I'd like to ask him: How can you be part of something you claim to hate?

'I'm thinking about how much I want to be rich.'

It's not true, but it's also not a lie. When I'm at my lowest, I come up here with my coffee and a banana, lean over the wall around the square of concrete that is our only escape from the building, and daydream about all the things I'd do if I had money. Real money, in fifty, one-hundred, two-hundred bills, not the 'welfare' I make at Supersaurio. Money isn't everything, but boy would it be a relief. A massive relief. I keep this to myself because as a kid I was taught it isn't polite to talk about money: we aren't supposed to ask for it, confess to wanting more of it, and most of all, show how important it is to us. We poor people are above it. Being a woman and having ambitions are two of the worst things that have ever happened to me. So, yeah, I wish I could tell Omar that I'm thinking about money, only without having to justify myself afterwards or risk seeming too practical or superficial. There are lots of different ways of succeeding, and for me one of them involves reams of cash.

85

'What would you do? If you had money.'

I watch him tap ash into the air. It falls, falls, falls for a moment that drags on and on until it touches the ground below us. I want to tell him to stop, that the ash could fall on someone's head, but then we'd get into a dumb argument about why these things matter so much to me and so little to him. The last time a similar topic came up, we both got so upset we spent the next few days avoiding each other. I know I shouldn't be keeping track of how long we didn't talk, but I do it anyway.

'I wouldn't be here, to start.'

If I had money, I wouldn't be working somewhere that leaves me feeling cold, frustrated and hopeless. I wouldn't be working at these offices. In purgatory. I'd like to atone for all the sins I commit inside these four walls so that one day I can walk out of here, clean and purged of all evil, ready for a *real* job. He smiles and takes another drag. He never asks or excuses himself with a *Mind if I . . .?* Or a *Is it okay if I . . .?* Those kinds of questions give the other person the opportunity to say 'yes, I do mind actually' and Omar comes up to the roof to smoke. That's what he said to me last time I mustered the courage to say something about it. Five foot nine of blunt honesty that came as a breath of fresh air in a workplace where the lingua franca is passive aggression.

'Well, at least you have a job.' He doesn't look at me, but the corner of his mouth quivers. I finish eating my banana.

'Yeah.' I chew quickly because I find it embarrassing to eat in front of him. 'Things could be worse. I could write op-eds for a living.'

'This morning I was reading something by that guy you can't stand. What's his name again?'

I roll my eyes.

'Don't send it to me. I get so mad I spend the rest of the day replying to him in my head, then I sit on the bus wondering why I let this stuff get to me when that's exactly what they want, they want us to get riled up and click on their stupid articles. It's a gross, fucked-up world we live in.'

'I'll ping it to you on Skype when I'm back at my desk.'

'Man, you know you're not a great person, right? Like, you're pretty awful. I'm not sure what Lucía 1 and Lucía 2 see in you. I bet they have no idea what a huge pain in the ass you can be.'

He finishes his cigarette, eyes glued on me.

'And calling your colleagues Lucía 1 and Lucía 2 is . . .'

His laughter is infectious, I hate him.

'How do you do it? It's like you're two different people,' I say cheerfully. 'In the office you're . . . like them. Outside you're, I don't know, normal. Which one is the real you?'

He puts his hand on my head and knocks twice, the same as my dad.

'When you're my age,' he begins.

'Thirty-seven.'

'Thirty-six.'

'Okay, sorry. Thirty-six.'

He clears his throat.

'Let's just say you have to play along because this is the only game there is. Everyone is playing this one. Sure, you could make up your own game, your own rules, but that takes a lot of work, a lot of sacrifice. And at the end of the day, you may find you've lost a lot more than you've gained, that it's all been for nothing.'

'Your serious voice is scary.'

'No more than that sweet, little voice you put on when you answer the phone. The fact is, you're not stupid, so you're obviously going to play the game. Your grandparents played it. And your parents. Everyone plays it. You're not special. Most people aren't. I play to win, or at least I try. But I know it's a fucking game. It's not forever. If I have to pretend for a little while . . . so be it.'

He looks down at my hands. I'm so sad that every bone in my body hurts.

'But I hate the game,' I say. 'It blows. When you win a round, you don't get to go on to the next level. You're stuck on the same one, playing the same round every day. Every fucking day! I feel like I'm being forced to do this, you know, like someone shakes me awake every morning and sits me down in front of my computer screen, and ties me to my seat, and I have to play the game because I don't have a choice, because not playing, not playing is . . . death.'

I unclench my fists, then clench them again.

'Listen. Matiqui isn't a moron. Hang in there. They're going to hire you full-time.'

'Pffft. If they do, Yolanda will have a meltdown.'

He elbows me gently.

'And don't you want to watch her blow up, in real time? Just give me some warning first. She's been getting on my nerves as well. Anyway, listen to what I say. I'm older than you.'

Yawn.

'What do you know, suck-up?'

22

May 2017

It's the first day of Ramadan, and I'm in the sixth-floor kitchen when Matiqui catches me on the verge of drinking some water. He looks at me in silence. I look at him looking at me. We open our mouths at the same time, then close them. He touches his tie, smooths it. If he could see his face right now, he'd crack up. Needless to say, I don't laugh.

'I saw nothing,' he says.

'I'm on my period,' I announce, like I'm talking about the weather: *It's baking today.*

'You're on your period?'

I point my thumb at myself, a real melting pot of cultures.

'That's why I'm not fasting.'

'I see.'

I close the bottle of water and look at him.

'I've tried to educate myself.' He pads up to me slowly, like a cat, as if he's frightened of me for some reason. 'Ramadan Mubraka? No . . . Karmi?'

'Kareem.'

Like Karim Benzema, one of the great loves of my life.

'That's right!' His whole face lights up with pride. I may faint today. 'Ramadan Mubraka Kareem.'

'No, no.' I shake my head. 'There are two ways of wishing someone a happy Ramadan . . . You either say Ramadan Mubarak, or you say Ramadan Kareem.'

'Right, okay, I think I get it. Is it like . . . Mmm. Merry Christmas or happy holidays?'

No.

'Yeah, something like that.'

'Fantastic. Well, feel free to eat and drink as much as you like. We'll all look the other way.' He starts turning toward the coffee machine. He's almost all the way round when he remembers something, and turns to face me again. 'By the way, is there anything I can do for you this month?'

'For me?'

'Yes, you. Does anything spring to mind? Whatever it is, all you have to do is ask. If it's in my hands, I'll make it happen.'

'Uh . . .'

We look at each other. I have his attention. My neck, elbows, and scalp begin to tingle.

'Well . . . I mean, I don't know if this is possible at all . . . But . . . Okay, since I'm not taking my lunch break, I was wondering if I could . . . leave early?'

'You mean, you want to take your lunch break later and leave at three instead?'

'At two.' My ears are buzzing from my own nerve. But he offered. He looked me in the eyes and said: *Whatever it is, all you have to do is ask. If it's in my hands, I'll make it happen.* 'I start at eight . . .'

'Oh, right, I forgot. Absolutely, no problem.'

'Yes?'

'Of course.'

'Really?'

He laughs.

'Really.'

That was easy, I think. I could get used to this. All of a sudden, I find myself believing in the basic goodness of humankind.

'Thank you so much.'

'You're welcome. It's no bother. At all.'

I decide not to harbor any negative feelings about him, ever again. I hang in there for another four hours.

23

June 2017

The days begin to unravel, the ends of some mixing with the beginnings of others. One morning it's Monday. Next it's Thursday, and I have no idea how I got there. Routine grabs me by the shoulders and pushes me from one place to another, like a machine. My day-to-day turns into a series of near-identical events that stretch out in front of me while also slowly clamping around my neck: I switch my alarm off at the same time every morning, eat breakfast while staring blankly at the same spot on the dining-room wall, walk from my house to the bus station, climb on the bus, do the usual seventy-five-minute commute to the office, spend six hours sorting through paperwork that Yolanda reliably drops on my desk without giving me so much as a glance, scan the documents, shred them while staring blankly at the machine that swallows any sheet of paper I feed it, get my stuff together at the end of the day, walk from the office to the bus station, climb on the bus, and do the usual eighty-minute commute home, where I hang out for the rest of the day. A few hours later, the alarm goes off and the whole thing starts all over again.

On Fridays I'm so tired I spend the weekend in a state of inertia that I can't seem to shake off. I still do the things I used to when I was happy: I go for runs, hang out with friends, read, spend time with family, write, mess around on the internet, buy dumb shit I don't need that makes me feel warm and fuzzy inside, binge-watch Netflix with zero chill. The exhaustion isn't visible, and I have no proof of it beyond my own first-person testimony, but when Sunday comes around, I feel the sky darken and the whole universe sink its claws into my flesh. Just one more week, I tell myself as I lie in bed, and I don't know if they're words of encouragement or mourning.

Days turn into weeks. I stare blankly at the ceiling night after night without complaining because, to be fair, there are a lot worse things than realizing you have no clue what you're doing or want to do with your time, with the weeks, the years your college professors promised would be the best in your life and that fly past while you stare ahead with a dumb, ridiculous look on your face, too chicken to do anything.

'Meryem.'

My boss's office is on the building's eighth and final floor, the executive floor. I've only been three times. You could hear a pin drop in there. It's like they're all ghosts. I stare at him for a second, unsure what to say. We communicate a lot by phone and email, but we hardly ever see one another in person.

'Hi.'

'Hi. How are you?'

We lock eyes; he's relaxed, I'm surprised. A stress bomb explodes in my stomach, and I open and close my hands, suddenly very nervous. An alarm is quietly going off in the back of my head. I think: *That's it*. I think: *He's firing me*.

I think: *I must have done something really bad for him to feel his only choice is to kick me to the curb one week before my internship ends.* I run through everything I've done in the last few days and smile faintly.

'I'm alright, and you?'

Besides Matiqui's, there are three more pairs of eyes glued on me. I'm not good with attention. I swallow, and uncertainty honeycombs my insides. If I have to stand up, I'm going to faint.

'Great. I was hoping to talk to you today. Could you follow me to my office?'

'Sure.'

I'm going to puke. In a momentary lapse of sanity, I turn off my computer screen after locking it, then turn it on and off again. My lips are still curled into a perfect smile, and my face muscles are fully detached from my internal panic. I think about that thing Isabel Pantoja said once: *Teeth, teeth, that's what really bothers them.* I almost laugh at my own wisecrack because my brain is a moron, a jackass that's constantly betraying me when I need it the most, but then I stop myself by discreetly pinching my thigh as I get up from my desk. THINK, I tell myself. THINK. WHAT HAVE YOU DONE? My palms are tingly. What's the worst that can happen? That he tells me to pack my things and get out? He'd be doing me a favor. If he fires me, then at least it'll be easier to feel sorry for myself. I can say I never gave up; I was let go.

'Is it always this loud in here?' he asks. I nod, too scared to open my mouth in case something really stupid flies out of it. 'And you don't have trouble concentrating?'

I start walking beside him and shrug, since I can't think of an answer. Yes, I do have trouble concentrating, actually, but you get used to it. You have to make the most

94

of what you're given. Wear ear plugs or headphones and read whatever it is you have to read, write reports, make phone calls, and block out the noise, pretend it doesn't bother you. I decide that if he asks me another question, I will throw up on his shoes. We leave the offices and walk down a hall to the elevator. I rack my brain for something to say because I don't know what to do with my arms or feet or eyes. I try not to look at his face, but then I do, and I see him watching me like he's waiting for something.

'Do you like coffee?'

'Coffee? Like, just coffee?' Huh? 'Oh, totally,' I course-correct. All my stomach muscles contract. I am definitely going to throw up, I can feel it in my throat. The nerves are about to yank me down and fold me in half. 'So much.'

Oh, totally. So much. Who says that? What a moron.

'In that case, why don't we go downstairs and chat about this over coffee?'

About *this*?

'Sure, why not?'

I hear myself speak and think about how childish I sound, how thick my accent is. My chest falls. We get in the elevator, and I check myself out in the mirror. A fucking lunatic, that's what I look like. We both smile when our eyes meet, and I try to breathe. I press 0 and clasp my hands in front of my body.

'I'm sorry I ambushed you like that. I don't like speaking on the phone . . . I find it a little impersonal.'

'I understand. It's totally fine.'

'Is this when you usually go down for breakfast?'

Just fire me already, I beg you.

'A little earlier, actually. I have a snack around ten. But since I take the bus, I eat breakfast at like six thirty.'

The elevator stops.

95

'That early? Where do you live, Vecindario?'

'No, Puerto Rico.'

'Puerto Rico?'

His surprise is humiliating. His tone makes my neck burn. The way he says 'Puerto Rico' like it's the last place he'd ever want to live. We walk out of the elevator, and I walk a little behind him out of embarrassment.

'I thought you lived closer. Have you considered moving?'

'To Las Palmas? Sure, but . . .'

We pass the security guard and head outside. It dawns on me that he has no idea how much I make as an intern, that this might be the fourth time we've spoken since I started here, and that our entire relationship revolves around work emails. I know nothing about who Matiqui really is. The man could be anyone. For all I know, he could have three dismembered bodies stored in his fridge, and I could be walking straight to my death, which I'd meet with sweaty palms and acid reflux because I've just realized I don't want to get fired.

'I can't afford to, not with what I make as an intern,' I say, now fully red.

'Right, that's what I wanted to talk to you about. Now that the audit's behind us, I've finally had a moment to look over what you've been up to these past few months.'

'Uh-huh.'

Here it comes.

'And I was thinking . . . I've reviewed your annual trans-action reports and litigation summaries. I also had a look at the documents library and file system you created . . . I know you have other plans and that you're still in school, but I'd like us to wrap up this internship.'

It's going to slip out. If I open my mouth, it's going to slip out.

'Am I fired?'

'What? No.'

Time drags on and on and on, moving so slowly I could cup this moment in my hands and squish it.

'I'm offering you a job.'

'Me? Why? I don't know how to do anything.'

The sun hits me in full as we stand outside the supermarket, and I squint. I can't see the catch, but I'm sure there is one. There must be. None of the other interns were hired, not the ones who were around longer than me, and not the ones who started after. Some were let go before the end of their internships. Others bought their own farewell cake, then went home at the end of their last day. Without cake. He laughs wholeheartedly, mouth open, a perfect chuckle.

'What are you talking about? You're a self-starter, methodical, very organized. You hit targets. I need someone who *does* things, not someone who just talks about doing them. I also need help staying organized. I'm never here, and I have too much on my plate. I want you to be my assistant.'

'Like . . . your personal assistant?'

What about Yolanda?

'*Like* the department assistant but also *my* assistant, in particular, yes.'

I swallow.

'So? You don't seem . . . happy?'

So? So. What's the salary? When does the contract start? Is it probationary, service, permanent? Would it be through the temp agency? Is the salary over minimum wage? How much? Will I get PTO? Health insurance?

'Yes, of course. This is great. Sorry. It's just that the sun is in my face, and I'm getting blinded. I'm really, really happy. Thank you.'

When I get home, I run upstairs to my bedroom and look at myself in the mirror by my desk. I'm not just an ordinary person anymore. I'm a person with a steady job. A worker. I smile, slowly, as I settle into this new reality, my new identity. As soon as the change sinks in, I fist pump and shout *inyourfaceinyourfaceinyourfaaaaaaace*. Not for one second do I stop picturing Yolanda's expression.

PART TWO

temp.meryem.elmehdati@supersaurio.com

Fandom: Supersaurio (Las Palmas – District 2)
Characters: Yolanda, Irene, Ligia, Meryem
Tags: TW Mobbing
Category: General
Words: 358

Glory Days

Before joining Supersaurio, Yolanda had worked as a realtor at Remax Carvajal for five years. She'd closed on properties in Ciudad Jardín, Tafira Baja, Santa Brígida, and Maspalomas, glory days when she'd drunk the nectar of professional success. She was bored to death at work now. Every day was the same, and she barely had anything to do. Yolanda had been at Supersaurio for fifteen years. She'd witnessed retail campaigns for Christmas, Carnival, Easter, Day of the Canary Islands, back-to-school, Halloween, Black Friday, then Christmas again. And yet time seemed to stand still.

A loud clatter snapped her out of her thoughts. Irene, Matiqui's daughter, turned toward her, face contorted by the shock of what she'd just done.

'I'm so sorry.'

'. . . Irene . . .'

Yolanda had only looked away one second. But that was Matiqui's daughter for you: curious, hyperactive, incapable of sitting still. In other words: insufferable. Yolanda had work to do. She shouldn't be babysitting a kid. That was a job for the intern, but for some reason Ferrán had called her instead. 'I need a favor,' he'd said, and who was Yolanda to turn him down? Now there she was, surrounded by cans of strawberry Clipper Zero. Dozens upon dozens of soda cans that had been stacked in a perfect pyramid were now strewn at her feet.

'I'm so sorry,' the girl said again. 'Please don't tell my daddy.'

'Don't worry.'

'Please.'

'Ligia!' Yolanda called to a woman at the end of the aisle. Yolanda was sure she'd heard her. 'Ligia!'

'You won't tell my daddy, will you?'

'No!' she snapped. Then she saw the look on the little girl's face and cleared her throat. 'No, don't worry. It was an accident.'

But Irene was already crying. Her eyes were glazed. Yolanda unlocked her phone, looked up the intern's number, and called her, annoyed.

'Good morning, Yolanda.'

'I'm on the second floor, in the soda aisle. Come down right now.'

'Bu—'

Before the intern could finish, Yolanda hung up and turned her attention to Irene.

'Don't cry, Irene. It was an accident. It's alright. Someone will clean it up. LIGIA!'

24

June 2017

Today's look: short-sleeved cotton dress with lapel collar and knot belt in the same material front buttons black flats clean hair (finally) light makeup so no one realizes I'm wearing makeup because I'm all natural and couldn't care less about my appearance. I just rolled out of bed looking like this and came straight here.

'Sorry, Maryem. Be with you in a second.'

I look at my hands. The three most hostile places on earth are, in the following order: an ER room where you wait hours to be seen by a doctor who will think, *This is what you came here for?*, a bank, and a temp agency. Years ago, my mom took me to the ER because I wasn't feeling well and had really bad cramps. I got my period in the hospital bathroom and nearly passed out in my seat while waiting for my name to be called. Nothing unusual here, said the nurse who eventually saw me. You shouldn't come to the ER over a little blood. I think of that nurse every now and then. I wish her the best.

Isabel, the woman I'm meeting at RANDSTAD agency, smells of vanilla and an unidentifiable citrus. The scent is so strong that I don't smile when she speaks; I just purse my lips and nod. I want to be flayed alive or lose my sense of smell, whatever comes first. After a while of me feeling like I'm on the brink of anaphylactic shock, Isabel turns to face me.

'So sorry, Meryam. Be with you in a minute. Please take a seat.'

Location: a cheap plastic IKEA chair on the other side of her desk. There are seventeen people talking on the phone and banging on their keyboards, all squeezed into cubicles scattered across the office. If I wasn't so addled from the nausea, I'd be laughing through my teeth like a lunatic. Who temps at temp agencies? Other temp workers, of course. I'd bet my life that RANDSTAD has all their employees on service contracts. Charming, isn't it? I think so. Lately, the only thing I find charming is under-the-table work (what table?). I used to think there were three types of people: salaried workers, op-ed writers, and the unemployed. Now I think there are four types: people on permanent contracts, temp workers, op-ed writers, and the unemployed.

'Maryam. Such a pretty name. Where's it from?'

A corner of my lip curls up.

'It's Meryem.'

'Excuse me?'

'Meryem. With an E.'

'Maryem?'

I slip my hand under my dress and sink all my right fingers into my right thigh. The dress is new. I bought it for this garbage. I'm a whole new person, a person with a real job. I have to look the part. This can't possibly be her natural odor. I feel like someone's shoving a bottle of Supersaurio-branded vanilla essence down my throat just to film my reaction.

'Me-ry-em. With an E, two Es.'

'Oh, sorry. I've never heard that name before.'

'No worries.'

'Well, it's a very pretty name,' she says again. She grabs a stack of papers, places it in front of her, and smiles. 'Where did you say it's from?'

When I woke up this morning, I had the audacity to tell myself I would have a good day.

'It's Italian,' I say, without blinking.

'Italian! Does it mean anything?'

'Love, life, and levity.'

She must know I'm messing with her. Her face lights up.

'Beautiful. I love it!'

In Imran 3:30, God says: *On the Day when every soul will be confronted with all the good it has done, and all the evil it has done, it will wish there were a great distance between it and its evil.* There are two angels with me at all times. I can't see them, but I know they're there. One tracks all the bad things I do while the other tracks the good things. When I fall asleep, the book closes. Some nights, I have insomnia because I'm convinced I will die in my sleep. What a horrible way to go. God doesn't punish people for their thoughts but for their deeds. One good deed translates into several good deeds, while one evil deed is only ever equal to one. I get sidetracked, I'm somewhere else, not in this cheap plastic IKEA chair. Lying, even a little white lie, is a sin, but it only counts as one evil deed. My mind drifts. I watch Alicia or Miranda, or whatever she's called – I don't care – move her lips. If I walk outside after this is over and give the first panhandler I see five Euros, I'll be awarded several good deeds (I'm not sure exactly how many, I'm not an expert or an imam). One of those good deeds will cancel out my evil deed. At least that's how I see it. If I were to die after leaving here – mowed down by a bus or a truck or a stupid fucking electric scooter as I'm crossing the street – and have to answer to God, then I'd say that, as I understand it, lying is allowed when a life is at stake and that, right now, my life is at stake: no matter where I go or what I do I always wind up having to explain who I am, where I'm from, and where exactly my mother gave birth to me. And no matter how I respond, there's always a follow-up question. Then another and another and another. Maybe this is my own personal jihad, the torture I must face on Earth so my soul will be cleansed, the battle I must wage until I am righteous enough to access Paradise, I don't know. I'm empty inside, Isabel, I'd like to say to her. Because of people like you, I am hollow, dead, a mouthless emoji, a perfect circle with two eyes that does not suffer, endure or harbor any expressions. I look at you and you look at me. I know I may not seem it, Isabel, but I am in fact extremely sensitive. Some of my friends joke that I'm like a robot because I never shout. Because I never get flustered or visibly angry. And yet, I do have feelings every now and then, and twenty-five years of non-stop *oh, what does your name mean, oh, where's it from, no, but where are you from, I mean, where are you from like originally* is beginning to get on my nerves.

'Thanks.'

'So are both your parents Italian?'

'Yes.'

'Amazing.' She really does seem amazed, what a trip. 'Alright, Marién, as you can see, this is a standard service contract. If you want, we can look through it together or you can take it home and read it there, then call me with any questions that come up, or even shoot me an email. What I do want us to look at now is this timesheet.'

I watched this clip where Seth Meyers interviews Uzoamaka Aduba, and she tells him about coming home from school as a little girl and asking her mom to please start calling her Zoe, because it's easier. Without skipping a beat, her mom turns to her and says that if people can learn to say Tchaikovsky, Dostoyevsky, and Michelangelo, then they can learn to say Uzoamaka.

'Sorry to interrupt, Amanda, but is there any chance we could go through the contract together right now?'

She doesn't correct me and say her name is Isabel, actually, not Amanda. If she feels any anger, she swallows it with a smile and nods. Fuck her. I let her stew in her shitty dumb perfume while I read the paperwork, and then, once we're done, once I've signed everything that needs signing, completed the occupational health and safety course on a 2000 desktop gathering dust in a corner of the office, and wrapped my head around the timesheet I'll need to fill out every day and get Matiqui to sign at the end of each month, I shake her hand and say, *It's been a pleasure, Manuela.* One time my dad explained to me that no matter how far you've strayed from the path or for how long, God will forgive you if you repent from the bottom of your heart. Even if your sins made it all the way up to heaven. Even if they were so great and plentiful they covered the surface of the entire planet. I couldn't figure out how to explain to him that due to a mix of pride and resentment, there are certain things I can't repent for from the bottom of my heart. I get that what I'm doing is bad; sometimes I just don't care. I hate many of my neighbors. I don't know how to turn the other cheek. All I'm good for is playing dumb. *Dear Gabriela,* I write to her the next day. *Please find attached the remaining documents.*

25

June 2017

Some of us Supersaurio employees have a secret. I hear it from Omar, who heard it from a former stock clerk he hooked up with at the 2013 Christmas party. He hooked up with her just months after his relationship of four years ended. The words *four years* flit around my head as we talk. *Four years with one person!* I want to scream. In 2013, I was someone with projects and dreams. Not anymore. Now I have zero projects or dreams, even though every time I log onto Instagram there's someone talking about one of theirs. A very special project that they're closely involved with but can't talk about because it's top secret. Winky face. But they promise all will be revealed soon. Winky face. When I log onto Instagram to post a selfie or reply to a DM only to wind up scrolling for hours, sucked into the app, I see lots of people with lots of projects, though no one ever explains how it is they can afford to spend all year traveling the world. Blessed in Bali, #suckstobeme, catamaran and sausage legs in Formentera, #summervibes, fuck them all to hell a million fucking times.

There's a storage room in the building that the managers lost the key to years ago. No one in charge had the time to deal with it, and the office staff never go to the basement, so barely anyone knows it exists. I hide down here sometimes. It's damp-smelling and crowded with boxes, shopping carts, a broken desk and chairs, out-of-commission computers, and a ten-foot-tall mildewy stuffed dinosaur. Sometimes I cry in his monstrous little arms. In what I can only call a collaborative network, those of us in the know make sure to always leave the key back where we found it. We do not talk about the storage room outside the storage room. It's like *Fight Club* but for crybabies. The day I see Yolanda smoking on the roof, *my* roof, I feel violated in some indescribable way and spend the rest of the day speechless, as if she'd seen some part of me that no one had ever been privy to before. I stop going up there. I make friends in the storage room: Sergio, a stock clerk; Carla, a butcher; Munir, another stock clerk. We smile when we see each other in the aisles because we're all in on the secret. Omar calls them my 'little communist friends.' When I think about Omar, the insides of my wrists tingle. I try to picture the stock clerk he made out with in Christmas 2013. She's probably stunning. I instantly regret it. One thing my little communist friends and I have in common is that we're pretty miserable at this company. And yet, we don't leave.

26

June 2017

From: Yolanda Mikhailov Yolanda.Mikhailov@supersaurio.com
Sent: Tuesday, June 4, 2017 1:55 PM
To: Meryem El Mehdati temp.meryem.elmehdati@super-saurio.com
Subject: to do list

Dear Meyreme,
Remember to finish EVERY assignment and input each company's information into PRIMA before you get started on anything else. Otero and Víctor are very busy with the HR investigation and can't be expected to answer your questions all the time, especially when the information is right there, you just have to look harder. You're making a bad impression, I don't think there's been enough communication between us. . I see from the email below that you've been getting new assignments from Ferrán. So let me remind you that you should still be doing everything you used to do as an intern, even in your new role.
    I trust you understand my position.

Rgrds,
Yolanda

I read Yolanda's email a dozen times, slowly exhaling through my mouth. I open and close my hands beneath the desk. 'You're making a bad impression,' I whisper to myself, her email glowing on the inside of my eyelids like it was written in neon. I read it again, frozen in place. I feel like if I breathe too hard I might explode into a thousand pieces. I take a screenshot of the email salutation and add it to my collection of the thousand different ways this person has managed to dismember my name.

In response, I write:

Yolanda, cut me some slack, will you?

Then I erase it by punching the delete key over and over, as loudly as possible; no one can hear me because they're all at lunch. Clack, clack, clack, clack, clack. It's so quiet on my floor that I get the itch to do something crazy, like tear the monitor away from my desk and hurl it out the window or go down to Yolanda's floor to confront her. 'I trust you understand my position.' I cackle through my teeth, like a nutso. It's the funniest thing I've read in years. I trust you understand my position is what I should be saying to her, I think, while mentally ripping out my computer and smashing it on the floor. I wipe my right hand across my lips.

I start writing, again:

Dear Yolanda,
You know, when I was a kid, nothing scared me. I'd throw myself off the swing mid-air and land knees-first in the sand. Sometimes it hurt, sometimes it didn't. I didn't care. I laughed like a maniac. I used to ask the dumbest questions. It didn't embarrass me at all. I'd put my hands into things just so I could know what was on the other side, on the inside. I was indestructible. That's how I wound up breaking one of my top teeth. When I saw my face, I burst out laughing. Which is why they're crooked and kind of weird, I know you've noticed. Now I have this recurring

dream where I try to talk but my voice doesn't come out. Someone is hurting me and I'm trying to say 'stop,' but there's no sound. All I can do is cry. I'm being chased down the street, but I can't call for help. Every dream is different but in all of them, I open and close my mouth, stammer, burst into tears. When I wake up, I've always got a crick in my neck and my hands are clenched. I stare at my hands in the dark room, then open and close them again and again. I'm strong, firm, and independent. I can scream if I want. I can speak up. It's just a dream. But I never speak up to you. I let you call me Mirian, Marian, Merian, Mereym. I let you hang up on me, give me the silent treatment, exclude me from everything in your power, send me shitty emails like the one you did today. Maybe it's because I can't risk losing this job, or because my parents have drilled into me that it's important to always be nice to others, no matter what. Be nice, be nice, be nice. No one ever remembers the nice things people do for them, only the mean ones. If I were to grab you by the hair one day and sweep half the floor with you, hallway by hallway, I doubt anyone would remember how I put up with months of you treating me like garbage. Sure, God may understand. But here, they'd call security, make a big stink, and I'd end up in the street, with no severance, because I'm actually on RANDSTAD's payroll . . . Still, if I knew God understood me, I would walk out of here satisfied.

Sometimes I think about this when you talk to me. You're standing in front of me and I'm watching you flap your lips, but I don't see you. I don't even hear you. I'm in another world, one where I put you in your place because, I mean, how hard can it honestly be to remember a six-letter word? According to God, everything that exists has a purpose. I'm still young, and I haven't figured out if you're proof of something or if you're my punishment, but never forget that this young person in front of you is at least a foot taller and twenty kilos heavier than you. I sure don't.

Five minutes later, I feel calmer and delete everything I wrote while thinking about what my life would be like if I'd been born into a family of means. If I could spend time on 'projects' instead of working like a dog. I hate my job, but oh, boy, do I need it.

From: Meryem El Mehdati temp.meryem.elmehdati@supersaurio.com
Sent: Tuesday, June 4, 2017 2:05 PM
To: Yolanda Mikhailov Yolanda.Mikhailov@supersaurio.com
Subject: RE: to do list

OK.

I hit send, then cry on the bus ride home.

Fandom: Supersaurio (Las Palmas – District 2)
Characters: Omar, Meryem
Tags: Slow burn
Category: Romance
Words: 386

'Para quedarte'

Omar looked at the paper flower sitting on his desk between the pencil case where he kept his highlighters and the framed picture of him and his siblings, Juan and María. In the photo, his hair was parted like he'd measured it with a pair of set squares, and he was wearing khakis, a white shirt, and tightly laced shoes. He was the youngest and most fastidious of the three. Meryem had made a quip about his style once. She'd pointed at him, laughed, and declared: 'For a guy whose mom does his hair every morning, you sure have a lot of opinions about my life.' He'd found it funny, like just about everything she said. It was silly, but he picked up the flower and twirled it between his thumb and index finger, as if it were a real flower. She'd made it out of a napkin from the cafeteria, folding it in half once, twice, then opening the square up and folding it again, into a triangle. Then she'd brushed away her hair and complained about something. Omar had replied, and Meryem had concluded: 'Once you realize your life's in the hands of a broken system, these kinds of choices – Nesquik or Cola Cao – stop mattering.' Her tone of voice wasn't so much serious as self-deprecating. Omar had noticed a while ago that most of what she said was done in the spirit of teasing or attacking herself with the kind of cruelty usually reserved for our enemies. 'That's why I don't care,' she said, pushing the flower toward him. He'd been distracted by her eyes, her neck, the silver chain she never took off.

'Cola Cao is owned by the Ferreros, and the Ferreros are—' 'Jerks?' He finished her sentence. 'Exactly. That's why I drink Tircao. Every Euro I spend at Supersaurio comes back to me.' Omar had grabbed the flower and inspected it. He'd smiled. 'It's usually guys who give girls flowers.' 'Sure, but I'm a feminist,' she'd replied. Back in his office, he set the flower on his desk. It'd been sitting there since. He picked up his cell phone, unlocked it, and scrolled down to their WhatsApp chat. 'Heading down for breakfast. You coming?' Two blue check marks. 'Okkkkkkkkkkkkkkkkk.' He'd treat her to a classic sugar donut. Her favorite.

27

June 2017

The music is so loud, the tabletop shakes. The water in my glass ripples to the rhythm of the song. Alonso's ex is crazy. Was crazy. I don't really know since I'm not actually paying attention. I have no clue what my face is doing right now because even though he's sitting right across from me at the table, I can't see him. He's told us like twenty, thirty times already that his ex is unhinged, batshit, a few fries short of a Happy Meal. If I'd stayed home, I'd be in my pajamas right now watching *First Dates* with my siblings. The thought puts me in a mood.

Next to him, Omar shifts his weight to his other leg. He raises his glass to his lips, takes a sip. Whisky. I look away, like I'm seeing something private, intimate. I try to concentrate on Alonso and his monologue, but his voice crackles and fades because I have no interest at all in anything he's saying. I've got nothing against men, but I swear most of them never shut up. The worst part is they have no sense of exactly how much they talk. Society has convinced us they're the quiet ones and we're the chatterboxes. I can't cite any studies at the moment, but come *on*. My face says, 'I'm listening, please continue,' or 'I'm listening, say more,' while my brain gradually loses its grip on the conversation until all I hear is a gurgle of sounds issuing from his mouth. I enter low power mode. I'm organic, eco. I don't know a lot of guys whose exes aren't or weren't at some point crazy. Not saying I don't believe them, only that it's a little sus. On the other hand, I do know people who are or were once very crazy, and they were all . . . would you look at that? Men.

'And she goes and changes all my Netflix and Amazon Prime passwords? She seemed so cool in the beginning,' he moans. His wavy hair swishes with him as he shakes his head. It's June, and he's wearing a turtleneck sweater and a headband, like he's a soccer star or something. It's tacky, but no one tells him.

'Without saying anything!' he continues. 'Without even telling me. I had to find out in the lamest way possible.'

His sense of style is supposed to convey the real him. He's a boss, but a cool boss. Modern, open-minded, and understanding. The kind who lets you leave half an hour early to pick your kid up from school, except then you'd better answer his Saturday- and Sunday-night emails. You'd better be cool back. The headband says you can talk to him, even if he's your boss, you can be open with him. Maybe the con works on some people. Maybe some of my colleagues admit to him that the closer they get to the offices, the more they drag their feet in the hope of delaying the start of their workday as long as they can. Or that they hide if they see someone they know from work in the wild, outside office hours. I'd rather put my hand through the shredder by my desk than tell any of that to any of these people, especially him.

'But whose name are the accounts in?' Omar asks.

After the IT woman gave me my new computer, I switched floors. I'm not behind the front desk anymore, far away from everyone else. I'm on the eighth floor. The executive floor. I'm *somebody* now. My desk is right outside Matiqui's office – all glass, door permanently shut. No one sees him without my express permission, which is basically just me nodding and saying: 'Sure, go on in.' Sometimes I put on a show and buzz him on the intercom even though he can clearly see me and the person waiting to talk to him through the glass wall. Now and then, I throw out a 'he's expecting you,' and feel spontaneous. Others, I just shrug and say: 'Sorry, let me see if he can fit you in tomorrow.'

My literal ascent to the eighth floor has almost put me at the same level as the rest of my cohort. I'm still a step below because I was hired through a temp agency, and they all know what that means: one false step and I'm out on the street – zero headaches and no severance. Still, we help each other out, and I can never decide which is worse, someone doing me a favor or asking me for one. Lunch has gone from being the only time when I could have a break to a strategy game where one mistake could make me someone's mortal enemy. I hate group dynamics, but I take part in them like everyone else. Matiqui says: 'After-work drinks this evening. I told Lucía to invite you.' I mingle with these people, my pseudo-bosses. I attend the after-work drinks. I don't know what bus I'm going to take home.

'So?' asks Lucía 1. There are six of us clustered around a high-top.

'Whatever, hers. But we shared them. She could've told me. Whatever. I'm telling you, she's a schizo.'

One day, Omar showed up at my desk with Lucía 1, Lucía 2, Alonso, and Francisco, and invited me to lunch. Now we're like a clique or something.

'So they're her accounts,' says Francisco-but-please-call-me-Fran-not-Paco-I-hate-Paco-just-Fran. 'She pays for them and everything, right?'

'You're such a dick, Alon.' Lucía 2 pretend-rolls her eyes. She nibbles on her canapé. I'm not here. I'm somewhere else. Far, far away. 'Men. Hey, Mery, do you think you could squeeze me in to see Matiqui tomorrow? I need him to sign some paperwork for me.'

She's talking to me. Apparently I'm Mery.

'Mmmm,' I pretend to think about it. 'It'll be tough. Why don't you give me whatever you need signed, and I'll leave it on his desk, then ping you once it's done?'

Alonso and Francisco start arguing, half joking, half serious.

'Ugh, you're the best. It's the quarterly tax stuff. You know the drill.'

I don't, but I nod. Lucía 1, Lucía 2, Alonso, and Francisco-but-call-me-Fran are all from the mainland, like Omar. Every Euro you spend at Supersaurio goes back to the island, but the higher you get up the corporate ladder, the clearer it becomes that the people in charge are all mainlanders. It doesn't make me mad, exactly – not at a company where HR claims to put people and their values above everything else but where almost no one can get my name right – I just find it funny. Maybe I don't count as *people*. Maybe my name isn't actually Meryem.

'No problem.' I smile.

'Hey, I've been thinking about you and the corporate magazine's young talents section.'

Omar looks at me. I look at him. He has the faintest smile. I'd like to wipe it off his face. To lean over the table and punch him square in the jaw and see if he still finds it all so amusing. I have this theory about myself: I was not born with the energy needed to function at full capacity in the labor market. I'm no good with people or taking initiative, at least not here, in this context, at after-work drinks. Leaving the office only to work another few hours that you don't get paid for. Whoever came up with that idea: pure genius. I have to constantly pretend, play a new part every day.

I'm not passionate about or interested in any part of what I do for work. Truth is, I'm not passionate about much. On very rare occasions, a feeling of serenity grips me and I spend the next few hours at peace with myself, though I've noticed this tends to coincide with the days I eat an entire XL chocolate-covered palmier in secret. A stack of thirty-three sugar cubes, all for my body alone. Sinazucar.org and their sugar-free recipes can suck it. The caffeine-sugar combo has me speeding like a racecar for the rest of the day, and by the time I get home, I remember none of what I've done for the last few hours. It's the closest I've ever come to doing drugs. I suspect the reason I'm pretty good at my job is not that I like it or am motivated by it but that I don't want to lose it. As the daughter of immigrants, I've got the whole meritocracy and hard work spiel hardcoded in my DNA, never mind that meritocracy is a big fat lie and hard work only benefits those who haven't lifted a finger in their lives. Why does a business assurance manager earn more than a cashier or a stock clerk? If every cashier and stock clerk were to vanish from the face of the earth, we'd notice immediately. If all the business assurance managers did . . . you get the idea.

Lucía 1, Lucía 2, Alonso, and Fran are head over heels for their jobs. Every new email gives them butterflies. Every hurdle is just another obstacle to be cleared, a game. For my part, hurdles either make me anxious, tired, or bothered. Another fence to leap over. Another obstacle to overcome.

Is precarity not punishment enough? When I get home, I'm so drained I can't think. All I can do is change out of my work clothes, pray, and go to sleep. I used to think I was a lot more than my job title, but these days I'm not so sure. Am I no longer capable of having any feelings and thoughts unrelated to my role at this supermarket?

'I don't get paid to think about work outside office hours,' I say. They laugh because they assume I'm joking. This is how most people react when I'm being completely serious. They crack up. They think I'm hilarious.

I know four things about Alonso. The first two: his ex is crazy, and he likes to read. I'm aware of the latter because he slips it into every conversation. He loves bookstores, literature, Tolstoy, Bukowski, Neruda, Dan Brown. He says this without blushing, the total airhead. His office smells like Loewe pour Homme and coffee. He has dozens of books strewn about and dirty mugs that he never rinses. Instead, the cleaning women collect them and put them in the dishwasher for him. I've seen them do it. And I'm sure he hasn't read even a third of what he says he has.

Alonso is the company's talent manager. When he called me to discuss my transition to personal assistant, I knew I could ask him about my new salary and job description because he was wearing *fun* socks. He tried selling me my new prison sentence with a ton of English loanwords and bland jokes. Beyond that, I spent the rest of our conversation dissociating. He gendered 'we' in the feminine instead of the usual masculine. Misogyny? Single-handedly eradicated. Some of the stuff we humans have to put up with just to pay the bills – it's despicable.

'You're just so funny.' The third thing I know about Alonso is that he's from Madrid. He brings it up a lot, especially when he talks about Gran Canaria and compares it with everything he's left behind slash misses about Madrid. I've been to Madrid a couple of times, and it's, like, fine, whatever. At least here we're not inhaling pollution every day. 'I'd love it if you could write up a quick bio for us to publish in the next issue. Something that really captures your essence: fun, fresh. You know what to do. We can take a picture of you at the entrance.'

'Sorry, publish it in what exactly?'

'The company magazine, of course.'

I laugh because I'm sure he's pulling my leg.

'Listen, we have no one else your age on staff. You're a perfect fit: you're both young *and* talented.'

'You're young,' Fran echoes. He pretends to count on his fingers. He holds out his thumb, then his index finger, and says, 'and talented. You're hired.'

'Define young,' Lucía 2 asks.

'Under thirty,' I say, half joking, half serious. Omar goes khhhfff kfffff with laughter, but no one notices. *What's so funny?* I want to ask him. *What's so funny? These people are* your *friends.*

As soon as you approach your thirties, a part of you is slowly erased. I see it in the people around this high top. Looking back, they can't pinpoint the exact moment they changed, even though they can tell they're different. They don't understand teenagers anymore, and their phone is now their enemy. The flame that burned inside them when they were young is snuffed out. I can see this in myself, too: I'm becoming more insecure, more tentative. I doubt everything. I never used to hesitate back in the day, I was unstoppable. Their hearts break in two and they begin to gradually lose everything they once found exciting. They have bills to pay, taxes to do, doctors to go to once, twice, three, four times

122

because that UTI isn't going away on its own. They grow up, go gray. It's just a theory.

'I find it hard to believe there's no one else under thirty at this company. The cashier I gave my money to yesterday can't have been a day over twenty.' It was true.

'Supermarket employees don't get to be in the company magazine,' he explains. His words hover between us. All six of us are supermarket staff. It takes me a second to understand what he means.

'You'd be perfect,' Fran adds. 'You have such a cool name.'

Dickhead, I think. You can't even say it properly.

'Thanks, but aren't we also technically employed by the supermarket?' I reply, pretending not to understand. Talent manager. I'd rather get run over by a taxi blasting the COPE radio station than send one email as a talent manager.

'We work in the offices, not in the supermarket itself. The magazine is only meant for the corporate side.' When Omar speaks, I have to make a conscious effort not to turn around and look at him. It's embarrassing. Pathetic, really. It's like we're always seeking each other out, though I tell myself I do this so I can hear him better. 'I'll forward you an old issue so you can check it out.' My heart starts beating very slowly. I give zero fucks about this magazine.

The fourth thing I know about Alonso is that the kind of money he has could bury us all. He could buy half the Supersaurio supermarket chain if he wanted. It's the type of wealth that comes with double-barreled names. That's why they've made up a job just for him. That's why he can come to work with his hair like that, wearing a headband. I'm not beaten down. I'm just exhausted. Maybe I'm anemic again.

'So what you're saying is there are two categories of employee,' I say. 'The worthless ones who work in the supermarket and us.'

'God no. Not at all.' Alonso sounds shocked and appalled. 'It's just easier to stay organized this way . . . There's the supermarket and the corporate offices. Relax, woman.'

Woman.

'I wish I could be a young talent,' Fran sighs. He elbows me playfully and in that moment I hate him with every fiber of my being. I'm not crazy. They're winding me up, but I'm not crazy. I know exactly what Alonso said. 'They should give you a prize. They should hold a ceremony and give all of you a prize. I'd love that.'

'A prize just for being born the year I was born,' I smoothly reply.

The only person I think understands me laughs through his teeth again, khhhhfff kfffff. I don't look at him. I'm mad for some reason, I don't know why. *There's no rush*, I hear someone say over my head. I drink the rest of my water, just to do something. Slow-ly.

'So, can I count on you? I'll send you an email with what you'd need to write. It's just a few lines, no sweat. We can go over it together.'

His email is in my inbox the following morning. I delete it unread.

28

June 2017

Every time I use my bus card, I hear the timebomb in my neck go buh-boom buh-boom buh-boom because every punch is one less ride between now and the moment I turn twenty-six and cease to be considered young. From then on, the pass will cost thirty-five Euros instead of the twenty-eight I currently pay. The thing that kills me, that jabs me right between the ribs, isn't the price difference but the arbitrariness of the age separating those who are young from those who are not. At twenty-six and one day I will be just as young as I was at twenty-five, eleven months, and twenty-nine days.

The problem is that the next bus pass you can get is the one for Canary Islands residents. If you're young, does that mean you're not a resident of the Canary Islands? Are the two mutually exclusive? What I want to know, what I don't understand is why there's a youth bus pass but no adult bus pass. In light of the circumstances, in light of the fucking economy pushing most people my age back into their parents' houses because they don't have a pot to piss in, does it make any sense to cut off youth before your thirties?

This time I miss the bus because I have to renew my bus pass and the line is so long that despite arriving thirty minutes before the 91 is scheduled to depart, I'm still one minute late. They've only got two people working on bus pass renewals at the San Telmo branch. Can you believe it? It's impossible to live in the Canary Islands and not feel like you're in a developing nation instead of Europe. I mean, come on, H&M doesn't even deliver here. I get to my parents' house and wonder how I look to them when they open the door: Do I look like a young person or like a resident of the Canary Islands? Whatever. I mean, at least I have a job.

Fandom: Supersaurio (Las Palmas – District 2)
Characters: Otero, Víctor
Tags: Horror (?)
Category: General
Words: 384

Gorillas in the Mist

The anti-stress ball had been a present from Yolanda. Otero's hand was so huge it made the ball look like a marble. This amused Víctor, who had one just like it knocking around somewhere, though he never used it. That afternoon, Otero squeezed the ball, peered over his computer monitor at Víctor and said:

'Call Merién.'

'Why?'

Otero released the ball.

'Just do it.'

Víctor turned toward his phone and pressed the third button down from the top. Then he put it on speaker.

'Hi, Víctor.'

'Heeeeyyy, Mérien. How's it going?'

Three floors above them, she laughed. Her laughter was very contagious. This amused Víctor.

'I'm alright. You?'

'Hi, Merién!' Otero piped in.

'You're on speaker, Mery.'

'Hi, Otero. So, how are you guys doing?'

'You know, alright. Sitting at our desks. Breaking our backs for that sweet moolah etcetera, etcetera. Hey, Mery. Didn't you forget to tell us something?'

Víctor propped himself up on the armrests of his chair to get a better look at Otero. What was he talking about?

'Uh . . . Something, like what?'

'Think about it.'

Víctor gestured at Otero, who shook his head.

'I think I don't know what you're talking about.'

'You sure?'

Silence stretched out between them.

'Have I done something wrong?' she asked after a while.

'Noooooo. No, no, don't be crazy. Relax, woman. You've done nothing wrong. Isn't it your birthday tomorrow?'

'Whoa, Mérien! Your birthday's tomorrow?' Víctor laughed.

'Oh,' she said. Víctor thought he heard her breathe down the other end of the line. 'Yes.'

Otero pretend-brushed some non-existent fuzz off his shoulders.

'You should be more excited. Tomorrow's your special day! How old will you be?'

'Twenty-three,' Víctor said.

'Twenty-six,' she replied. 'Guys, I've got a meeting with Matiqui right now. Sorry. I'll call you later.'

'Hold up. A meeting with Matiqui? About what?'

'Huh?'

'What's the meeting with Matiqui about?' Víctor leaned over the phone.

'It's with the Quality Control team. I'll call you later. Bye.'

'Wait.'

She didn't. Otero and Víctor glanced at one another.

'Doesn't that seem weird to you?'

'I don't get this chick.' Otero gestured with his hand. 'I can never tell what she's thinking.'

'I mean about the meeting with Matiqui and Quality Control. Shouldn't we be in it?'

'Fuck.'

They jumped to their feet.

128

29

July 2017

The evening before my twenty-sixth birthday, I walk into my parents' restaurant, drop my purse and laptop bag on the table where my siblings and I usually eat, and announce:

'I'm done.'

It's Monday, and the restaurant is busy.

'The world's bullshit,' I say to my audience of two. 'The wheel never stops turning, whether you're under it or not. I'm getting old. It doesn't matter if it runs you over because they can always replace you. Capitalism is a broken system that beats you down and strips you to your marrow until you go crazy, or worse yet, start believing it's the only option, and you're the one that's the problem. You're just not cut out for it. You don't work hard enough!'

'Do you *have a dream?*' my brother asks. He's the tallest of the three.

'We can't mess with her today. She has diplomatic immunity.'

'Every day, I do things for my boss and every day he wants more and more and more. I don't have time to think or feel. I'm like a machine. A fucking robot. Yes, Matiqui.

Thank you, Matiqui. Sure thing, Matiqui. Of course, put your foot on my neck whenever you feel like it, Matiqui.'

I slam my fist on the table but misjudge my own strength and hurt my hand. I sit in front of them, feeling a little humiliated. My sister holds out her hand and I put mine on top. She massages it a bit, then gives it back.

'We love it when you go all Maduro on us.'

I give them a long, hard look. They're twins. I couldn't stand the sight of them when they were born. They were always together – crying, sleeping, eating, and shitting themselves in tandem. My parents, who'd learned their lesson when they named me Meryem, called them Samir and Lilia. Soon they became Sami and Lily.

'I hate it when you talk like you're the same person with the same thoughts.'

Once they were a bit older, they decided I was their favorite person in the world. As kids, we played the games I wanted to play, watched the TV I wanted to watch, went to the places I wanted to go to. I was delighted, obviously.

'We do have the same thoughts.'

My parents' restaurant closes on Fridays and Saturdays. Their friends told them they were crazy to do that, that they could make as much on those two days as they did in a whole week, but my parents didn't care. Things have gone well for them in the twenty-seven years they've been open. At first it was just them and three waiters. A few years back they expanded, hired more people, and got Facebook and Instagram accounts. The twins and I manage their socials because our parents are convinced they're too old to make sense of it.

Since opening Marhaba, they've been interviewed three times: twice for a local network and once for a Norwegian TV documentary. The restaurant's main clientele has always been cab drivers, neighbors, and people from the north end of the island who come to Puerto Rico on vacation. In the last few years, the influencer boom, the rise of 'ethnic' things, and the impulse to discover hidden gems around the island have brought a flock of morons to the restaurant who are obsessed with the authenticity of multicultural food. These days, it's not uncommon for us to get tables of ten to twelve people who wander around the restaurant taking selfies, filming the cooks, and doing Instagram lives while inhaling their food like they've never tasted a spice in their life.

'What am I thinking right now?' Lilia asks.

'You're thinking: If I don't become the best mathematician in all of Europe, I'm going to kill myself.'

'Suicide is haram,' I glance around for my parents. I can't see them. 'Chacho, I'm hungry. Are we eating or what?'

'Does it count as suicide if I cross the street with my eyes closed?' Lilia asks.

Sami is studying Chemical Engineering. Lilia is studying Mathematics. In the context of my family, I am the village idiot. Whenever my parents and I bump into a khalti, she always asks after the twins. Always. Everyone in the neighborhood knows them: they're polite, open, friendly, extroverted; they are, in other words, odious. The words *chemical engineering* and *mathematics* always seem to surprise the person we're speaking to. Chias, that sounds so hard, some of them say. Wow, rabbi, so smart, say the others. Then comes the anticlimax. What about you, Meryem? I'm a translator. Oh . . . interesting. No one gets how hard it is to be born into a family of Maghrebi immigrants and *not* study medicine or engineering. It's what everyone expects from you, just like they expect your parents to fiercely oppose you dating an atheist or, worse yet, to marry you off to a first cousin before you've even graduated from high school.

131

With time, my attitude toward the khaltis has changed. I used to wonder why they never made an effort to integrate. As a student, I'd get off at the Puerto Rico bus station and see them in the park, always in packs of six or seven, with their respective progeny, all in the same uniform: head scarf, djellaba, strong Maghrebi accent. It bothered me that they took up so much space. I used to think: how hard can it be for them to call less attention to themselves, for them to be quieter, and stop sticking their noses where they don't belong how are your parents doing howareyourbrotherandsisterohwhereareyoucoming fromatthistimeofdayohthat'ssofarI'msureyourparentswished youwerecloseryou'realwaysmovingaroundsomewheredifferent everyyearoooohh, scrutinizing me, making me feel judged. And I judged them back: that's right, I'm not like you, I want more for myself. I want to be more than just a mother. I want to have a life of my own, to be able to go places when I feel like it, to not have to shoulder things like a husband a house kids the groceries I bought at Spar, to have bigger concerns on my mind than just gossiping in the park with other women just like me. It was very stupid of me. I know that now.

'Finally! We're your children, and we're HUNGRY.'

My sister throws her arms in the air at the sight of my parents, and my mother laughs. They look so much alike that I feel like an alien. Black hair, dark eyes, pale complexion. I'm the only one in my family with brown hair. Maybe I'm actually adopted, and they can't bring themselves to tell me. Maybe that's why I suck at numbers.

'It seems our children don't know where the kitchen is.'

'*Your* children don't know where the kitchen is.' My father touches my shoulder, then sits next to me. 'I don't think I've seen you in a couple days.'

This is his way of telling me he misses me. My dad doesn't say things outright. He makes gestures, does little acts of service. Instead of saying *Sweetheart, I missed you*, he calls and stays on the line with you for two hours while you do your thing and he does his. Instead of saying *I love you, be careful*, he picks you up, no matter what time it is or where you are.

'That's what we get for living in a broken system,' I reply. 'I went to see an apartment in Arenales today. Do you know where that is?'

'Yeah.'

'Near the big lighted fountain?'

'Exactly.' I feel the beginnings of what will become a full-blown headache in an hour or so. 'So, I see the apartment, which is a total shithole.'

My mother turns to face me. She has The Look.

'I mean, it's a horror show. Awful. A hovel. Put José Antonio Ortega Lara in there, and he'd beg his kidnappers to take him back to their rathole. The bed is ten steps away from the kitchen. The water pressure's a joke. The electric stove is small and filthy. There's *one* window in the whole place . . . But I tell myself, it could be worse, right?'

Juan, one of the servers, comes by to take our order. The twins go first.

'I can't afford to be picky. Rent is €500. It's the cheapest place I've found near work. Five hundred for the first month and another five hundred as a security deposit. But when the landlady sees my pay slip, she decides it's not enough. She says the apartment is meant for couples. Even though the bed she has in there is a single? It was so depressing.'

'Five hundred seems like a lot,' my mother says. I ask if they have any harira left, and Juan says yes. I order harira and a bottle of water. 'Do you have a list of other apartments to see?'

133

'She has an Excel spreadsheet,' my brother says, poking fun at me. 'She showed it to me the other day.'

'I can't wait to leave home and not have to deal with you anymore,' I say. 'Or your shadow.'

'Hey, he's *my* shadow.'

'Don't lose hope. The apartment wasn't right for you, that's all.'

My parents' faith is unwavering. You can make plans and chase dreams all you want, but God does it better. If something isn't right for you, it simply won't happen, no matter how hard you try or how much you work for it. You have to have faith that what's meant to be will be and vice versa. What feels like the end of the world today may be a blessing in disguise tomorrow. We're mere mortals who can't see beyond what's in front of us. My parents moved here on their own, took whatever jobs came their way (my mother worked as a photographer and shop assistant; my father as a handyman, a stock clerk, a waiter, a cook), then had my siblings and me, and opened Marhaba. There were tears, there were sacrifices, but by my age they already had everything I do not have. Plans for the future, a car, a house, a business. It's something I struggle with. To close my eyes, leap into the void. Now and then, my faith wavers. Not because I don't believe but because I'm not perfect. I'm just human.

'Does anyone have anything to share while we're all here together?' my mother asks.

'Me. Before Meryem starts talking about capitalism again,' my sister blurts out.

Despite myself, I laugh.

30

August 2017

Asshole in beige slacks, Stan Smith Adidas, and cowboy shirt: you did a double-take on the two girls walking ahead of me in their private-school uniforms, then called out HOTTIES, making them walk even faster, you steaming pile of shit, I hope a bus runs you over at the next crosswalk. Maggot.

3 1

August 2017

My favorite dish in the whole world is my mother's potato tortilla. People are often surprised when I say this because they expect something exotic, like couscous, roast lamb with prunes, or chicken tagine, but my parents made sure to raise me, their firstborn, fully immersed in Spanish culture. Anyway, one day I get home feeling depressed because Yolanda called me stupid in twenty brand new ways and what do I see in the living room but a picture of a first communion dress my father bought me years ago. I stare at it, frozen still, then teleport back to the day I'd come home on the verge of tears because all my friends at school had beautiful white communion dresses that made them look like princesses while I had nothing, just sesame cookies and a henna tattoo on my right hand that a few of my classmates obviously made fun of. My parents drove me to El Corte Inglés that same afternoon and bought me a first communion dress even though it had no place in our lives. Then my mom took a gazillion photos of me in our living room and the communal courtyard with her nineties' analogue camera. The only time I wore that dress again was to a family wedding. I do remember feeling like a princess. As I stare at that photo, it dawns on me that maybe the reason Yolanda is so cruel is that she doesn't have anyone in her life to fake a communion for her. I yell: 'Mooooooooooooooom, what's this photo doing here?'

32

August 2017

One August morning Matiqui calls to say he's under the weather and will be working from home. I decide to make the most of this and laze on the rooftop. It's 24° Celsius in Las Palmas de Gran Canaria. Neither cold nor hot, because of the panza de burro clouds blanketing the sky. I watch them pile up, pushed to this end of the island by the trade winds, and predict rain in Teror later in the day. I know it's technically summer, but it barely feels like it to me. I still haven't eaten ice cream on Avenida Marítima or gone to the beach. I haven't been on vacation either because I don't get PTO through the temp agency. Every day I don't work is a day I don't make money, so I stay right where I am.

In summer, I always think about my grandmothers, especially my dad's mom and her house in Morocco. Every time I remember her, I get this image in my head: a cliché of white walls and a roof terrace. Cows, chickens, a trio of cats that belonged to my family but we never got around to naming. We used to call them ktot, which just means *cats* in Arabic. My family and I aren't 100% sure, but we think my grandma swore at some point that she'd been born in that house and planned to die in that house when her time came. Which is why we made the pilgrimage to her village every summer. It was a lot more than just a visit, it was a full-on pilgrimage involving multiple pit stops and complicated highways.

Hundreds of thousands of kilometers separated the real world from our destination. Millions of hours of highways and tollbooths, eight lifetimes bumping down pitted backroads that connected the last traces of civilization to my grandma's house. She lived in a village, a real village with hundreds of stories, all astonishing. There was the quarrel between neighbors over a dingy parcel of land that left several dead, the eloping brides and grooms, the accusations of witchcraft, the decapitated roosters, the curses and santería at Fatimita and Mohsinito's wedding, the djinn sightings at the well, in the village square, and on the path to the only mosque within hundreds of kilometers. To this day, all my attempts to devise a response protocol for djinn sightings have failed: no one wants to speak to me about djinns or consider what they'd do if they ever saw one. They just want to avoid them at all costs.

Even though I haven't been in years, I'm sure that the village – mine, my parents' – is exactly the same as it was the last time we went there. It probably has the same smell (earth, clean water, grilled corn, hashish), the same colors (green, dark yellow, brown), and the same people (elders, small children, young couples who've returned to the houses they inherited from their families). In the summer, I always think about my paternal grandmother and her home because it's near the anniversary of her death, and the sadness is a gut punch.

She follows me around all summer like an ear worm tucked in the very back of my head. I know the melody, the lyrics.

Sometimes I think I can't feel her anymore and that I'll finally get to just miss her from the safe distance of time; others, she's a recurring, intrusive thought, a wave much bigger than I'd bargained for that drags me by the ankles into the high seas.

The walls of that house tell countless stories about my childhood and early teenage years, at least the ones I've chosen to remember, though some are beginning to slowly fade away. With time, I've learned to forget and leave behind the more embarrassing anecdotes, my episodes of sour face and eye rolls. The bored slump of my shoulders every time we had guests. I wish I could say I remember my grandma's voice, how she wore her hair, what she smelled like, her clothes, but I've forgotten it all and mastered the art of torturing myself over it. What I remember are her facial features, how hard she cried when we left, her hands, her love of coffee, which she always drank black.

If only I'd visited more often. If only I'd asked more questions, called and written more frequently. I never thought she'd die before her time. I just assumed I could go there whenever I wanted. The place was mine, my family's. It would always be there.

Another summer I didn't go to the village is when my grandma's house stopped existing. My uncle chose to do a full renovation, so I chose never to set foot there again because I had nothing to go back for. In my family, almost nothing is inherited wholesale: it's all divvied up between living relatives. The couple, the children, the siblings, the aunts and uncles. The parents. He didn't ask anyone for permission. He just razed it all to the ground, then built something new and alien, something completely divorced from my past. Not only can I not forgive him – I don't want to.

When I was a kid, my parents used to joke that our family was so big that if we split my grandmother's house between us, we'd each get a single tile. That's when I picked *my* tile, and every summer I'd make sure it was still there, intact. The tile became my summer obsession. I'd play with the cats and touch my tile, go to the well and touch my tile. A lot of my memories were linked to the rooms of that house, which is still there, even though it's not standing. In the garden, in the stables. They all come flooding back to me around summertime. I know it's technically summer, but it doesn't feel like it to me. This year, I'm not going to our village either.

33

September 2017

Omar takes the whole month of August off. When he gets back in September, he's slimmer and a lot more tan than usual. His eyes sparkle. I don't tell him that last bit, I'm not totally insane. The thoughts I have about him shoot off in a million directions: some days I miss him, others I'm overjoyed that I get to work in silence without our Skype chat constantly blinking at me in the taskbar. We bump into each other on September 1 at the supermarket entrance. I open my mouth to ask if he's been waiting for me like the psycho I know he is, but the second I'm within earshot he starts talking.

'What took you so long? I've been waiting forever!'

'Why?' I ask, walking right past him. He catches up to me with one long stride. 'I'm not a temp anymore, kid. I get to show up when I feel like it . . .'

He starts talking to himself, doing both sides of the conversation.

'Hey, Omar! How was your vacation? It was great, thanks. What about yours?' His voice is too high-pitched when he does me. 'The worst, I've missed you . . . Things aren't the same when you're not around. I was crying – sorry, I just remembered you don't speak proper Spanish – *I cried* the whole time you were gone. Down in the dumps every day, talking to no one . . .'

'The only way I'd ever say something like that is if you threatened my entire family.'

'But you'd say it.' We walk into the building, stand at the elevator.

'Under duress, yes.'

'. . . but you'd say it.'

'Hey, Omar! How was your vacation?'

I smile at him, even though I don't want to.

'It was great, thanks. What about yours? You're looking tan. It suits you.'

'The worst,' I say. The elevator dings, and I walk in on autopilot, like someone who's done the same thing every day for years. 'I've missed you . . . Things aren't the same when you're not around.'

He laughs.

'*I cried* the whole time you were gone. Down in the dumps every day, talking to no one.'

'Stop. You don't sound convincing at all.' He's like a sunflower, following me with his eyes. I press the eighth-floor button, then the seventh.

'What can I say? I'm a terrible liar. You do know lying is a sin, right?'

We look at each other in silence, then both say at the same time:

'How are you?'

'You really think my Spanish isn't good?'

We look at each other again.

'No, I don't think your Spanish isn't good.' He reaches for his backpack straps and tugs on them. 'I really like the way you speak. It's sweet.'

143

'Because it'd be kind of weird for someone from Andalucía to make fun of the way another person talks . . .'

'My mastery of the Spanish language would make your head spin. I'm the Lionel Messi of dialectics.'

I laugh.

'How are you?' I ask, this time in earnest.

Fourth floor, fifth floor, sixth floor.

'Great. It was good to get away.' He walks out of the elevator, and I catch a whiff of his cologne. My palms tingle. 'I didn't want to come back.'

'No shit. I wouldn't either.'

'I'll message you later.'

His smell clings to my nose. It's burning me up.

'I did, you know,' I say to his back as he leaves.

'Did what?'

The doors are closing as I confess:

'Miss you.'

As the doors slide shut and the elevator moves up, I look at myself in the mirror and hear Omar saying: 'I heard that!'

'Insanity: madness, dementia, or loss of reason. In Civil Law, insanity is cause for a legal person to be constrained and placed under guardianship. In Criminal Law, it is exculpatory as the insane person is considered to be in a mental state in which, due to a lapse of judgment, he or she cannot take responsibility for their actions,' I read later on the Spanish Wikipedia page. Sounds like an accurate diagnosis for what I am currently experiencing.

34

September 2017

'Who wants to see Snape in his underwear?'

It starts out as a joke. Sirius is bored, and Snivellus and his hooked nose scurry out of the castle, black cape billowing behind his furious gait. The perfect victim, Snape stands for everything James despises. What better way to humiliate someone so desperate for the respect of his peers? James formulates this question off-handedly, as if it took him no effort to use the spell Snape himself had scribbled in the margins of his dusty old Book of Potions. Beside him, Sirius laughs, and his laughter makes James feel taller, smarter, cockier.

'Come on, Prongs.'

He says this with gusto, barking it in his ears. *Come on, Prongs.* For your mother, for world peace. Remus frowns. Peter stays silent. Several of their schoolmates laugh, crowding around them. They yell, applaud. They love whatever it is Sirius has just lit, which instantly combusts. Snape deserves it, of course. The inveterate ass kisser is always snooping around, sticking his slimy nose where it doesn't belong. Who cares if the excuses James gives for what he's doing are a little basic? He hates the guy with every part of himself, and this hatred gnaws at his stomach. Lily shows up and fixes James with her eyes.

'Leave him alone!'

James's wand trembles almost imperceptibly. He wants to say something clever. Instead, he takes one step forward, then touches his hair, ruffles it around. Sirius laughs again, this time wide-mouthed, and turns to Lily, incisive, pensive, *Padfoot*.

'Who made you James's boss, Evans?'

Lily takes her hand to her robe pocket. James knows she is also going to pull out her wand.

'I don't need any help from a mudblood.'

Snape's response stops her in her tracks. Lily presses her lips together, suddenly livid, and James springs forward.

'The only muddy thing here is Severus's unwashed underwear. What do you reckon, Sirius?'

'Underwear off!'

The spell glimmers, then lashes out. Snape hovers in the air for less than a second. He squirms, red with rage, and in response slashes James's nose, who

And in response slashes James's nose, who. Who what? I reread the page, stop. Click-clack, click-clack, Yolanda struts down the hallway, red high heels, red blazer, hair pulled back in a tight bun. For a minute, I think I'm hallucinating, that she's a mirage. I lose the thread of what I was writing, all my attention focused on her. She's a vision. Satan. She strides past my desk and heads straight to Matiqui's office. I'm tempted to take a picture of her with my phone because I can't believe her look. I want to capture this moment for all time so I can revisit it in the future. There's probably some detail I've missed. She stops in front of the glass door.

146

Her reflection bounces off my face. We stare at one another, her back to me.

She could've called and saved herself the trouble. I don't smile, I don't move, I just watch her watching me. She slowly turns around, chin raised just slightly, and gestures at me with her hand. She doesn't walk up to my desk. She's a red creature standing before me. A demon, a djinn.

'How can I help?'

I'm friendly, charming. My long-term plan is to smother her with kindness, to drive her up the wall. To never let her know if I know something, or why, for her to always be unsure of what's going on with me. To save every insult she deploys in the HR folder. (I've got proof on the Google Drive.) To show up at the HR office one day with a huge stack of paper and accuse her of workplace harassment. To watch her cry. None of my favorite online retailers delivers to the Canary Islands. I am a patient person.

'Where's Ferrán?'

'He's not in today. He's working from home.'

I could've been a Yolanda. Some of my classmates at university were poorer than me but pretended not to be by dressing in boat shoes and beige tones. Dark blue Zara Man sports jacket, hair carefully brushed back. Twenty-four-hour clowns. The whole 'a poor mindset won't make you rich' attitude may have held water in Law School or Business School, but it didn't in our department. Instead we laughed at them. Since then, I've checked out these phonies' LinkedIn and Instagram profiles: they're entrepreneurs. Literature and the internet saved me as a teenager. It may sound like an exaggeration, but it's true. If not for books and cyberspace, I'd be a whole different person. A fascist, or worse, a liberal. I'd say dumb shit like: 'Hard work will make your dreams come true,' or 'I'm not racist, I'm organ-ized.' When I see Rocío Monasterio on TV I always get the sense that her human form is on the verge of splitting open and revealing a sixteen-foot lizard. Pure hatred and venom. It's the same feeling that blows on the nape of my neck when I'm in Yolanda's presence, except in her case the lizard is smaller. A wall gecko.

'I need to talk to him. It's important.'

It must be eating her up inside to have walked up two flights of stairs only to not find what she was looking for. Yolanda doesn't believe in elevators. They're for slackers and pinkos. I try to look at her straight-on but can't. It's like studying an extremely detailed painting. You can't figure out where to start, and you'll go crazy from trying.

'You can call him. He is working . . . just from home,' I say, in case she didn't hear the first time.

'Please check his calendar and tell me what meetings he has today.'

She steps up to my table, click-clack, click-clack. I pinch myself on the thigh, clench my jaw to keep from snickering. I'm dying inside. I think of all the times she's made me cry. I breathe in through my nose, slowly, then out through my mouth.

'He doesn't usually have meetings on Fridays, which is why he works from home.' My voice quivers.

'Okay, I'll call him.'

My right eye starts to twitch, and a tear sears my water-line. I'm buckling from the effort to suppress my laughter.

'Okay.'

Click-clack, click-clack. Two weeks ago, I got home feel-ing sad and tired, so I signed onto my old fanfiction.net account and reread some of my pieces. Even though there were hundreds of mistakes, I felt better. In my comfort zone,

148

if you will. My happy place. Now I write during lulls at the office, when Matiqui isn't in or my coworkers have forgotten I exist because I'm not standing directly in front of them. Click-clack, click-clack. I could write a whole book about the infuriating sound of her heels, or about her red suit or her hair bun, which is so tight it's even giving *me* a headache.

'What're you doing?' she asks.

A lone tear rolls down my cheek. I wipe it, rest my arms on the desk. *Knitting*, I want to tell her. *What do you think?*

'Working,' I say with a smile.

I have this theory about Yolanda. This time, we look each other dead in the eyes, and I can tell she's trying to work out what I'm thinking. *I hate you*, I visualize in my head. *I hate you, I hate you, I hate you.* When she leaves, I peer at my reflection in the glass walls of Matiqui's office and take off my glasses. I wipe my eyes with the palms of my hands and cover my mouth. I wonder if anyone's ever died from sheer self-restraint. I delete everything I'd written in the document on my computer and stare at the blank page for a while. Then, I start typing: 'The morning Yolanda met her nemesis . . .'

35

September 2017

'Come on, smile for the camera. I want to post it on Instagram, so the pic has to be, like, at least half-decent,' I ask.

'But I *am* smiling,' Omar complains.

'Then smile differently. The way you're smiling now makes you look like a psycho.' He gives me the finger but smiles anyway. To his right is a sign that reads HERMANOS BETANCOR, my favorite churrería. 'Perrrr feeeeect. Should I tag you?'

'I don't have Instagram.' I show him the photo. He seems satisfied. I put my phone back in my jacket pocket. 'Not too bad, if I say so myself,' he says so himself.

'So I guess you think you're not-too-bad-looking, huh?' I ask. 'There's a free table over there, in the back. Hi! Can we take that table?'

The man behind the bar pushes up his glasses.

'Sit wherever you like, mi niña. Be with you in a minute.'

Today, I am having A Good Day. The sun is shining. The temperature is a perfect 20° Celsius, neither hot nor cold. Day thirteen of my cycle, I can do no wrong. Yolanda's sick. Matiqui's on vacation. My hair's getting longer and shinier every week. It's A Good Day.

150

'I mean, have you *seen* me?' he asks.

A few days ago, Lucía 2 elbowed me at lunch while I was busy inhaling half a kilo of spaghetti in tomato sauce, then raised her eyebrows toward Omar, who was microwaving his lunch. Is shouting when a conversation doesn't go as planned a sign of character? No. A sign of character, of a strong personality, is brazenly heating up half a kilo of spaghetti under the watchful eyes of the people who will sit beside you at lunch. It's dumping the entire contents of your Tupperware on a plate and scarfing it down. It's being unfazed when somebody asks, 'Are you eating *all* that?' and replying, 'Yeah, why?' while continuing to consume your lunch. I followed Lucía 2's eyebrows to the guy who, hours earlier, had slapped my hand away from a bag of potato chips and said, 'they're ham.' Baby-blue shirt, bottle-green sweater, jeans. Perfectly coiffed hair. Supersaurio's very own bullfighter, Jesulín de Ubrique, I said once to mess with him.

'What's going on?' I whispered.

'Doesn't he look hot?' she whispered back.

I bit the inside of my mouth so I wouldn't laugh in her face. Omar's a good-looking guy, that's not why I laughed. He's blond with light eyes, a big nose. Sometimes, he'd roll up his sleeves while we're chatting, and I'd get distracted by the contrast between his arm fuzz and his skin, by his hands, by the untamable swirl of his hair. I didn't think of Omar as a good-looking guy. No, to me Omar was the bark of laughter when he answered the phone, even though I hadn't said anything yet. He was the comma he never spaced out from the next word. *Hey, Meryem.* He was the 'bleh, what a gross, fucked-up world' that he could say aloud while I could only hiss it through my teeth because no one ever disagreed with him, but they did with me.

'Yeah, I dunno,' I said after a while. 'I mean, I guess he's kind of good-looking. But he's blond.'

'And that's a bad thing?'

Lucía 2 is also blonde.

'Beats me. I don't trust blonds. They're up to something.'

Back in the present, where he is right there next to me, I shrug. Given the choice between death and fessing up to certain things, I choose death.

'You're such a pain. I see you every day. It's like you think you'll die if you lift a finger.'

He laughs.

'You know, I could absolutely kick the bucket one day.' He unbuttons his trench coat and places it on the empty chair to his right. The first words out of my mouth when I saw him this morning were: *Hey there, Inspector Gadget.* 'I have a question.'

'Shoot.' I drop my things sloppily on his trench coat, just to annoy him, and sit across from him.

'Are there any social media platforms you're *not* on?'

'TikTok. But listen, you're the weird one here. You're not on Instagram, or Twitter, or Facebook. You're not anywhere. How can you even live like that, like an animal?'

'They don't do anything for me.'

'Aren't your friends on social media?'

'Sure, I guess, but they don't use it as much as you do. It doesn't really interest them.'

'*They don't use it as much as you do.* Please show some respect. I've got close to four thousand Twitter followers.'

On the bar TV, a Romeo Santos song starts playing. This may be one of the best days of my life.

'Four thousand crazies who read everything you post.'

'Nothing you say can change how I feel about the four thousand crazies who read everything I post. Also, I've got even more followers on the fanfiction site.'

I don't tell him just how much the internet has rewired my brain. I've lost the ability to focus – there's always a new notification. All I can do these days is react to visual stimuli. This thing looks cool, that thing makes me laugh: re-tweet, like. This thing pisses me off, that thing offends me: report, block. If one of my posts doesn't get a certain number of likes, I beat myself up for hours, wondering where I went wrong. I compare myself to the people I follow and to the people I read. There are days when doing this makes me feel pretty terrible about myself, but that doesn't stop me. My focus is scattered across nothing and everything at the same time, hanging off a thousand different bits of content that I'm not interested in or that are bad for me, and yet there I am, scrolling. Sometimes I don't remember picking up my phone. All I know is that I've wasted two hours of my life poring over Instagram pictures of people I don't know. The photos are endless; they parade in front of my eyes, guzzling my time like it's no big deal. It's not like I don't know what's happening. The urge to leave it all behind and focus on my real life, the life I can touch, the people around me – it cracks in my face like a whip. I tell myself: *I'm done*, delete every account, pull an Irish exit – bye-bye Instagram, bye-bye Twitter, bye-bye Facebook Messenger – and last a day, or two, or three if I really put my back into it. Then, the FOMO dribbles down my neck. What exactly I fear missing out on is a mystery. The discourse. What's going on. So I re-activate my accounts . . . It's a vicious cycle.

'More than four thousand followers?' We look at each other. 'Do you know *every* song on the planet? This is insane.'

'Relax,' I reply, using the same tone as Romeo Santos.

He laughs.

'You know what I find funny? A couple days ago you were about to have me arrested for something ridiculous. Remember? You went all radical, far-left feminist on me for something that just slipped out?'

'When?'

He imitates me.

'*Here, have your eyes back. I found them glued to my tits.*'

'Please, I do not talk like that.'

'You *100%* talk like that. It's a lot of tchhhhhztchhhhhz, like static.'

I point at him.

'I think you might care too much about what I say.'

'On the other hand,' he says, ignoring me, 'you know every reggaeton song under the sun, back to front. But those lyrics aren't very feminist, are they? Do your internet followers know *that* about you?'

'You're literally a man pushing forty getting into an argument the internet put to bed in 2008. I refuse to educate you. Google it.'

We size each other up in silence.

'What's your favorite thing about the internet?' he asks after a while.

I mull over his question while the server, who has finally remembered we exist, comes over to our table. We order two churros with hot chocolate.

'Anything I can think of or that's happened to me has already happened to somebody else,' I tell him. 'I just google it and bam, a hundred million hits at my fingertips. Before, when I was younger, I used to feel . . . alone. Actually, I don't know if *alone* is the right word. Cut off. I always felt a little uncomfortable, no matter where I was. Then I started meeting people who cared about the same things, and I saw that I wasn't a total weirdo, I was just from a really small town. Does that make sense?'

He sits with my answer.

'Yes,' he finally says. 'I've never heard of that other website you mentioned.'

'What website?'

'That other one where you have tons of followers.'

'Oh.'

The server places two churros with their respective hot chocolates in front of us. Omar's face does a one-eighty.

'These aren't churros. They're porras.'

'They're churros.'

'Meryem, they're porras. Churros are thinner, and they're . . . they're shaped like hoops.'

I refuse to give in.

'What does it say on that sign out there? Churrería, right? Not "Porrería".'

'You're something else.'

'No! Wait. Don't touch anything! I have to take a pic for Insta.' I move the plates and cups according to a vague set of aesthetic criteria, but the light in the café and the metal of the table are hideous. The photo doesn't come out as nice as I wanted. 'Okay, done.'

The churros are so delicious that neither of us says anything for a while.

'Tell me about that website.'

I chew my churros with deliberate slowness.

'Fanfiction dot net,' I finally say. 'I write fanfiction in my free time.'

'Cool. I don't know what that is.'

I wipe my mouth with the napkin.

'I write stories based on other people's stories. Books, TV shows, movies . . . I started doing it as a teenager with

155

Harry Potter, not about Harry but about his parents. Then *Twilight* came out.'

'The one with the vampires.'

'Exactly. I got obsessed with those books. I was sixteen. Between eleventh and twelfth grade, I think I wrote like seventy fanfic pieces.' I smile at the memory of those years and how happy I was. 'So, the deal is you write stories and post them on the website, and tag them so that other people can find them. So, if the fic is . . .'

'Fic?'

'Shorthand for fanfiction. I'm talking kind of fast, huh?'

'No, keep going.'

Something about the way he moves his chin makes me feel self-conscious.

'Continuuuuuee.'

'Okay, fine. So, let's say the fic is about Edward and Bella. What you do is you tag those two characters. If it's a sad fic, you use the tag "Drama." If it's funny, you use the tag "Humor." And so on, until you've given readers as much information as possible. That way, if someone's looking for a comedic fic with Edward and Bella that's R-rated because of the language or because there's sex or whatever, they can—'

'Oh, so there's sex.'

'Of course. There's anything you can think of. It's like the original author doesn't exist anymore. You don't need their permission. Whatever you come up with is free game.'

'What if the author decides to sue you because they don't like what you're writing?'

I shrug.

'Then they'd have to sue thousands of people all over the world. So good luck to them. Nobody makes money writing fanfic. I don't think there's anything wrong with borrowing characters and letting your imagination run wild.'

'Okay, so you said you have all these followers on that website. How do they find you?'

'Because readers recommend your work on fanfiction forums, or someone who's already popular saves you as one of their favorites, or because you happen to be writing one of the few Spanish-language fics about a specific couple in a specific world. I had this seven-chapter fic about Paul and Jessica from *Twilight*, and someone read it, liked it . . . and recommended it in "The Best of the Best." Next stop, hall of fame.'

'You know, you'd sort of casually mentioned writing before, but I figured you just had a blog or something.'

'Umm, Omar . . . You do know what year it is, right? No one has blogs anymore.'

He reaches across the table and touches one of my bracelets, carefully going over each link. The feeling of his fingers on my skin makes the back of my head tingle. I swallow.

'My sister has a bracelet just like yours.' He looks me in the eyes. 'Where can I read your fics?'

'Nowhere. I don't want you to read them.'

'What? Why?'

'Because there are two worlds. The real world and my fanfic world. My life here and my life online. They never mix.'

It'd be catastrophic, my own personal Armageddon. The last thing I wrote this morning on Twitter was: 'Shouting Allahu Akbar down the office corridor in the hopes we get evacuated and don't have to go back to work.' I picture Otero and Víctor reading my posts and stifle a shiver, though I don't know if it's because of the mental image or because Omar's hand is still around my wrist.

'I promise not to show anyone. You can trust me.'

'I know I can trust you. I do trust you. It's not about that.'

He pulls my hand toward him.

'Meryem. I want to read your ficfans. Your fanfics. Your stories.'

Past Meryem and future Meryem scream. Present Meryem thinks about Lucía 2 elbowing her at lunch. About her eyebrows. Doesn't he look hot? Hunched over the table across from each other with our hands on the table and the air stinking of fried churros, I think: No, he doesn't look hot. He looks dangerous.

'No.'

That evening before I turn off my computer and go home, I see a message from Omar on our Skype chat: a link to my fanfiction.net profile. The last time I updated my bio was in 2010.

36

October 2017

What I don't get is why something that's supposed to be a fundamental right hits my paycheck like a cluster bomb. I read: 'Stunning, newly refurbished 25m² loft featuring living-dining room, bedroom, and bathroom. The apartment is in perfect condition, unfurnished, just steps away from Paseo de Chil, in Triana's commercial district, close to supermarkets, pharmacies, and all bus stops. Rent: €700 / month. Renter is responsible for water and electricity. One month security deposit, first month's rent, and broker's fee. Only serious candidates will be considered: proof of income required.' I think: *It should be illegal to pay €700 a month plus utilities to sleep in the kitchen of a 25m2 shoebox*. Then I close the page, furious.

I try to get on with my life, but start obsessing over the pictures of that rathole and what they're charging for it. 25m² with a single window. *Stunning loft*, say the total dickwads. Days later, I read: 'The Bank of Spain recommends spending no more than 35% of your monthly wages on rent.' My head is scrambled for ages. I can't stop thinking about it, but I don't give up. I keep looking. I visit a 'move-in-ready studio with all the finest details. Located in León y Castillo, near Plaza de la Feria, don't pass up the chance to live in this all-inclusive penthouse. €650 / month plus utilities. Fully equipped kitchen. Unfurnished. 22m². No separate bedroom. Two-month security deposit, broker's fee, and first month's rent.' The woman from the real estate agency gestures a lot with her hands. If I choose not to pass up this chance, I'll have to cover her fee. My face telegraphs zero emotion when she explains this to me, but a fire ignites in my chest. Why should I have to pay *her* fee when I'm not the one engaging her services? A two-month security deposit for a 22m² unfurnished hovel. At least I have the freedom to choose, I guess. Like, do I *really* want a bed, or do I *need* a sofa or should I buy a futon instead and pay €700 to basically live like I'm in solitary in a correctional facility. My bank starts bombarding me with spam for loans. The first call I get, I'm offered €20,000. The second, €30,000. For whatever project I have up my sleeve, says the loan officer. I should seriously consider it. I could use the money to go back to school, buy a car, refurbish my house. I hang up because that last suggestion really annoyed me. What house? I nearly shout down the line. What fucking house? I'm hounded by mail, through the bank app, at the ATM. €40,000 right at my fingertips, just one click away. I develop a colossal grudge against my bank and all things related to it. I consider taking the money and running. I watch Santander executive Ana Botín become a feminist icon, and sit in front of the TV, stunned. I think of all the women working at Santander who will lose their jobs in the coming months because its branch offices are closing, and of the long lines of elderly people who don't know how to use ATMs and have to pay a fee to take out money (their own money!) with a teller at the counter. Would they come

160

find me in my grandma's village if I decided to run off with those €40,000? Would they stalk me there and demand it back? €47,000. No paperwork needed, just a click. Makes a girl want to do something crazy.

A steady rage grows inside me and builds up, little by little, in my guts. I can't seem to get rid of it, no matter how hard I try. It creeps up my shoulders, puts its hands around my neck and squeezes, squeezes, squeezes, enough that I can always feel it, wherever I am, whatever I'm doing. It doesn't asphyxiate me completely or incapacitate me: I'm still functional, operating, I can work. Days pass, weeks. I don't do anything about it. I wouldn't know what to do. I stare down at my hands. Open them, close them.

In early October, I move to a two-bedroom apartment on Calle Arena, a ten-minute walk from work. I pay €615 a month, plus utilities. The water heater half works, and the fridge is so ancient it can barely keep anything cold. All my belongings fit in two Leroy Merlín moving boxes and two suitcases that sit beside me in the backseat of my parents' car. They make a point of helping me clean my new apartment, but the place is minuscule, and it takes us almost no time at all. Entryway-kitchen-living-room. There is no sofa or kitchen table or shelving. A tiny, windowless bathroom. No TV. The bedroom looks out on Calle Arena. There's a Stradivarius clothing store, a La Madera café, and a restaurant within walking distance. Right under my apartment, there are three luxury boutiques, a stationer's, and a hair salon. €615 a month plus a one-month security deposit. Because I deal directly with the landlords, a pair of retirees, I don't need to worry about the broker's fee. It's sheer luck, though a part of me can't help feeling canny. Checkmate, I beat the system. Obviously, I'm an idiot. I can hear all the buskers playing their violins, flutes, guitars, and saxophones

161

on Calle Triana for pennies. At first I tell myself it's charming. I treat my parents to lunch because I don't want them to leave, and when they do, when we say goodbye and they walk out the front door, I'm flooded with a sadness so deep I sink to the floor and scroll through my Twitter timeline, heart things on Instagram, reply to messages on WhatsApp. My home is no longer my home. Now it's my parents' house, the place where I grew up and don't live anymore but sometimes visit on weekends. I become a person without a home of her own. When I cry, it's to the muffled soundtrack of a busking saxophonist.

My landlord, an older gentleman who lives on the floor below mine with his wife, my landlady, seems friendly at first but soon shows his true colors. He starts taking my mail hostage and only releasing it when it suits him: He is the villain of a TV movie on Antena 3. I briefly contemplate moving, but I don't want to lose the security deposit and I don't want to go apartment hunting. It seems like a crazy thing to do when it took me so long to find this place. It's just mail. And he does eventually give it to me. A few months later, he starts coming upstairs and knocking on my door to talk. I open the door the first couple times. The third time, I pretend I'm not home. It turns into this weird dynamic: every so often, he shuffles upstairs, bangs on the door, waits a second, then shuffles back down to his apartment. I don't tell anyone about that either. He's probably just lonely. In need of some chitchat. Women can justify anything if we try hard enough.

37

October 2017

One evening I get home, leave my things on the floor near the front door, and drag my feet to the living room. I sit on the sofa and let it swallow me up, just for a minute, five minutes tops. I wind up lying down with my knees draped over the armrest – I may as well get comfortable. I enter an infinite loop that involves reading tweets and scrolling through Instagram. Next thing I know, the sun's set, it's night-time, the day's over. It's 7:08 p.m. Today, I've had a life between 6:40 and 7:50 in the morning; the rest of the time, I've been working. I don't realize I'm calling Omar on the phone until I see his name onscreen. I know I'm calling because the thought of calling him popped into my head, but it doesn't totally register, like when you get up to go to the bathroom without making the conscious choice to get up and go to the bathroom. You just do it. He doesn't answer. I close my eyes and stretch out on the sofa. I think: *If I go to sleep now, would anyone judge me? In my work clothes, stinking of corporate spirit.* Omar calls me back.

'You rang?' he asks.

I close my eyes.

'Yes.'

'Oh! I thought it was a butt dial.'

'No, it was a finger dial. I mean,' I clear my throat, 'I thought of calling you and my finger dialed your number.'

'Is there something wrong?'

'No, why? Are you busy?'

'No, I'm just sitting at home watching the cooking channel.'

I laugh.

'What's on?'

'Jamie Oliver's committing crimes against humanity.' He pauses. 'I would've picked up anyway, even if I was busy.'

'Okay.'

'I'd have said, I can't talk right now because they're making cod au gratin with garlic mousseline and escalivada on TV, but I'll call you when it's over.'

'How polite of you.'

'What can I say? I'm old school, a gentleman.'

I laugh through my teeth. Neither of us speaks for a while – somewhere between a minute and three hours.

'What's for dinner?'

I hear him take a breath, like he's thinking.

'I don't know. Why? Want to come over? I've got stone bass.'

'You eat more fish than anyone I've ever met. It blows my mind. Is it an age thing?'

'It's called making the most of discounted catch at the fishmonger.' I hear him switch off the television. 'We could also have chickpea salad with pico de gallo.'

'Sure. I mean, I don't know. I don't mind, really, both options sound good to me. What can I bring? I have a ton of ginger ale. My fridge is in critical condition. I've got a single head of mushy cauliflower. You can have it if you want it.'

'No.' He laughs. 'You can drink ginger ale, but I'm not touching the stuff.'

'But it's delicious.'

'I like that for you, but not for me.' Which is exactly what I said about his shirt today. 'Are you really coming over, or are we just kidding around?'

'I'm really coming over. Aren't I? I mean, I thought we were being serious. Were *you* kidding around?'

'I was being serious. It's no trouble setting an extra place for you at the table.'

'Alright. Okay. I've got to shower, but I can be over at eight, eight thirty or so. Send me your location.'

'Okay.'

'Okay.'

'I'm hanging up now.'

'No, I'm hanging up.'

I hang up. I open my eyes, get my butt in the shower, then take four cans of ginger ale and the sad cauliflower to his house. Turns out he lives right on Paseo de las Canteras, on the boardwalk.

38

October 2017

On International Day Against Breast Cancer, Supersaurio is awash in pamphlets with pink ribbons. No corner of the supermarket is spared from images of women wearing pink bandanas. Playing on a loop on the loudspeakers is a recorded message of the company bragging about how much money they've donated to cancer research and inviting customers to add their own little grain of sand. Employees are asked to pin a pink ribbon on their clothes. Pink shirts are handed out to all the female employees, and we get an email alerting us to a Pink Run being held in just a few days. No one goes to the Pink Run, but we keep the shirts because we're woke. At noon, all the women on shift go to the meeting room in our pink shirts and pink ribbons for a group photo that someone in HR posts on the website.

Since Supersaurio is not feminist or misogynist but equal opportunity, somebody complains about the fact that the men didn't get a shirt. They want to divide us, I hear, to pit men against women. All discrimination is wrong, even the positive kind. Well, fuck, I guess men are to blame for the fact that women get breast cancer now. Who wants to divide us? I don't know. Probably the pinkos. Soros, Obama, Mediaset. Sitting on the office-bathroom toilet seat, I open my bank app and check my savings. Ten more months, I tell myself. Ten more months, and I'm finding something else.

39

November 2017

In the video, a group of friends claps at a party. They sing, all together: 'Puigdemont, we're gonna lock you up!' Alonso laughs as he plays it on his phone. A guy in the group smacks a tambourine to the beat of the song. They go on singing: 'Puigdemont, we're gonna lock you up with your buddy Trapero. He's gonna be your compañero!' One person plays the guitar while another sings in the middle of the circle. I'm horrified, enthralled. Lucía 1 and I stare at the video in silence until it's over. Alonso hits play again. He thinks it's the funniest thing in the world.

'It's so good,' he says. 'Everyone's lost their mind.'

'Um, I gotta go. I have a million things to do,' says Lucía 1. She gets up from the table. It was just the three of us. I'd bumped into them while I was getting coffee at the cafeteria and couldn't think of an excuse not to sit at their table. 'I don't know why I let you rope me into watching this crap. Anyway. Later.'

As I watch Lucía walk away, the song gloms onto my cerebral cortex. *Puigdemont*, sings the djinn that follows me everywhere I go, *we're gonna lock you up*. I look down at the cup in my hands. I don't know how I feel about what I just saw. It's amusing, but I'm unamused.

'Do you think she's upset?'

'No, I don't think so,' I reply. 'There's a shareholder meeting this afternoon. She's just busy.'

The first part is a lie. The second is true. I don't know if she's upset, but I do know the video unsettled her enough that she wanted to get away from Alonso. She'll never admit this to him because women have been raised to believe we're crazy, that this thing we've found so unsettling isn't actually a big deal.

'I mean, come on, you've got a sense of humor. You agree it's funny, right?'

'Sure.'

'Sometimes I have a hard time understanding you women,' he continues. 'You're really unpredictable, what with all the mood swings.'

'I guess.'

I consider lifting my hands to my hair line and tearing my skin off in strips, right in front of him, just so he'll shut up.

'Anyway, Catalan independence is a complicated issue.'

'So is everything else.'

'You don't like me, do you?'

I blink.

'What makes you say that?'

He shrugs.

'I'm not stupid. You have actual conversations with other people. All you do with me is nod and agree.'

I don't sigh, but I'm about to. He's not stupid? Debatable. Do I always agree with him? Of course. He's my boss. I clear my throat.

'I find the idea of having an actual conversation with you intimidating,' I lie. 'You're a boss.'

A talent manager, whatever.

'But I'm a good boss,' he objects. 'We're practically the same age. I don't waltz in here like, *I'm your boss, you must respect me* . . . do I? I'm different . . .'

A millionaire who needs validation from a personal assistant. My life is just one long fucking episode of *The Office*. On top of everything else, I'm supposed to play therapist to a guy who basically owns the company I work for?

'I mean, it's compli—'

'Besides, Omar's a boss too. And you talk to him, even though he's higher up than me.'

'It's not the same.' I look at my hands, at my cup of coffee, which has gone cold. All my internal organs are contracting, entering high alert. 'He can't fire me if I tell him to go fuck himself. You can.'

He mulls over my response in silence. Those may be the dumbest words to have ever left my mouth – but I've got glasses on, my hair's done up in a perfect ponytail, and I'm wearing a suit jacket.

'I wouldn't fire anyone for cracking a joke. That's not the kind of boss I am.' His voice sounds weird as he says this, like he's about to cry from the frustration.

I daydream of having a life where my only worry is what kind of boss I am. A receptive, extroverted, cool boss. A boss who rides her bike everywhere, recycles, and tells her employees to take a mental health day if they need it. I don't know how to explain to Alonso that I find his mere existence sickening because it represents everything that's wrong with this world. A normal person, a civilian like myself, can't be friends with a Boss. Who in their right mind would be friends with their direct superior? It's wild that such a small segment of people could own so much, covet so much more, and leave only the tiniest sliver for the

170

rest of us to fight over like a pack of starving dogs. If I had money, I wouldn't put on the charade of going to work. I wouldn't need anyone's validation. And I wouldn't want it, either. Yet, here I am, comforting a man who's got money to burn. *People don't avoid you because you're their boss*, I think. *They avoid you because you're not a person, you're what you believe a person should be.*

My phone starts vibrating on the table. I see the word MATIQUI flash onscreen. To think some people don't believe in God. I grab my phone like it's a lifebuoy or an aid package airdropped from the sky. To think some people choose not to believe in Him because they can't see Him. Please.

'Sorry. Gotta run. Duty calls!'

I flee.

40

November 2017

'You rang?'

'Hi, Meryem. Could you come to my office for a minute? I need your help with something.'

All that's standing between me and Matiqui is a glass wall. It takes a lot for me not to roll my eyes every time he buzzes me. I can see him through the wall, he can see me. What's the point?

'Sure thing.'

'Great, thank you.'

I stay quiet for a moment.

'Okay.'

When I walk into his office, he gets up and steps away from the computer.

'I need to convert an Excel spreadsheet into a PDF, but I don't really know how. I'm hoping you do.'

This really weird sensation starts dribbling down my back, but I don't have time to sit with it.

'Sure thing.'

Out of all the phrases I regularly say to Matiqui, 'sure thing' is by far the one I use the most. Can you come in half an hour early on Thursday? Sure thing. Can you stay an hour later today? Sure thing. Can you check this stack of papers for typos? Sure thing. Can you do the work of two people for two weeks while Yolanda's on vacation? Sure thing. Can I put my boot on your neck while you whimper? Sure thing.

'It probably isn't all that complicated,' he says, 'but, for the life of me, I can't remember how it's done. No matter how many times people explain it to me, it just doesn't stick.'

I hope he saves me the speech, I think. It'd be less degrading that way. I sit in front of his computer and look at Excel.

'Young people probably don't even need to be taught this stuff anymore,' he continues. 'It's like you're born with the knowledge.'

In the time it takes him to say this, I convert the file into a PDF and get up.

'Done.'

'Amazing, thank you.' He looks at the file, checks that it is in fact a PDF, and smiles. 'What would I do without you, Meryem? You have no idea how often I ask myself that.'

I automatically smile in response. I feel like I'm made of plastic.

'Anything else I can help you with?'

'No, thanks. Everything's under control here.'

Nothing's under control, I'd like to tell him. You don't even know how to print things. You're a functional deadweight. I'm the one who reminds you about your husband and daughter's birthdays. I pick up your cat from the vet. I know your allergies. You make five times what I do and yet somehow still can't convert a stupid Excel spreadsheet into a PDF. At the interview for the internship, I lied about knowing my way around Excel, but I've been learning from some

Indian guys' YouTube tutorials. You don't have shit in control, I'd like to scream, but instead I give him a thumbs-up with my right hand. All good. I head back to my desk.

I'm burning up. The temperature rises little by little – one degree here, another degree there – until eventually I feel smothered, defunct. I make dinner and watch TV. Sometimes I manage to read. I listen to the radio while tidying up. I make plans and then flake on them because I just don't have the energy, again. I eat yesterday's leftovers at my desk out of a Tupperware container, and I walk. I walk home and then back to the office. I work, work, work. My job starts taking over my life. I don't have time to see Carmen, I don't have time to see Teresa. I can't seem to remember what I wanted to do, what my initial plan was, what the next step will be. Though I'm aware of time passing, it doesn't fully sink in – it's like time isn't passing for me but for another Meryem. Omar now takes up seventy per cent of my mental real estate. I talk to him more than anyone else. I can't see myself from the outside, I don't have time to think. I'm starting to feel that I could disappear any minute and no one would notice.

Fandom: Supersaurio (Las Palmas – District 2)
Characters: Dácil, Antonio
Tags: -
Category: General
Words: 168

Comrade, Join Us

Antonio was posted at the end of the hall, glancing around, keeping watch, covering Dácil's back. Dácil got on her tiptoes and stuck a poster smack in the middle of the break room bulletin board. It wasn't much, just an A3-sized sheet with her union logo and the phrase UNDER CAPITALISM, MAN EXPLOITS MAN in block letters. COMRADE, JOIN US. As Dácil stuck up the poster, she worried someone would see her. A few of her colleagues were resistant to that kind of messaging. Two weeks earlier, she and Antonio had joined CC OO, Workers' Commissions. She was scared of getting fired out of the blue, as had happened with some of her other coworkers. Dácil had two kids and a mother who relied on her income. Another supermarket chain had laid off 16% of its staff. As soon as the poster was secured to the board, she zipped her jacket uniform all the way up to her neck and rushed out to Antonio.

'Done?' he asked.

'Doneso.'

41

December 2017

The only time Omar catches me crying, I'm hiding in a corner of the storage room with my head on my knees and my eyes closed. I try not to, cry during work hours, that is. Firstly because it'd be humiliating to be seen like this, and secondly because it's unprofessional. But when I can't hold it in, I sneak down to the basement. The only time Omar sees me crying he says, *Meryem?* and I think I'd rather be low-key flayed alive, strip by strip, than look him in the eye, so I pretend not to hear and instead go on crying. Crying in peace should be a universal human right. There should be a law that guarantees our right to privacy when we're at our most vulnerable, that forces others to look away and pretend they haven't seen or heard us, except in cases when we expressly request their support, attention, or whatever we may need in that moment. I like crying alone. I don't like being hugged, or comforted, or checked in on. *Are you okay?* he insists. I think, *You must have shit for brains. Can't you see I'm not okay?* Then I say, *Yeah.* I say, *Don't worry about it.* I say, *I just need a second.* The thing is, a second lasts a second, not five minutes or ten. It's not enough time to take a deep breath in and out, to splash some water on your face, to leave. I don't move my arms away from my face, but I make a concerted effort to stop crying. What happens instead is that I start wailing even louder, and he says, *Oh, no*, but I'm sitting there on the floor and his distress makes me so mad I feel like I'm going to explode, like my skin is stretched so tight that I don't fit inside it anymore, and I can't get the words out: Yes, I'm fine, no, nothing's wrong, I shouldn't even be here crying because I'm supposed to be at a team lunch but it was canceled last minute and nobody warned me because the person who was supposed to not only didn't do that but invited the rest of the team out somewhere else without telling me so I stood outside the supermarket waiting for everyone for ten minutes until I realized they'd left without me because Yolanda suggested another place without letting me know and I just don't get what her deal is why she despises me I don't get it but I'm sick and tired of it so as soon as I'm done crying I'm going back upstairs and telling my boss that I can't take it anymore Yolanda wins and I quit I'm out of here so long King Kong see you later alligator good luck finding someone who can put up with this bullshit because I've frankly reached my limit. All this is stuck in my throat, but when I open my mouth to speak, nothing comes out. My face is red, my neck is red, my eyes are red, and all the words I can think of to explain what I'm going through are teetering, slipping through my hands and off the tip of my tongue. In the end, he asks, *Do you want me to leave?* And I say, *Yes*, and then, *No*, and then, finally, *You should probably go*. And he does. When I decide I've let enough out, I stand and wipe my face on my shirt sleeves. I cry against

177

the filthy toy dinosaur that lives where we all float down here. I'm an idiot, I think I'm so clever except I'm constantly reminded I'm not. *I'm sorry you had to see that*, I say aloud, addressing the ten-foot dino I've just covered in snot. Humans are such assholes, I explain.

The next morning, there's a grease-stained paper bag on my desk. I open it carefully, like I think I'm going to find a frog, a snake, or dog shit inside. Instead, it's a croissant from Colomar, perfectly golden. I stick my nose in the bag, take a whiff. My eyes well up. Marital status: Day 29 of my cycle. I switch on my desktop and see two new messages in my Skype chat with Omar. The first is: 'It was me.' And the second: 'It's not poisoned. It's from Colomar.' I don't talk to my boss that day, and I don't quit my job. I calmly eat the croissant at my desk. I pull it apart and bring it to my mouth piece by piece. A while later I reply 'thanks' and take everything that happened the afternoon before, squish it between my hands, and store it away. He says: 'You're welcome, gorgeous.' I kind of avoid him for the next few days. I'm scared I'll punch him, or worse, kiss him.

42

December 2017

One day you're young. Next thing you know, you've started thinking of yourself as a business venture. You're both the CEO, COO, and CFO of your own life. You must increase your productivity – go on, feel guilty about not making the most of your time all the time, about the fact you don't have a single minute you can spend doing nothing, because when you do nothing you get thinking, and you know that what you end up doing when you get thinking, right? nothing – cut expenses, make better use of the resources at your disposal, diversify your assignments, optimize results across the board, never mind that you don't have the faintest idea what it's all about or what exactly you're doing with your life. You have no employees to threaten with layoffs if they (we) don't meet certain targets, so when you get out of the shower and look at yourself in the mirror, you beat yourself up over everything you should've accomplished by your age, things that, unlike your friends, you're still nowhere near attaining.

You feel time going tick tock tick tock tick tock in your ears.

I used to think becoming an adult meant unlocking some kind of inner peace that would put an end to the unease that sometimes settles in my stomach. Now I know that human beings are these weird, pretty awful creatures who fear each other and that being an adult basically consists of trying to eat healthy and delivering paperwork to organizations that either treat me so-so or talk down to me. Sure, the staff are just human, though most of the time they don't seem it. For me, being an adult was supposed to be about relishing my independence, my profession, my own money. Instead, it's meant never not thinking about the laundry that needs to be done, then ironed, about the sad lettuce that's been sitting in the fridge the last couple of weeks, about how to avoid my landlords because I'm scared they'll try to raise my rent if I answer the phone.

So, one day you're young. Next thing you know, you're constantly tired. Every day a different part of your body aches and you feel like you've been beaten to a pulp, even though you've done nothing since morning because you don't know how to be a good CEO, COO, or CFO of your business of one. You try to remember the important stuff, like the monstrous cauliflower you bought in a fit of guilt and anxiety because you're fat and eat terribly and there are twenty-five calories per hundred grams of cauliflower, which means you can fill up on it without gaining weight. If you eat a hamburger while feeling very, very guilty, do you still put on the weight? You tell yourself you'll eat the cauliflower before it goes off, that you mustn't forget because if you *don't* eat it, you'll have to throw it away, which will just make you feel bad, so please, eat it. It's not going to last past tomorrow. Either roast it in the oven or blitz it into soup but eat the poor thing already – it's gone this weird color, it's basically half spoiled, it's clearly soft and inedible, what if you eat it and it makes you sick? You can't get sick. You can't miss work. Fuck your fucking life.

Fandom: Supersaurio (Las Palmas – District 2)
Characters: Davinia, Alicia
Tags: -
Category: General
Words: 261

It Won't Take a Minute

Davinia massaged her right wrist while waiting for Alicia to close the register. A woman in a bright pink track suit stood behind the person whose groceries were on the conveyor belt. Davinia cleared her throat and said:

'Ma'am. Excuse me, ma'am, but this cash register is about to close.'

'Pardon?'

'This cash register is about to close. Look,' she said, pointing with her not-bad hand at the sign Alicia had placed on the belt.

'Oh. But I've only got three things. It won't take a minute.'

Davinia raised her eyebrows.

'Please use the next register. This one is closed.'

'Honestly, it's only three little things. Look,' she said, opening her reusable cloth bag.

'Ma'am, I've told you twice. This register is closed. Please use the next one.'

Every day, Davinia had wrist pain. Joint pain. Pain in her back and neck. Before each shift, she took pills to help her through the physical and psychological exhaustion. After each shift, she took *more* pills. When she didn't, she felt like her head was about to burst. Alicia had just scanned the last item on the conveyor belt.

'Come on, mi niña, you don't mind scanning these three little things, do you?' the woman asked, addressing Alicia.

181

Alicia said nothing and pointed at the sign to her left that said REGISTER CLOSED.

'So rude! I guess this is the thanks I get for helping you keep your job by coming to a human cashier instead of self-checkout. Never again.'

'I couldn't thank you enough,' Davinia replied, tired. And she meant every word.

43

December 2017

A supermarket is a museum. Food, cleaning, hygiene, and beauty products are exhibited on its shelves according to a perfectly devised system. The deli meat shall never be placed near the detergents, nor the dairy products near the alcohol. The newsstand is always at the entrance. The items near the register should never cost more than three Euros. On each floor, two security guards patrol the aisles. Like all non-places, the supermarket is an environment defined above all by the absence of communication. Customers need not interact with another human being unless they want to. We've installed self-checkout machines so they can scan and bag their own groceries, then go home. This is not the customer's final destination. We are a mere circumstance, a transaction. People don't come here to socialize, they come here to buy things. *Veni, vidi, purchasi.* The fluorescent lights shall greet and accompany the customer to the end. The background music barely registers; the customers know these songs so well they can hum along to them without even listening. The customer will remember not a single face, not a single name.

Omar is chatting away in front of me. He pours sugar into his coffee and mixes it with a wooden spoon, takes a sip. I look at him, he looks at me. I make a show of fixing my shirt, sitting up straight, crossing my arms. I say:

'On a scale of one to ten, how would you rate your experience at Supersaurio?'

He cracks up, but he's been here a long time.

It's eleven and a bit in the morning. The only people in the cafeteria are the two of us and three women from Logistics. I know he's trying not to laugh because his shoulders are shaking even though his expression hasn't changed. Omar has a mark right below his right eye. Every time I get the urge to say something about it, I wuss out, I don't know why. I guess I don't want him to think I notice these things, that I notice *him*.

'There's not one day I come here that I wouldn't rather stay home,' he says after a while. He wipes his face with a napkin and crumples it up. I can't possibly have a crush on this guy – I hate blonds. And bald people; I don't trust them. The only exception to this rule is Zinedine Zidane. 'But lately, I've actually enjoyed coming to work a lot more.' He manspreads under the table. 'The workdays are more manageable, I'm having an okay time. So I'd rate it a four. What about you?'

I pretend to think it over.

'A one.'

'Come on. It's not so bad. You just like to complain.'

'My parents told me that we learn to put things in perspective as we get older. Is that why your hair's so white?'

'You're such a dumbass.'

'Why? Also, the only reason I'm not insulting you back is that I was brought up to respect my elders.'

184

I think of the women from Logistics and how they might view our conversation. I open my mouth to say something else, like *it's a joke* or *you know it's a joke, right?*, but he leans toward me, and I shut up. I think of his ex, the one he was with for four years, who packed his lunch and looked like Emily Blunt. Emily Blunt! I couldn't stop laughing when he told me. Not at him but at me. At my face like a slapped fish. When he asked what was so funny, I didn't know what to say, so I replied: 'Nothing, I just think it's funny that you're a modelizer.' I'm always on the defensive, ready to make fun of him. For a frac-tion of a fraction of a second, I'm sure he's going to send me to hell but instead he touches my face. He holds my chin. The most embarrassing thought in the world flashes inside my head in neon colors: *He's going to kiss me.* But the gesture lasts less than a second, maybe two, three at most, even though I can feel all the energy in my body rush to my feet and back up to my head. I don't totally get what just happened. Run, I think. Get up, feed him some excuse, and run.

'I don't know why I even hang out with you.'

I hate his mumbly El-Turronero accent with my whole being. So much that it clouds my vision. My insides get spongy. I'm liquid, malleable.

'The question is why *I* even hang out with *you*. Gotta go.'

'You have to go?' he echoes. I wish I could bury my hand in his face to see if I have the same effect on him as he has on me. I feel small and ridiculous, like he knows something about me that I don't. He checks his watch, his stupid iWatch. This fucking guy. 'But you just got here.'

'Yeah, but I have to go do something . . .'

'Alright.'

But I don't get up. I stay right where I am. I feel like if I move one millimeter, something bad will happen. A tsunami will hit the Canary Islands. Zinedine Zidane will leave Real Madrid again. My accent will no longer be the sexiest accent in all of Spain. My skin will turn to dust.

'I need to tell you something,' I manage to mumble. SUPERSAURIO! *Best prices on the archipelago!* blares on the loudspeaker. *Here are this week's super sales!*

'Are you okay? You look like you're about to pass out.' He laughs through his teeth. 'Go on, say something. You're making me worry.'

I don't like your stupid face, I'm about to tell him. You have this really weird mark below your eye. I breathe through my mouth. Your nose looks like a banana. ('Guess I've got a good banana, then,' he'd quip back.) I hate that I always know what he's going to say. I hate it all. I make a huge clatter as I get up from my chair, like I really am about to pass out. I'm a wild horse, the strength of a thousand suns roils in my chest. I look at him.

'That is one of the ugliest shirts I've ever seen in my life,' I mutter. 'This is a serious establishment, not a funfair.'

He thinks it's hilarious.

'You're not being a great person right now.'

'Yeah? So sue me.'

'But hey,' he says, except I'm on a mission, a mission to get away from him ASAP. I put distance between us in record time. I activate safety mode and operate without any of the features I was born with, not even ones I've developed with age: I move by instinct alone. As soon as I'm at my desk I'll be safe. I switch to second gear, then third; I step into the elevator, hit the button. Close, I say to the doors. Close, close, for the love of God, close. As soon as they do, and the elevator starts moving up, my nerves settle and my stomach turns upside down. I call myself a dork, again and again. Starting on the third floor, I call myself an idiot. From there to the eighth floor, I'm a dumbass and a moron. Only when I sit at my desk and see my reflection in the monitor do I remember I left my key card and photo ID on the table downstairs. My eyes are wide open. Several times throughout the day, I touch the exact spot on my chin he'd touched earlier. I don't ask for my card back. It takes me two days to work up the courage to go get it from him.

44

December 2017

'I don't know if I'm making any sense.'

The second Teresa's front door closes, Carmen starts taking off her bra. We scramble inside like starving dogs, like a pack of rabid hounds. Teresa tosses her sneakers in the space behind the door, then heads into the living room and drops her bags onto the table. I follow her and lie back on the sofa.

'You're making perfect sense. The old man's got a crush on you.'

I object: 'He is *not* an old man!' My objection is overruled. 'Plus, I mean, *does* he have a crush on me? I don't know. I just got the sneaking suspicion he was moving in on my lips,' I say again. I copy what he did, emulating him to a tee. I reach out my hand, touch my chin. I need to paint a clear picture so they can accurately assess what happened, like the international observers they are. 'I'm probably overthinking it.'

'Mmm . . . I'm pretty sure I have a lump in my boob,' Carmen says behind us. I get up slightly from the sofa and look at her. Both her hands are cupping her breasts. 'Can you check for me?'

188

'Come here.' She sits next to me, and I grope the breast she thinks has a lump. 'This is kind of awkward. I don't think I've ever touched a boob before. Here? I can't feel anything.'

'It's just a boob. You have them too. Teresa?'

When I hear the fake shutter sound, I turn around and see her taking pictures of us. I give her the finger.

'Your friend may have breast cancer, and you're over there playing paparazzi?'

'I'm just documenting the moment.' She slips her phone back in her pant pocket and kneels in front of Carmen. 'Okay, let me see. Oh, I have little lumps like that too. It's nothing to worry about. You know, Carmen, you've got really nice tits.'

'You think? Let's see yours,' she mutters, still a bit worried. Eventually, she decides she believes us and pulls her shirt back down. 'Send the old man a tit pic, Mery. Be empowered!'

'I've never understood why you have to be naked to be empowered. Like, can't I be empowered with my clothes on?' I ask, but I don't know if I'm actually interested in an answer, or if it's more of a general complaint about something I've just remembered.

'Don't be ridiculous.' Teresa sits on the floor. My next apartment will have parquet flooring, I think, like hers. 'So did he kiss you or what? The old man.'

'He's not old, fuck's sake. He's thirty-seven. He didn't kiss me. He touched my face . . . Like he held it. Ugh, I don't know.'

'Thirty-seven,' Teresa echoes. The way she looks at me, it's as though she's just noticed I'm sitting right there in front of her. 'He's basically in diapers.'

Something about what she's said really rubs me the wrong way. 'Hey.'

'Listen, how would you feel if your sister told you she was being wooed by some dude twelve years older than her?' She's being a friend, I think, taking the wheel when I can't see straight. 'A guy your age, for example. Lily's eighteen now . . . Think about it.'

I want to tell her I *have* been thinking about it. That I've been thinking about it, and about him, and about me, and about his hand on my face, about his nose and his shirt collars, about the two of us sitting in the emergency stairwell whispering in the dark, about how if he said, Let's do this, I'm not sure I could stop myself from saying, Okay, let's do this, about how stupid and ridiculous it makes me feel because I used to be smart and now suddenly I'm not.

'Let's try and be positive,' Carmen suggests. 'Set aside our cynicism, our years of life experience, and just be positive.'

Teresa puts my feet in her lap.

'Let's imagine that this, ahem, *guy* is a decent person and not a hyena who sniffed out your youth and charm and decided to suck you dry—'

'I swear it's not like that. He's . . . he's the person I talk to the most. You know, I love being alone, doing my own thing, but . . . it's like how I feel around you two. I don't know, I enjoy being in his company more than being on my own. Dear God.'

I can't find the words, so instead I stare at my hands.

'Noooooooo, Merymeeeeeeeer. You're fucked.'

I take a deep breath.

'I'm super fucking fucked.'

Fandom: Supersaurio (Las Palmas – District 2)
Characters: Alonso
Tags: Horror, hurt
Category: General
Words: 101

Madrileñan Psycho

His eyes zeroed in on the mirror, Alonso pulled up his fly after peeing and pointed at his reflection.

'You're a leader,' he said to himself.

He nodded and ran his hands through his hair, brushing it back.

'You have a commanding presence,' he reminded himself, his reflection glowing in the white, fluorescent bathroom light. 'You optimize your team's skills. You help your employees shine.'

He nodded again and ran his hands down his shirt, smoothing it.

'You don't limit your challenges . . . You challenge your limits.'

He made a weird noise with his mouth, then exited the bathroom.

45

December 2017

The dress code for this year's Christmas party is *black tie*. I go to excruciating lengths to doll myself up. Today's look: bottle-green floor-length halter-top sleeveless sheath dress from the party-wear collection, eyeliner on fleek or on point or whatever it's called on Instagram, that's what I am tonight, and hair loose because I don't know how to do mine. When I arrive at the hotel where the party is being held, I see Lucía 1 step out of a taxi in a flowy black dress, like Audrey Hepburn in *Breakfast at Tiffany's*, and think I'm going to pass out. I have dinner with my team – Matiqui, Yolanda, Otero, and Víctor – at a table that could easily fit another five people. I listen to them go on about their Super-saurio stock and the loft in Triana that Víctor bought so he could flip it and make a killing. When Otero and Matiqui talk about their kids and their plans for the winter holiday, I make a bit more of an effort to join in on the conversation. I glance under the table at my phone when Yolanda starts chatting about all the work she's having done on her house. I look at them and think: *Help*. There are sixty people swimming around the largest room of the Santa Catalina hotel.

When my nervous system decides I can't take it anymore, I pretend to go to the bathroom and walk outside.

There's a text from Omar on my phone: 'Smoke?' I spot him, then sit next to him on the stairs. Marital status: Day 23 of my cycle.

'You got a haircut.'

'You like it?'

'You look like a neo-Nazi.'

'Well, you look beautiful.'

'Thanks.'

He laughs.

'Did you just accept a compliment? Excuse me while I take your temperature, make sure you're not running a fever.'

'It took me two hours to get ready. Believe me, I know how good I look.' I brush my hair away from my face. 'I am sweating . . . buckets, though. Barrels. Freaking silos.'

'Guess I must make you nervous.'

'You have no idea.'

It's the truth, but he laughs through his teeth, like he's not taking me seriously. I can hear the music inside. The boom boom boom teleports me to last year's Christmas party where the band played nothing but old Maná and Edwin Rivera tunes. It's only been a year, but the past twelve months have felt more like a decade or two.

'You always look beautiful.'

'Debatable.'

'I see you every day,' he reminds me. He doesn't speak again for a long while. He finishes his cigarette, drops it on the ground, and carefully stubs it out with his shoe. I think: You have a crush on a guy who litters. If my hands weren't shaking, I'd be laughing at myself. 'I realized yesterday that you're the person I talk to more than anyone. A lot of the time, knowing I'll see you is the only thing that gets me out of bed and into work.'

193

He's drunk and missing his family, I think. I don't know how to say what I want to say, so I choose silence. He's eleven years older than me. We work together. This is what I'd tell Teresa if she were in my position. I'd say, *Run, abort mission, mayday mayday*, she can't see the tsunami because her head's underwater and by the time she feels the first tremor, it'll be too late – the waves will have swallowed her whole.

'I like spending time by myself,' he continues, 'but lately I've enjoyed talking to you even more. I don't know how . . . I don't know if you even want to hear this. And you don't have to say anything, okay? Things between us can go on like usual. I don't want, I mean, my intention isn't to . . . I don't expect anything. If all that happens is we keep up our regular banter, I'd be happy with that too.'

When I walk into the party, my heart's beating so fast that I'm pretty sure I will throw up if I stop moving. There's a dancefloor where the tables used to be and everyone is mingling. Colorful lights glow above the heads of people dancing and huddling around the open bar – red, blue, red, blue, green green green – and flash to the beat of the music, which is so loud even the floor is thumping. A DJ come from God-only-knows-where is remixing Spotify's global hits. *This* is what the company chooses to spend its money on. I'm quitting, my mind's made up. This is what's going to happen: I'm going to thank Matiqui for the experience and give him my two-week notice. He will thank me back and continue sipping at his whiskey. It will be quick and painless. I'll go home to my parents' and sleep for ten uninterrupted hours, then wake the next morning feeling rested. I won't have a single plan for the future, but at least I'll be at peace. I don't want success anymore, or happiness. I don't want to be a strong-minded, independent woman. I just want to be left alone. I hide in the bathroom and videocall Teresa and Carmen. I prop the device up on the sink and start splashing water on my neck and arms while my phone goes ring-ring, ring-ring. Teresa answers first. Two seconds later, Carmen gets on the call.

'I'm quitting,' I blurt out, zero context. 'Tonight. I can't take it anymore.'

'Your job?'

'Yes.'

Carmen turns off her camera, then turns it on again.

'Sorry, I'm with the dog, I hit the button by mistake. Why're you quitting? What's going on?'

'Did one of those slimy assholes touch you!?' Teresa is suddenly raging, expecting the worst.

'No, no. It's not that.'

I wipe my hands on my dress.

'Omar told me he likes me.'

They both say, at the same time:

'NOOOOOOOOOOOOOOO.'

'YEAAAAAAAAAAAAAAAAAAAAA.'

'Plus, I just can't take it anymore. I really can't! I was having dinner with my team, and these people, they're all just so . . . fake. They sat there talking about how they bought an apartment here and a house there. Meanwhile, I'm working for literal pennies doing two people's jobs. Then this *guy* goes and says he has feelings for me. I have to quit. The supermarket staff have their own separate Christmas party, like they're, I don't know, pariahs or something. Can you believe it? SUPERSAURIO IS A FAMILY, they say. My butt. I need to quit this place because if I stay a minute longer, I might turn into one of them and start believing I'm somebody when the truth is I'm nobody: I just have a shitty, pointless job and if I disappeared tomorrow, no one would notice.'

'*We* would notice.'

'. . . and Omar . . .' Teresa adds.

195

'Whatever, yeah, my parents would notice too, but that's not the point. It doesn't matter. I just need you to tell me everything will be okay.'

Carmen clears her throat.

'Of course everything's going to be okay. The world isn't ending. You're just quitting your job.'

'Right.'

'And if the world does end, that's okay too, because then we're all dead,' Carmen says.

'Right.'

'Did you say anything to Omar?'

'Yes. Yeah. I said, "check check, received, read." Anyway. Talk later. I have to go ditch this hellhole.'

But when I finally find Matiqui standing in a corner of the room with Otero, he stops me before I can say anything and asks me to sit down.

'Listen, Meryem, I'm no good at this,' he begins. 'When I started at this company, it was just me and Otero. Remember those days?'

'Do I remember!? Eighty-hour weeks, my man. How could I forget? Mery, can I get you a drink? A beer, maybe?'

I'm going to pass out, I can't take it.

'No, thanks. I, uh . . . I was just leaving,' I say quietly. They don't hear me. Otero walks to the bar, leaving me alone with Matiqui.

'It isn't easy being someone's boss. Not one bit. You trust me to direct you, to guide you, and I do my best, I really do, but there are days when . . . I won't try and deny it,' he says, 'there are days when I wonder if I'm doing a good job or if I'm just a disaster.'

I have this theory about men and how much they love talking about themselves. Now is not the time. I'll think it through some more later, once the world stops spinning.

'I know you and Yolanda have had your ups and downs.'
I make myself look at him. I look in his eyes. I look, look,
look. 'Being a woman in this world . . . it's complicated.
She's not a bad person, Meryem. Things haven't been easy
for her at the company. She had a rough start. That's what
she told me.'

'Uh-huh,' I manage to get out.

'You women aren't always . . .' He searches for the
right words. He looks at me, looks, looks, looks. I refuse
to help him out of the hole he's digging himself. I'm not
paid enough. 'I think you struggle to support each other. I
recognize I'm not entirely blameless either. I'm your boss. I
should've stepped in sooner.'

I can hear my blood thumping in my ears. Boom,
boom, boom. Slow and steady. My hands are tingling like
crazy under the table, so I open and close them – once,
twice, three times. I don't know if out of embarrassment
or rage. I struggle to separate my feelings, tease them out,
analyze them. I know I don't want to be sitting here. I
know that I will keep sitting here until he's done talking. I've learned that growing up is about pretending, day
after day, hour after hour, that you don't want to just go
home and be on your own. I see Omar, I see his mouth,
I see that I could've kissed him instead of standing there
in silence.

'I made you a promise a few months ago. Remember? I said
that as soon as I could bring you on on a permanent basis, I
would. I'm not the world's greatest boss, far from it . . . I work
too much, I'm extremely meticulous. Which can be hard on all
of you. But I try to be fair. I try to keep my promises.'

Spit it out it, I tell myself. Just open your mouth and spit
it out. Two words. *I quit.* It would hurt, like when I wax my
own mustache and have to white-knuckle the edge of the

sink, convince myself it's not that big a deal. It's never that big a deal, really.

'Otero and Víctor are really happy with you. When I get to the office in the mornings, the lights and AC are on. It's been months since I've had Accounting breathing down my neck about expense reports and estimates. Because they're always perfect. We're never short a single receipt. Ever since you took over the budget, we've cut expenses by 14%. You have a great attitude, you're a quick study. I know you're younger than all of us, that we must seem ancient to you, but . . . we'd love to have you on the team.'

Spit it out.

'Thank you, Matiqui.'

'I've spoken to HR. Our starting offer is €30,000 net. There's room for growth, especially if you keep up the good work, but I'd like to give you more responsibilities first. You don't have to say anything right now. Sleep on it. The salary is negotiable, too. I want you to be comfortable, happy.'

My ears start buzzing at the words '€30,000.' All my principles vanish in a burst of colorful, dazzling light that momentarily blinds me. '*Yes, absolutely,*' I immediately blurt out. Yes. I'm a sellout, I live in a rotten, capitalist system, in a world where people lease themselves out for several hours a day in exchange for a paycheck. Sometimes you're out of luck and get subsistence wages; other times, you're given a decent salary, decent enough to do what you *want* instead of what you can or should. I say yes to Matiqui, then throw my arms around him. I hug him as if he weren't my boss and he laughs and hugs me back as if I weren't his employee. And as I'm hugging him, I see Omar across the room talking to someone else, and I become electric, I'm a feeling, and I have a person, I'm someone who sets out to work every day like she's setting out to war, because the minute she started

198

doing so, she ran out of time to feel or think, someone who works even when she's sad, even when she's miserable, even when she realizes she's falling in love. When I eventually fill my friends in on what's happened, I'll tell them that, in my defense, I was drunk, possessed, so happy I couldn't think straight, I miscalculated, I did not properly self-boycott. I'll say: a remix of 'Salvaje' by Fuel Fandango was playing, and I shouted over the music at Omar I HAVE TO TELL YOU SOME-THING, and he stepped away from whoever he was talking to and asked WHAT'S UP?, and I said IT'S SO CRAZY YOU'RE NOT GOING TO BELIEVE ME, and he said YOU'LL BURST MY EARDRUMS IF YOU KEEP SHOUTING LIKE THAT, then put his hand on my back and gently pushed me to the door, and in that moment, I felt this fire creep from the spot where his hand touched my back all the way to my fingertips, and I was wild, unstoppable, I wanted to tell him what had just happened, to shout it in his ear, but the music was so loud, the lights so dizzying, and I don't know who grabbed who, if it was me or him, but I had this laundry list of reasons why I could never be with Omar, and the list just went poof in my head, chas, gone, I couldn't remember it, I forgot every single reason not to be with him. I don't know who kissed who first, and I'm not sure it matters because all the perfectly rational arguments for why I shouldn't touch him or go near him or kiss him teetered and then fell, fell, fell, vanishing. As we're kissing, I think nothing, hear nothing. He leans in and follows me and and and and everything's happening so fast. I can feel people's coats hanging behind me, above me. He says: 'We're in the coatroom.' We move apart, in silence. I see him wipe his mouth with the back of his hand, and my wrists and knees buckle, as do the cogs in my brain. I clean my lipstick off his chin. My hand on his face. His face beneath my palm. His eyes boring into me. My reflection in his eyes watching me watch him. And this time, when we kiss, it's so much better because he takes such care, he's so delicate with me that I'm convinced every moment until now has been a hallucination. Maybe it didn't happen. Maybe I'm at home dreaming. Maybe I've just woken up, and I'm lying in bed perfectly still, staring up at the ceiling. But the music makes the walls shake, I can feel it on my skin. His hands are on my face, and he's touching me like he doesn't think any of this is real either, like it's all just a dream. It's the first time since I met him that he's laughing *with* me. I exhale, breathless.

'Wow.'

PART THREE

meryem.elmehdati@supersaurio.com

46

December 2017

There's a ticking timebomb in my chest. Tick tock tick tock tick tock. My anxiety is the red wire, and my inner voice is the blue wire. I open my hands in front of me. Close them. Yesterday's fuckup is the yellow wire. I waver over which wire to cut first. Outlook's progress bar freezes at 49%. I stare straight through it, tick tock tick tock. Every day, Matiqui comes in at 8:35 a.m. on the dot, not one minute before or after. He stands beside me and says: 'Good morning, Meryem! Beautiful day, isn't it? Just wonderful.' Or amazing. Incredible. Superb. Then he walks into his office.

The tension I feel as I wait for him to get here makes my left ovary ache. It's 8:33 on the morning of the DAK (Day After the Kiss). I can feel it throbbing beneath my skin, the pain. I don't know if it was there earlier and I just didn't realize or if I've done this to myself out of pure nerves. I have a complicated relationship with my period, which has this annoying habit of rocking up whenever it feels like it. Some months, it's right on time. Others, not so much. The last time I went to the gyno, he insisted the only way to fix the issue (to fix myself) was to take birth control. Bad period pain? Here, have some birth control. Acne? Birth control. An irregular cycle or facial hair? Ditto. All roads lead to hormones intended to shut off a part of your body that isn't working like we think it should. No one has the time to explain that the blood trickling out of you on day 28, after you pop the last pill in the blister pack, is not your period but your body hemorrhaging from deprivation, nor that these pills are in large part responsible for your mood swings and weight gain. They don't tell you that taking birth control may increase the risk of life-shortening breast or cervical cancer. This much is true, though: you will not get another pimple. When I hear the elevator, I sit up straight, fidget with my hair, my shirt collar, the keyboard. My blood is thumping in my ears, in my wrists, tick tock tick tock, I feel like my skin is going to give, that I'm about to explode. 8:35 a.m. Matiqui stands next to me and says:

'Good morning, Meryem. Beautiful day, isn't it? Just stunning.'

I force a smile. I've spent the last few hours navigating hundreds of thousands of hypothetical scenarios: Matiqui saw us kissing and is deeply unimpressed. Matiqui saw us kissing, and I'm getting fired. Matiqui saw us kissing and honestly doesn't care. As far as he's concerned, it's great news. I'm not getting fired, but he is going to make me blush a lot. I'm not getting fired, but he wants me to make sure it never happens again. Which I'll agree to. I made up my mind yesterday: Omar and I must never speak again. Omar and I must never see each other at work again. I really like Omar, and he really likes me. His physics and my chemistry and both our anatomies do this weird thing when we're in the same space, and if I had a different brain, if I were a whole different person, someone capable of enjoying life without beating herself up, for example, a normal person, a person who isn't *unwell*, then maybe we could kiss some more. But I am not normal, I do not know how to enjoy life; it takes me forever to get my thoughts in order and make decisions because I am not allowed to get it wrong.

'By the way.' He retraces his steps, briefcase in one hand, brand-spanking-new iPhone in the other, suit tailored to his six-foot frame – I know because I have access to his medical history. 'Last night, you . . . You looked lovely last night.'

'Oh, thanks.'

'Did you have a nice time? I know these things aren't easy for you.'

I don't correct him. I don't say: 'Actually, these things aren't not easy for me. I get along with people just fine. Take you, for example.' Instead, I shrug.

'Yeah, it was fun.'

I think of Omar's hands on my face and swallow.

'Perfect. Macarena will call you to schedule a meeting in the next few days.'

'Great.'

He points at me with his iPhone.

'Very well. Excellent.'

The night of the kiss, I experienced a full five minutes of peace. I thought of nothing. Said nothing. I put my jacket on, left the hotel, waited on the steps for a taxi. Omar was going back home to Rota the next day to spend Christmas with his family. My brain was too mushy to think clearly, so I said: 'You scare me.' And I got the impression he understood where I was coming from, that he understood me, because he replied: 'You scare me too.' He closed the taxi door behind me, then placed his hand on the window. We didn't touch while saying goodbye; we were just two bundled-up people in nineteen-degree-Celsius weather on a December night in Las Palmas de Gran Canaria staring intently at each other. The panic started in the taxi. At first it just spattered me like fine rain, and I ignored it, but soon it had soaked me to the bone. By the time I got home, my teeth were chattering, and I was white as a sheet. I couldn't tell if it was because of the fifteen Euros the driver charged me or the kiss. The kiss, the kiss, every time I drifted off that night, he was right there, in my dreams, him and the hems of the coats grazing the top of my head, an ocean of sleeves trying to snag the back of my neck and pull me up, up, up. The kiss, and the gleam in his eyes – I don't like light-eyed blonds, I don't trust them. I dreamed he texted me in the morning: 'Just left the party. Want to take a walk?' And I said yes because I felt just the way I told my friends I did: scared of myself and of that alien substance that had coated my brain. I woke in the middle of the night, then fell back asleep and dreamed of him again.

When my alarm went off in the morning, I realized it hadn't been a dream at all but a real text exchange. Message received at 3:25 a.m.: Just left the party | Want to take a walk? Message sent at 5:16 a.m.: Sorry | fell asleep . . . we can get breakfast tomorrow morning if you want | when's your flight. Message received at 6:18 a.m. 10:15. Two blue checkmarks. I'd fallen asleep again.

We don't see each other for fifteen days.

Fandom: Supersaurio (Las Palmas – District 2)
Characters: Munir
Tags: Horror
Category: General
Words: 58

Fear and Trembling

Munir dry-heaved while wringing out the mop, this time kind of aggressively. The bucket tipped over and almost fell. Munir let out a frustrated sigh and mopped over the gross puddle of puke that had forced them to close aisle 7 – Dairy. He'd been at it for twenty minutes. He wasn't paid enough. They'd never pay him enough.

47

December 2017

Macarena's hand is very soft.

'Meryem.'

We give each other a firm shake. She's wearing a peach-colored suit and a spotless white silk shirt. I'm in jeans and a black cotton tee with the words HOT GUAGUAS under a large ball of fire consuming an intercity bus. It seemed funny when I bought it. I look at her, she looks at me, smiles. Now, I'm questioning my choices. Her teeth are so white I feel dirty and feral.

'Something to drink? Water, coffee, tea?'

I think of Nadia, her assistant. Her name isn't Nadia, it's Davinia, but Macarena's predecessor convinced her that Davinia didn't look good in her email signature, that Nadia sounded more refined, more professional. She's been at the company for seven years. I see her restocking Macarena's office in the early morning – Evian water, coffee capsules, bags of organic natural slim-effect eco green tea – just like I do every day. Once, I took a bottle of €1.88 Evian and drank the whole thing before Matiqui came in, just to see what it tasted like. Vile.

'No, thanks.'

She scares me.

'Go on, take a seat. There's so much to talk about! How are things with you?'

Her office is identical to Matiqui's. I'm seconds from apologizing for what I'm wearing. It's dress-down Friday. I begin gently gnawing on the inside of my right cheek and take a seat at the same time she does.

'Fine, thanks.'

'Matiqui told me you're serious and reserved. I don't want you to worry. This is a safe space, you can express yourself freely with me.' She takes out a folder and places it between us. 'Everything you say in here, stays in here. It's strictly confidential.'

No one who really knows me would describe me as serious and reserved. I cross my legs.

'Okay.'

'Fabulous.' Smiling, she pushes her glasses up. 'How do you feel about your experience at Supersaurio until now?'

All 260 bones in my body ache, every day, I want to tell her. Monday through Friday, I walk here from Triana. I cut through San Telmo park and take the pedestrian crossing near Sakura City Restaurant. The traffic light stays green for about five seconds before it turns red. All your senses have to be on high alert when crossing. No one cares about pedestrians. Not the assholes in their Ford Fiestas or all-terrain cars. Not the cabbies, bikers, or cyclists. Not even the bus drivers give a damn about pedestrians. Each and every one of them will do whatever it takes to avoid idling for a whole five seconds, even running pedestrians over and tearing down a city street at eighty kilometers an hour. I can count on one hand the number of times I *haven't* fantasized about throwing myself in front of a moving car or bus while waiting for the pedestrian signal to turn green. *That's* my experience at Supersaurio, Macarena. I didn't want to bring it up, but you asked.

'Well . . .' I swallow. 'Umm. I had a hard time fitting in at first because most people here are a lot older than me.'

I don't tell her that in order to fit in, you and the group you want to fit into have to make an effort. If, for example, someone twice your age yammers on and on about how they're throwing a birthday party and then invites everyone but you, how are you meant to fit in? If that same person, say, puts half their energy into cornering, excluding, and trampling all over you while the rest of your coworkers look the other way, how are you meant to fit in and, more importantly, why would you want to? If most of your colleagues act like you're either invisible or a lost cause, why, Macarena, would you ever want to fit in?

'But I think I've managed to find some common ground with my team and carve out a space for myself. Does that answer your question? In terms of what I've gotten out of the experience, well, Matiqui and the others are about two decades older than me, and I used to worry I wouldn't . . . be up to their standard, I guess, but I get the sense they're pleased with my work. Maybe. It's been a very rewarding experience.'

'They're delighted, in fact. What exactly have you found rewarding about this experience?'

It's like her smile is made of putty. I picture myself hooking one pointer finger into each corner and pulling just to see how far it stretches. I hate them all, I think. I'm punctual, respectful, I do everything they ask of me, and I do it well. What more do you want? How much of myself do I get to keep? I can never tell whether I belong to me or to the people around me. I smile when I don't feel like smiling, laugh at things I don't find funny, share my time and space with people I'd rather not be around. What else must I sacrifice for the sake of a paycheck, I wonder. It's Friday, and I'm so tired, I feel like my words are glommed to each other, that I'm not speaking clearly.

'Excuse me?'

'Why is it rewarding? What have you learned?'

I stopped crying in the bathroom as soon as I heard someone else crying in there. Instead I went on the roof and wept while staring out at the oil platforms visible from my hideout. Then I found out Yolanda also came up to the roof to cry, so I started heading down to the storage room. When the photocopier jams, I open whatever door the screen says to open. I don't call IT. Imagine having to drop what you're doing to help someone with a paper jam. I interact with the Finance department exclusively by email, with Logistics by phone. Naiara has pushed every one of her department's interns to the brink of hysteria and continues to do so. No one ever raises any concerns because she meets her targets.

'Well . . . three years ago, I had no idea what a shareholders' meeting was. Now, I plan them. Even though I got here knowing a thing or two about international commerce from my undergraduate studies, I didn't—'

'Your degree is in Translation and Interpretation, isn't it? I had another look at your CV and cover letter earlier today.' She pulls two sheets out of her folder and sets it between us. 'Before the internship, you were in a PhD program. Do you ever feel you're being underutilized here?'

I see myself switching on the office lights every morning. Sometimes it's early enough that I catch the cleaner on her way out. My life looks so different from how I'd pictured it years ago that sometimes I feel the shock of it tingling under

211

my skin. Every so often, Matiqui calls me outside work hours with dumb questions. I never complain. But I do feel a certain rage. If I don't pick up the phone for any reason, he sends me ten- to twelve-minute-long voice notes on WhatsApp. It grows little by little, that rage. I try my best to ignore it.

'No, I think limiting yourself to your degree and planning your future based entirely on that one thing is kind of naïve.'

I look her in the eyes. I'm dead, I think, hollowed out. There was a time when I thought people would notice. That they'd tear off my mask and eject me for being an imposter. At least I'd tried.

'It's true that when I first started working here, this isn't what I pictured myself doing. But this is my job now, and I'm good at it. These are the most important years of my life. I can go back to a PhD, but I can't ever go back to this age.'

Everyone lies, and everyone's scared of being found out. Before stepping into a meeting, Matiqui always waits for me to give him a thumbs up. Thumbs up, everything will be A-okay. Somehow, I always wind up in the elevator next to someone who's just itching to tell me about their weekend – everything they did, everywhere they went, their little bungalow in the south. *Mogán is so beautiful.* See, the reason I'm serious and reserved is that I'd rather slash my own wrists than tell anyone in here about my life outside work. To some, silence is as good as death because then they'd have to listen to their own thoughts, tuku tuku, and how do you *not* drown yourself when you're sharing a mortgage, three children, and a minivan with a person you despise? Better to unload on the poor fool standing next to you in the elevator. Another fucking Monday, another fucking morning of meetings that could've been emails. Macarena, in her peach-colored suit making my head judder like a washing machine, asking me stupid questions she knows I'm going to have to lie about. People are always asking for the truth, but then when you give it to them, they can't swallow it. It's too bitter, too salty. Not like that. Sugarcoat it for me. It's hilarious. *How much groveling must I do so that you'll let me keep working here?* I'd like to ask. It's all the same to me.

'You know, you remind me a lot of myself when I was younger.'

I think back to the time Omar and I were on the roof, legs exposed to the sun. In my memory, my face is basically glued to the phone because I can barely see the screen in the glaring sun. I read to him: 'On his radio program, *Es La Mañana*, Federico Jiménez Losantos responded to a tweet from Pablo Iglesias. The two had been on the talk show, *Intereconomía*, before Iglesias founded Podemos. Federico said on his show that "everyone is stupid at least once" and reminded him of what he'd told him on *Intereconomía*, "I didn't know who you were but as soon as I heard you talking like a diehard Bolshevik, I said you reminded me of myself back when I was a douchebag." Yet, "I've never been as corny or nasty as you."' *I can't stand the guy, but he makes me laugh*, Omar said then. His eyes got so small when he smiled that I had to look away. I thought I might die. I didn't, obviously. No one dies from catching feelings.

'Do I?'

I bury my right fingers in my thigh.

'Yes, absolutely.' She pulls out more sheets from her folder. The woman is prepared. 'You know your own mind. I like that. It's something we really appreciate in my department. Did Matiqui explain the terms of your new contract?'

'Vaguely. He just said it was changing and that I'm being brought in-house.'

'Okay, perfect. We're switching you to a different category. In order to do that, we need to change your title.' She smiles, I smile. *See?* I want to tell her, *I too can become a weapon of mass destruction.* 'I want to talk to you about insurance, retirement plans . . . Are you sure you don't want something to drink?'

I used to know my own mind. There were two sides: them and me. I'd come here to spend nine hours punching my keyboard and talking on the phone with people who owed me reports, paperwork, receipts, hotel reservations, then go home and start all over again the next day. I knew exactly who my enemies were. Now, I'm not so sure who I am. I hate being here, and yet I won't leave. My interests aren't the same as when I started. They're like theirs. Like my enemies' interests? My enemies are the others, everyone who isn't me. If I get health insurance through my employer, will I still go to bat for universal health care – 'for those who need it, but . . .'? If I buy Supersaurio stocks, will I start thinking of their losses and gains as my own? The more privilege I have, the more privilege I'll want and the less willing I'll be to let other people, who haven't worked as hard as me, access that privilege. I know this tune. A line that has always been clear to me will begin to disappear; the more money I make, the more terrified I will be to lose it, the more I will owe the company, the more grateful, docile, and robotic I will become. How could you bite the hand that feeds you? I'll cease to be me and become Macarena instead. At some point in my life, I will look a twenty-six-year-old woman in the eye and say: 'You remind me of myself when I was your age.' I'll be wearing the blazer. My suit will be so expensive and my teeth so white that the twenty-six-year-old will feel physically sick.

48

December 2017

On New Year's Eve I have dinner with Carmen and her girlfriend Mercedes. They live in Ciudad Jardín, near Doramas park, in a two-story house that looks straight out of Instagram. The smell of roast chicken steals into the dining room, where Carmen and I are making snow-pea salad.

'Maybe I'll just up and quit, who knows?'

Her curls bounce as she laughs. In our teens, I used to jokingly call her *Cabbage*.

'You're going to quit now that they've finally given you a contract, health insurance, a real salary?'

I carefully julienne the snow peas. I've had my head on backwards for weeks, three or four thoughts spinning round and round from the moment I drag myself out of bed to the moment I crawl back in. I haven't said anything to Omar, of course. I don't want him thinking I'm all mixed up. Carmen and Mercedes' dog, Dana, curls up by my feet under the table.

'I don't know how I'm meant to look that man in the face when he gets back. What do I even say? Or do?'

'Whatever it is straight people say or do.' I stick my tongue out at her, mortified. 'Chill. The guy's like fifty million years old—'

'Thirty-seven. He's thirty-seven! I can't believe what an idiot I'm being!'

'It was just a couple of silly kisses in the coatroom. Don't be such a drama queen.'

I take a deep breath, look at her.

'A couple of *really good* silly kisses,' I correct. The knife I'm using goes sht sht sht as I finish slicing the snow peas. Carmen and I spent all morning hopping from grocery store to grocery store trying to track them down, first the one in Vegueta, then the one in Central, always by foot because Carmen walks everywhere now, she's an ecofriendly human addicted to counting steps on her smart watch. 'How am I meant to even look at him? I don't remember what I said, what I did. I remember nothing. What if I'm a bad kisser?'

'Meryem. Come on.'

'I mean it! I hadn't kissed anyone in, like, forever. What if I've become a terrible kisser? What if he swallowed a spider while we were kissing but was too embarrassed to say anything?'

Carmen doesn't dignify me with a response. She just carries on with what she's doing, though I can tell she finds it all highly amusing. Maybe I'd find it amusing too if I hadn't totally lost the plot, gone cuckoo bananas, if my nerves weren't at breaking point.

'I think it's safe to say that the fact that he's still texting you means you're not a terrible kisser.'

He is still texting me. We're constantly chatting these days, no matter the time. Every time my phone lights up, it's him. The DAK, he'd written me a pretty long message, saying 'Hey | I think I more or less know what you get like

216

by now | and I think maybe | well I wonder if | I don't know | I hope not | but I think you might be feeling embarrassed | about last night | god knows why | but just so you know | there's no reason to be.' At first, I didn't have a clue how to reply. Eventually, I chose honesty and wrote: Yes, I'm embarrassed. 'There's no reason to be, really,' he replied. We never brought up the issue again, though it was still there, like when you've got something stuck between your teeth and you keep poking at it with your tongue.

Dinner is phenomenal: roast chicken (halal) à la Ottolenghi, mashed roast sweet potatoes, snow pea salad with dill and lime, and a three-chocolate tart from Guirlache. We'd spent the afternoon cooking with these friends of Carmen and Mercedes who I really like even though I can't keep their names straight. Shortly before midnight, Omar texts me. At 11:53 p.m., he says: 'I wish I could toast the New Year with you.' At 11:55, I say: 'Even with non-alcoholic champagne?' At 11:58, he replies: 'Even with non-alcoholic champagne | even with sparkling water | you're the best thing that's happened to me in years.' I start breathing funny after reading his text, like my lungs are full of cotton or my chest is squishy. The last time I liked someone, like for real liked someone instead of just settling, I wound up so hurt it felt as though I'd been sliced right down the middle. Like I spent months hemorrhaging blood. Like I went everywhere with my guts hanging out. No one seemed to notice, though. Not a single person. It was surreal. I decided then and there never to let my guard down again. If you let yourself harden, nothing can touch or hurt you. You don't suffer, you don't feel anything, and for a while, it's amazing – being invulnerable, impenetrable, a cactus in the sun. But sooner or later, you realize that being alive means exposing yourself to hurt and disappointment, not because you're a

217

masochist and enjoy pain, but because the opposite of that is being dead. At 11:59, I type, I type, I type, then delete everything. At midnight, I text back: 'Happy New Year :), I had no idea you were so corny.'

49

January 2018

Click-clack click-clack, Yolanda struts up to my floor, click-clack, she's in her Ralph Lauren get-up, hair in a tight bun, tight-lipped, maybe this is her armor, I think, maybe this is the only way she gets to feel like a badass bitch, like a girl boss who can bend the world to her will, I get excited – alright, let's do this, it's another day – and as always she walks right past me like I don't exist, she's a woman on a mission, and that mission is to see Matiqui, and when she doesn't see him, when three seconds before reaching his door she realizes his office is empty (it's Friday, if only she listened to me, if only she paid attention all the times I've told her that our boss does.not.come.into.work.on.Fridays she'd have saved herself a trip), swivels around, looks at me, and swallows.

'Hello, Miriam.'

'Good morning, Yolanda.'

Click-clack click-clack click-clack. Sometimes I dream I'm being chased down a long dark hallway and I run and run and even though I don't see her, even though all I hear is that noise, I know it's Yolanda.

'You finally did it. Congratulations.'

I pretend not to know what she means and throw her a look of utter incomprehension. I've had some years of experience.

'Did what?'

'Managed to stay.'

Fuck you, I think. Fuck you fuck you fuck you a million times over with the force of a thousand suns.

'Only thanks to you and everything you've taught me,' I reply, and I feel myself expand, getting bigger and bigger, so huge I tower over her, look down from way up high, and she tries to look back up at me but can't because she needs to shield her eyes with her hand because I am glowing, I am luminous, because the terrified person being chased down the hallway is now her, and the person doing the chasing is none other than me. 'I hope that one day I get to repay you for all you've done for me. I really do.'

She doesn't say anything else. She just nods and leaves, click-clack click-clack. Every day, it's a struggle not to scream back at her but now I know that she knows I know how badly she treats me, that I've known all along and chosen to do nothing, all so I could get here and look down on her like I am now, that's enough for me. I'm ten feet tall, like Saurito, and I feel untouchable.

50

January 2018

My father comes from a poor family. Super poor. Seven-siblings-nine-mouths-to-feed poor. I've never heard him complain. I never hear him complain about anything. One day, he points at my sneakers and says: 'They're filthy.' 'It doesn't matter, Baba.' I don't have time to argue with him about this kind of thing, it's not important. They're just a pair of gross, dirty sneakers that I'll wear until they fall to pieces, until they're riddled with holes or the soles come off. I'm not losing any sleep over it. He doesn't push, but the next time we see each other, he brings it up again. He says: 'Meryem, why don't you wash your shoes? They're filthy.' I brush it off, I say, yeah, sure, I'll get around to it.

My paternal grandmother was obsessed with cleanliness. She was always saying, 'We may not have much, but it's all spotless!' whenever we went to her village in the summer, the village in the mountains, millions of kilometers from civilization, with zero Wi-Fi and barely any reception, the one with the house that no longer exists and the tile that's been lost for all time. I have this theory: every family has a vulture flying circles around it. My grandmother was always well groomed, well dressed, put together. My grandmother had three boys. The eldest went to the United States, the middle boy went to Spain, and the youngest stayed. He's the vulture.

My dad doesn't bring it up again. Then one day, as I'm getting ready to go to Las Palmas, I notice my sneakers aren't muddy-water brown dusty-floor brown just-plain-old brown but white again, and I can picture it perfectly. I close my eyes and see my dad quietly handwashing them in the sink of our roof terrace, see him carefully removing each lace and dropping them in a bucket of soapy water, see him calmly scrubbing my dumb sneakers with a brush. My dad, a man with a mustache, who takes it in his stride when his kids tell him, 'Don't worry about it, Baba.' I don't mention it when I say goodbye to him, but I cry on the way to the bus station, walking down the hill, the one where the Los Danieles restaurant is, I cry, quietly, with my headphones on, then wipe my face with both hands, and sniffle, then walk faster so I won't miss the bus. I don't mention any of this to my dad, but I make a conscious effort never to let my sneakers get that filthy again.

5 1

February 2018

A young woman tells her partner that people are born alone and die alone. I read the label on a can of food that's caught my eye: Hering – Zarte filets in Tomaten-Creme. What a stupid thing to say. No one's born alone. Our mothers either push us out or else have one or two pairs of hands prying them open so we can be pulled out. SUPERSAURIO, *the best prices on the archipelago!* blares a voice on the loud-speaker – a voice now rooted in the deepest-set part of my brain – followed by the first chords of Juanes's 'A Dios le pido.' In my modest experience, being a woman constantly involves some kind of bodily pain; it starts in your teens and continues until the day you die. It's crazy, if you think about it. When it's not my tits that ache, it's my uterus, or my head because my uterus is about to start aching, or it's my lower back because I'm on my period, and yet I'm not supposed to complain because it's all totally normal, it is widely accepted that our bodies hurt and that's that.

I wonder if any supermarkets in Germany sell Spanish products because Spanish people are assumed to live there. I seriously doubt it. Only Canarians are sad and starved enough to grovel for three measly cents from a country that wouldn't hesitate to squash us at the first opportunity. The fabric of our economy is entirely dependent on tourism, so we will continue sucking on Europe's teat until we puke, but they and their moms can eat their stupid Zarte filets in Tomaten-Creme. I'm not touching that stuff with a ten-foot pole. I take a picture and send it to Omar. On my fridge is a postcard he sent me during the winter holiday. I see it every morning and night.

When he gets back from vacation, we have The Talk. The Talk consists of me moving my hands and arms a lot and saying that I want us to start off as friends and then, maybe, we can become more than friends, because I'm just not comfortable skipping over the friendship part straight to the *more than friendship* part, but I understand if his cruising speed is a little faster than mine because I'm a little chikili-cuatre-out-of-my-mind, and I accept that, and promise to never again, under any circumstance, objectify and / or kiss him. He says okay. That he wants to be friends as well. He doesn't get mad. He doesn't punish me with a thick, gloopy silence. He doesn't change. The relief makes me exude so much energy that he asks if I'm okay. It takes me hours to realize that I'm so used to negotiating my desires with men that I always speak from this weird place, one where my priority is not to be heard and respected but to make sure the man I'm communicating with doesn't get mad and explode with rage.

Besides, life isn't meant to be lived alone. When you buy fresh pasta, it comes in packets of two portions, not one. Two. You can tell it's not quite enough, that your plate is only half full, but on the packet it says these eight servings equal two portions that equal about 750 calories. I guess maybe being fat is worse than living alone but not as bad as dying alone. Inside me a clock goes tick tock tick tock; every egg I flush down the toilet is a missed opportunity. Imagine chipping away at a mortgage for thirty-two years on your own because paying rent is basically throwing away money, except, if you think about it, the house whose down payment you spent a full decade scrimping for won't actually belong to you until you're deep into your sixties. If there were two of you, it'd take a lot less time. If you don't have siblings or other relatives, a neighbor may end up calling the cops because your apartment reeks and when they kick down your door, they'll find your 49-kilo corpse in the living room (because you never ate both portions of fresh pasta). In my religion, it's believed that when you die, your soul stays with your body until you're buried. I'm not sure what happens if your body is charred or mutilated, I've never had the courage to ask because what if the answer is horrifying? You can't just un-remember or forget what you already know. I see myself dead, waiting for someone to find my body in a twenty-three-square-meter rathole, queen-sized bed basically in the kitchen because I was too poor to use whatever eggs I had left, and I laugh through my teeth while waiting in line at the register. When it's my turn, the cashier looks at me funny.

52

February 2018

I have this Twitter account no one knows about. Not one soul in the entire universe. I signed up in 2008 just to try it on for size, then forgot all about it until 2011, when I went on Erasmus and felt like the loneliest person in the world. I went with this girl in my class who I got along with really well right up until we went on Erasmus together, which is when I found out she's a total jerk. Her name is Pamela. Pamela seemed normal enough in class, the kind of person you could talk to or go on a year abroad with, but it happened that when she drank she turned into a raging bitch, and even though she forgot the things she said and did when she was drunk, I didn't because I don't drink. I would've left it alone were it not for the fact that all people seem to do on Erasmus is drink.

I did my year abroad in Belgium, which felt like an intriguing place – it wasn't England or France, it was Belgium. And what did I know about Belgium? Nada, which is why I went. I went to Belgium because it's a member of the European Commission and the European Parliament and, I think I've mentioned this before but back then I was a person with dreams, silly as that may sound. I truly believed that with hard work and sacrifice, you could live your dreams. Anyway, so I went to Belgium to improve my low-rent French and to study near the European Commission and the European Parliament because I could picture myself translating or interpreting for them, whichever one I wound up being good at. The only spots my college had available in Belgium were at the University of Liège. I googled Liège, and the first hit was a news article listing it as the second most dangerous city in all Europe. Someone with all her ducks in a row quack quack might have been discouraged. Not me, though. Of course, back then I didn't suspect I was crazy either. The first city on the list was Charleroi, also in Belgium. I figured it couldn't be all that bad. I mean, I'd survived school in Arguineguín. No way was it worse than that. I didn't tell my parents. Then, in late August, I packed my bags, cried in the airport like a baby, and took off.

My secret Twitter handle is @cheriecoco because it's the song I heard the most that year: 'Chérie Coco' by Magic System. It was funny like something that isn't funny but actually really messed up, like when a guy gets handsy with you 'as a joke' and everyone around you laughs, except you don't think what he did to you is the least bit fucking funny. But you laugh with them anyway and suck it up, then cry a little when you're alone because you really should've said something, or done something, you should've left. But you didn't. That year, they played 'Chérie Coco' at every party, every bar, at the only club I went to in Brussels. Moussier Tombola's 'Logobitombo' also played around the clock, just like 'Chérie Coco.' The lyrics were catchy, kind of demented, the dance moves jumpy and contagious, people would climb up on the bar, table, on anything within reach, just to hype up the crowd.

Around mid-December of that year, a man stood in the middle of Place Saint-Lambert and took several hand grenades and a combat rifle out of his backpack, intent on eliminating anyone in his path. He killed six people before turning the gun on himself. I was taking a French-to-Spanish scientific translation exam when I heard screaming and the rush of people running for dear life. I heard the explosions, the gunfire. It wasn't like in the movies. There were no heroes. They locked us in the college building and made us hide under our desks. The first thought I had was about the test: Would we have to take it again the next day? Which made me laugh, obviously, so I pinched myself hard enough it left a bruise. We were there for hours. I got a 19/20 on the exam. For months after, I didn't hear 'Logotibombo' played anywhere. No one was in the mood to sing along to – machine gun to the right, machine gun to the left.

In those days, I was constantly on Twitter. At first, so I could follow news of the mass shooting. Later, so I had somewhere to spew my unfiltered thoughts. Nobody knew who I was. I could be anyone, say anything. Once I started working at Supersaurio, I stopped using Twitter for news and began using it to vent to my audience of zero. @cheriecoco could express thoughts like 'Kill me now.' I experienced true freedom. Then came the followers. The re-tweets, the likes, the locked accounts quoting my tweets, the guys sending me washed-out, unsolicited dick pics, the guys with soccer players or Pepe the Frog avatars who called me 'Arab' as an insult, the websites that stole my 140-character-and-later-240-character tweets and uploaded them to lists of the funniest things that year, or month, or on Eurovision. I flew too close to the sun. I thought a woman could be funny on the internet and not pay a price. I set myself on fire, then made my account private.

228

53

March 2018

'Personally, I think it's *the* tragedy of the twenty-first century. They're coming after families now. We get no support. None. It's like they hate us.'

I glance over my glasses at Otero and choose the most sensible course of action: I dissociate. The *real* tragedy of the twenty-first century is seeing all these people hurtling forward just so they won't have to be left alone with their own thoughts for ten sorry minutes. Did you see me hold a gun to anyone's head and say HAVE CHILDREN? I don't remember doing that. Pretty sure I didn't force anyone to take out a thirty-year mortgage, buy a car that runs on diesel fuel, and have two or three kids. At work, they tell you how lucky you are. You still have your freedom! Enjoy it while it lasts because things get a lot harder once you're a mother. Women go part-time when their parental leave runs out. Men . . . don't. Funny that. Women leave company parties early to put their kids down. Men don't. Makes you think. At seven thirty at night, there are still some men in the office, despite them having children. I'm not passing judgment, just stating facts. Who's looking after their little ones? Beats me.

No matter where I am, I'm surrounded by people who've mortgaged my future just so they can maintain a lifestyle that was never going to be sustainable in the long run. I don't see anyone getting riled up about that. Another thing I haven't seen is anyone asking themselves if maybe, just maybe, they're taking more than the world can offer. Like the bungalow in Maspalomas that they rent out year round, except for the Easter holidays because that's when they go south; the two cars they're always double-parking or else parking on the literal sidewalk – sorry I'll just be a minute I'm picking my kid up from school um okay no need to get like that asshole it's just a minute while I wait for my kid you fucking jerk – the trips to Japan, Peru, weekends in Madrid to watch *The Lion King* or *Blood Wedding* or or or. I'll have to grow old on this tiny sliver they've deigned to leave me, to make do with rancid scraps that I've got no choice but to shove in my mouth, whether I want to or not. And on top of everything I have to sit here and listen to some dude lecture me on why people my age don't want kids? Cool, just what I needed.

I study the restaurant menu. When Matiqui asks me to plan lunch or dinner for the team, I pride myself in choosing only the best establishments. Qué Leche, Deliciosa Marta, El Santo, Segundo Muelle, Pícaro, Bevir. I consider it a moral duty to claw back my surplus value by taking us out in style, no regrets. Matiqui's Amex card goes sshhww sshhww whenever I swipe it on the machine. It's against company policy for anyone but him to use it, but for all intents and purposes, I am Matiqui's shadow. Yolanda gently elbows me.

'Yes?'

'You're a young woman,' Otero calls out, 'tell us what you think.'

'What I think . . . about . . .?'

'Don't you think people your age are too focused on dumb things like, I don't know, riding bikes and making vegan cheese instead of starting families?'

For the first time in months, I look Otero in the eyes. I give him a hollow, blank stare. Men like him move through the world convinced they're the lone surviving wolf in the pack. If *they* don't fix things, then civilization as we know it will spiral toward its decline. The truth is they're just a bunch of topless dudes screaming at the TV, but no one has the courage to tell them. It's much easier to go along with it – yeah, yeah, it's just wrong, terrible, you're so right, you're Superman, a gladiator, with your blade you have vanquished a lion, an entire battalion, things really are different, aren't they, dear lord, what a mess, uh-huh, yeah – anything to avoid a tantrum or an ear-bleeding lecture. And still, I get the teensiest thrill out of it. They're barking, Sancho, which means the world's changing and they're shit-scared.

'People my age aren't having kids because they're riding bikes?'

He laughs. He thinks I'm funny. He thinks a witch cursed me at birth. Sure, I'm funny, but it's only because most of the people around me don't believe I'm being serious when I speak my mind.

'No, of course not, but I think it's obvious that because they're in favor of things like . . . I don't know, to give you an example, like advocating for more women in STEM . . . right? Because of that, they're pushing back the decision to have their first child.'

A waiter comes to take our order.

'And you're saying women make this decision on their own?'

'Please elaborate,' he says.

'Elaborate on what?'

(3 glasses of Petit Bourgeois, 1 glass of Les Abeilles, 2 bottles of sparkling water, 2 bottles of mineral water, 1 Coca Cola Zero with a lot of ice and lemon.)

He shrugs.

'On your idea, your point. Your position, I guess.'

There are four pairs of eyes trained on me. I scratch my forearm nervously.

'I don't have anything to add. I was just wondering if what you're implying is that women make the choice to have or not have children *on their own*. I mean, I don't see any guys my age begging girls to have babies with them.'

A while ago, I heard the PP politician Celia Villalobos go on TV and tell the youth that we need to start saving for our retirement now, now, NOW because we can't count on there being any retirement benefits left for us in our old age, that we should set aside at least two Euros a month – a coffee or pack of rolling tobacco. A real genius of finances and Candy Crush, that woman. I can't *believe* no one ever thought of that! So, you're saying that if I start setting aside two Euros a month *now*, by the time I'm sixty-five – or sixty-six, maybe sixty-seven, sixty-eight (who knows, they may increase retirement age to seventy in the coming months) and even then we probably wouldn't be able to fully stop working and be forced to take on a side gig as a cashier, dishwasher, or Glovo courier – I'll be a multi-millionaire who doesn't need benefits? No one else on the talk show questioned her statement. *These* are the people railing against us, wondering why we don't buy property and start families. Fucking Boomers.

'Anyway, even if these guys existed, even if there were men my age going around begging women to make babies with them, I'm not sure where they, or the baby's mom, or the baby itself would live.'

232

'I mean, if you want it enough, then you make it happen. Tighten your belt a little, save up . . . get a mortgage. It isn't *that* hard. When I was twenty-seven, I could walk into a bank and get approved for a mortgage for 100% the purchase value, and I made less than you. 27,000 gross. My parents co-signed. 150,000 smackeroos, pim, pam.'

His voice reaches me like it's coming out of a car wash.

'Is that the place in Tafira?'

'No, we only moved here about ten years ago. The house in Tafira cost a little more than that.' He laughs, ha ha ha, with his mouth wide open, like an animal.

Median cost of a detached house in Tafira: €300,000.

'You tell me we're not popping out kids like we should and that this is tragic, and I'm telling you it makes sense and these are the reasons. Next thing I know, we're talking about your mortgage and how your parents were your guarantors. Cool cool cool,' I mumble, laconic.

He opens his mouth.

'C'mon, woman, you're not alone. When you buy a house, it's with a partner. You work together, help each other out.'

My imaginary partner and I are skiing down an idyllic slope. We have an au pair who speaks German to the kids – we pay her in cash – and a beautiful golden lab that the little ones play with on our porch in Massachusetts. His mother is always finding an excuse to drop in on us, she's always 'in the neighborhood.' He's a doctor, and I write women's erotic literature under the pen name Larissa Baker. I make more than he does a year, and he pretends not to mind. Matiqui clears his throat.

'You asked for her opinion, and she gave it. Let's change the subject.'

'Don't mind Otero, Mery. He always gives everybody a hard time,' Víctor says.

233

The one person I don't hear a peep out of is Yolanda, who just watches. I carefully run my finger along the edge of the table.

'I'm sorry, but your understanding of how things work is patently false and also totally ridiculous,' I say.

'Ridiculous?'

'Yeah. I don't know. Not everyone wants the same thing. When was the last time you rented an apartment? I just feel like it's really out of touch for anyone to think that you just have to tighten your belt a little and get a boyfriend to be able to afford a duplex in Tafira Alta.'

'Everyone here lives in a duplex,' he says. Yolanda stays quiet and props her elbows on the table. 'One day, you'll grow up and have a duplex of your own.'

'What makes you think I want to live in a duplex up in the mountains like the rest of you?' I laugh. 'Is there only one way of doing things? Plus, there are three people at this table who don't have kids. How come I'm being singled out? Víctor is your age and has a grand total of zero children. Same with Yolanda.'

'Don't get your panties in a twist. We're just talking.'

'I just haven't been able to convince any women what a huge catch I am,' Víctor says.

A pair of hands sets a glass of Coca Cola Zero with a lot of ice and lemon in front of me. I swallow. I don't want my voice to shake.

'Every time I say something different or disagree with you, you tell me not to get my panties in a twist, *we're just talking* . . . My panties are not in a twist. All I did was answer a direct question.'

* * *

234

A few hours later, Matiqui leaves his office and walks up to my desk. It's Wednesday, which means he has to be out by four thirty to pick his daughter up from swim class because his nanny is visiting family in Peru. He gives me a long look. I think: *I will not apologize. I will not.*

'Don't mind Pedro. He just likes riling people up. He's not a bad person.'

Future Meryem will get the urge to stick her head in a burning hot oven when she remembers what Present Meryem said.

'But not being a bad person is the bare minimum,' I reply. 'He smiles and acts like his questions about very basic, obvious things aren't offensive. He says, "we're just chatting" or "we're just having a conversation," and if you object or point out his behavior, then you're the one whose panties are in a twist, and—'

I see him smile.

'Maybe I overreacted.'

'No, not at all. You're absolutely right.' He shrugs. 'What can I say? Sometimes we end up working with people who aren't like us, and we have to find a way to . . .'

He swishes his hand.

'. . . Cope.'

'Yeah.'

'Don't ever apologize for speaking your mind, Meryem.'

Ferrán Matiqui. Forty-eight, gay, married to an IT tech, parent to a little Asian girl they adopted eight years ago, director of Compliance at Supersaurio Supermarkets S.L. My boss. I wonder how many times he's had to hold his tongue and pretend he didn't hear anything.

'Okay.'

'Alright.' He raps his knuckles twice on my desk. I think of Kevin Spacey. 'Alright then, see you tomorrow.'

'See you tomorrow.'

Maybe that's the secret: to become unflappable, stony, virtually inhuman. I don't tell Matiqui that I'm sick and tired of how some people have to fight back or cope while others get to barrel right through us like bulldozers.

54

March 2018

I have this theory about men: it never occurs to them to just leave women alone. They're like cavities. You act like they don't exist until they're rotting on the inside, and then you need to get the whole tooth removed. Am I generalizing? I have male friends, I think I know what I'm talking about. No, I'm not a misandrist. But. It doesn't matter how long you've known the guy, at some point he will size you up and sort you into one of two categories: category one, would fuck; category two, would not fuck. Since it never occurs to them to just leave women alone, nine times out of ten, the answer is that they *would* fuck her. It's crazy. Peg-legged, wild-eyed, bald, they don't give a damn.

In the past few years, some guys my age have started doing a lot of work on themselves. They've engaged in self-reflection, self-examination, self-compassion, self-restraint, self-criticism. Sadly, what I haven't seen them do is self-destruct and leave us the hell alone. Funny that. New masculinity, old masculinity, toxic masculinity, store-brand-gluten-free-biodegradable-with-traces-of-dairy-and-tree-nuts-masculinity, handle with care. Imagine having to spend hours thinking about whether it's gay to wear a pink shirt or not watch the soccer game. Maybe I'm being unfair. Maybe they really can't help themselves, and I just don't get it. The thing is, it literally kills them not to be the center of attention, I swear. International women's day? What about international men's day? So we're hysterical, are we? What other choice do we have when we're constantly facing off with guys catcalling us on the street or pulling over in their car when we're walking home alone at night and laughing when they realize they scared us. Where are your friends? Do you need a ride? They're either purposefully brushing up against us on the bus, or in the elevator, or in line at the supermarket, or they're squeezing every last drop of life out of our bodies and ruining us emotionally because they can, because they're bored, because they don't know how to be alone, because we're women and they're men, and women are kindling and men are fire and then the big bad devil huffs and puffs and blows it all away. The wheel turns, and we're right back where we started. Tell me who in their right mind wouldn't be hysterical. Who?

Smile, go on, why the long face? You know what happens when you ask a man to calm down and not be hysterical? He gets furious. NOTALLMEN is basically just two or three men. My grandad, my dad, and my brother. I wouldn't put my hand in the fire for anyone else. Frankly, I wouldn't do it for them either if they weren't my immediate family, if I wouldn't rather get burned than prove that YESALLMEN. If I'm just a girl standing in front of a drunk asshole asking him to please move because I want to leave the bathroom he's got me cornered in at a bar I used to love but will no longer be patronizing because of him, then why should I have to put up with dumb jokes about how women always go to the bathroom together?

238

Why can't I go out for a run in the middle of the night while listening to music without being scared some man will snatch me on my way home, have his way with me, then drop me in a well or a ditch, or wherever he feels like it? Yeah, Mom, don't worry, I'm home now.

I grew up being bombarded by how much men love women. I don't know if you've heard, but men are, like, obsessed with women. Maybe you didn't realize, but they're totally crazy about us, we blow their freaking minds. But here's the rub: they have preferences. Men want women to be made-up but not too made-up because they mustn't know how long it took us to get ready; we need to look natural, like we just woke up like this, with perfectly drawn eyeliner and extra-long lashes. Men want women to be sexy but not so sexy that we're provocative. They want us to be sexy without knowing it, to be outgoing but shy, to have a strong character but speak in a purr, to be curvy but slender, to have big tits and ass but a wasp waist. We have to be unaware of our beauty, modest because otherwise we're vain, and if we're vain, we may not be that beautiful after all.

55

March 2018

Matiqui enlists me to help organize International Women's Day. When he tells me this I feel pathetic, like a servant being passed around without anyone asking her opinion. Did you have a massive list of things to do today? Well, tough luck, I've decided you can handle this other headache too. But don't worry, he adds, you'll have help. This is how I wind up being part of the company's PTA, a clique of middle-aged women who basically function as an in-house Sicilian mafia. Though I consider myself a prisoner of war, I don't breathe a word or raise any objections. Yolanda and another colleague have been arguing for the past two minutes. The rest of us just watch. Today's look: collared romper with long cuffed sleeves and hidden inseam side pockets (*look, pockets!* I tell everyone) as well as patch breast pockets with buttons, purchased on sale, dirty hair in a ponytail, three zits on jaw heralding yet another egg soon to be flushed down a toilet. Location: meeting room.

'I'd pass around gifts. Tokens of appreciation. Something like a desk plant,' Lucía 1 says. There are two days until March 8, and 76% of the workforce identifies as female.

'I love that. What about a succulent? Something easy. I'm totally swamped.'

Yolanda clears her throat.

'We're not passing around the gifts this year. It's distracting for everyone, and it takes too long.' She joins her hands over the table. 'Ideally, we'd have them come collect their presents somewhere.'

'Yes, you're absolutely right.'

'We'll have to give men and women separate time slots, or it'll get too crowded.'

A short silence.

'Men? It's International Women's Day,' I eventually pipe up.

'We can't exclude them just because they're men.'

Is there a hidden camera somewhere? I hope we're being recorded. I'd love to be featured in a viral Twitter video.

'We wouldn't be excluding them. It's International *Women's* Day,' Lucía 1 says.

'I'd feel uncomfortable knowing that we—' Yolanda tries to reply.

'We can give the men something on International Men's Day.'

'Not all men are fathers.'

'Not all women are mothers.'

'Miriam . . .'

I close my eyes. She means me.

'It's Meryem.'

I don't notice the others looking at us. My father's always telling me to be nice. I bite my tongue.

'Mery-em.' She stares at me a long while. I don't think I've ever hated her as much as right now. 'Do you want to weigh in? I thought you were here to help.'

'On March 8, I'm joining the strike,' I say. 'But instead of giving the women tokens of appreciation or gifts,

241

I think we should donate that money to an organization for battered women, for example, or something like that. I just thought of it right now, but if people are interested, I could find out more information and present it at the next meeting. If you're interested, of course.'

Of course they're interested. Physically, I am sitting in my chair with one hand folded over the other on the table, but in my soul, in my spirit, I am way, way, way up high, so high I may never come down again, I might just stay up here. How does anyone say no to an idea like that? No, frankly we *don't* want to give a hundred Euros to an organization for battered women on International Women's Day, we'd much rather give a succulent to every employee, man or woman. I wonder if it's ever dawned on these women that they organize every single company party, function, and event. Yolanda stares at me in silence, pondering what I've just said. She smiles a little, and I smile back. Teeth, teeth. They also clear up after every event, make sure everything goes to plan, worry about how people will get home. None of the men ever volunteer to help, ever. Are they not pissed? Do they never ask themselves why?

56

March 2018

'Yolanda mentioned you weren't coming in on Thursday?'

It's 8:35 a.m. and Matiqui walks past my desk, remembers he meant to ask me this question, and backtracks. You rat, I think, and picture myself dragging her down the hall by her very tight bun.

'Why wouldn't I?'

'Something about a strike? I need you here on Thursday. We have a meeting with PRISMA.'

We look each other in the eyes, him standing and me seated. Poor man with his briefcase, last-generation iPhone, suit, and €328 shoes. He's staring down at his screen. This conversation is a formality.

'Well, they've called for a countrywide strike on March 8. I'm planning to come in in the morning, then leave at eleven thirty . . .'

'Do you feel discriminated against as a woman here at Supersaurio?' He pries his eyes away from his phone and looks at me. There's no hint of anger in his voice, only surprise. It's like he's seeing me for the very first time. 'I wish you'd said something.'

Some men don't harass women or catcall them. They're good men. They pull their feet up when you sweep between the sofa and the coffee table. They empty the dishwasher. They cook dinner hundreds of times. They don't believe you're any less than them. At the same time, they also don't ask themselves why nine out of the company's ten executives are men. They're good people. They'd never lay a finger on a woman. They honestly believe that everything they've achieved in life has been through grit and hard work and that you're only not right up there with them because you're not good enough. It's not that I hate them, it's that I find them exhausting. No one should get a prize for being nice.

'I wish I'd had the chance to, but Yolanda clearly felt it was important for her to tell you herself.'

He doesn't raise the issue again.

57

April 2018

Just as I'm leaving work one Friday, Omar writes to me on
Skype to ask about my plans for the weekend. I say I'm going
down to Puerto Rico, obviously, and he replies, 'Obviously,'
and I see him typing typing typing until finally he says,
'Hey, if you're not doing anything tonight, do you want to
grab dinner? I can drop you off at your place after,' and I
read and reread his question, and it's so casual, so I'm-not-
saying-anything-just-asking that I have to remind myself I
already have plans for dinner and a movie with friends, but
then he says he's going on vacation on Sunday, and we won't
see each other until he gets back, so I cast aside feminism,
sisterhood, and two life-long friendships and say, 'Alright
then,' deciding in that moment that I too can be casual and
uncomplicated – cool, even.

In my apartment bathroom, I peer at my face from up
close, study myself. I inspect my nose (too big), teeth (my
incisors are kind of crooked and stick out a bit), eyes
(recently I noticed my left one wanders when I'm tired or
not wearing glasses), chin (weird), skin (dull, yellow). I
put up my hair, then let it down again. I wish I knew how

to do my hair like beautiful women: braids, updos, side parts. I study myself from different angles – straight on, in profile (my gut's swollen) – and try smoothing my dress. I am a twenty-first-century woman, I tell myself. I am a strong, smart, independent woman. I have a full-time job. I pay my own bills. I need for nothing. I don't need anyone to like me. I don't need a man to like me. I don't need *him* to like me. I wish I were a little taller, though. And maybe ten kilos lighter. I wish I had finer features, whiter teeth, a thinner waist, that my legs were longer and slimmer, my hair thicker and brighter. I wish I sounded like a woman instead of a cartoon. I wouldn't mind sacrificing some of my brains for beauty. This last thought shocks me so much that I pull out my phone and text Carmen: 'If you could be twice as pretty but 15% dumber, would you?' I have several texts from Teresa asking if I'm having a good time even though I stabbed them in the back and telling me to call if I need an excuse to get out of dinner early. Her last text is a string of peach and eggplant emojis. I blush. 'I haven't even left the house,' I write. 'I'm scared,' I add. I see her instantly read the message and text back: 'Why?' Even though I'm worried she'll think I'm crazy, I say: 'I can't hear myself think when I'm around him.' I wash my hands, wet my face and neck. I look at myself in the mirror, like really look. I picked the wrong dress. I hike it up a little, look at myself again. It's like I've been hit by a tornado. My eyes are gleaming, I look mad. I wish I didn't have a face or body. I wish I could communicate exclusively by voice, like Siri or Alexa.

We agreed to meet outside Teatro Pérez Galdós, and even though I'm there ten minutes early, armed with a book to read while I wait, I spot him on the theater steps. I stand in place, about a hundred meters from where he's sitting. I consider texting to say I'm under the weather, that I won't make it to dinner, sorry. Once I told him in passing that I hate waiting for people because it makes me feel like my time isn't as valuable as theirs.

'Excuse me. Do you have the time?'

As he turns to look at me, he smiles, and I can't help smiling back. I realize that when we met, the world didn't stop turning. There was no flash of blinding light. I didn't lose my voice. Life went on as usual. Now, we look at each other, and I can't say who approached who first, but we start walking and talking, and it's not like in the movies, I don't feel swept off my feet, reduced to a speck of dust. All I get is this flash of heat around my neck and the awkwardness of not knowing what to do with my hands, my arms, with myself in general. I suspect he noticed first and that I've spent months turning all this over in my head – chewing, digesting, taking it in. Like a lobster, I don't realize I've been cooked until I'm served on a platter.

58

May 2018

The way we started arguing was so dumb, I still can't make sense of it, no matter how hard I try. I know that when I walk up to my apartment hours later, I slam the door, then just stand there, leaning against it. I tell myself: 'You *will not* cry over a boy.' I throw my handbag, scarf, and jacket on the floor and leave them there in a messy pile, then shout OK GOOGLE PLAY THE SPOTIFY PLAYLIST LISTEN TO THIS WHEN YOU NEED SOME REGGAETON and OK Google replies OK MERYEM PLAYING THE SPOTIFY PLAYLIST LISTEN TO THIS WHEN YOU NEED SOME REGGAETON. Then I get in the shower because for some reason I think I'll only be able to deal with this once I'm clean. The shower doesn't help. I decide to text him, but when I open our thread, he's already typing, so I wait, wait, wait. He stops, then starts again. I think of ringing him but feel ridiculous, like I'm fourteen years old and sad because Raul, the class otaku, didn't sit next to me on the bus ride home. *Screw him*, I think, then sink into the couch and switch on the TV. I hold out for five minutes, then turn the TV off again, grab my phone and keys, slip on my shoes, and head to his place. I stand there, outside the entrance to his apartment building on Paseo de las Canteras, too chicken to push the buzzer. I tell myself it's only pathetic if he knows I'm here, so I decide to leave, except instead of leaving, instead of heading home with my head held high, I pull my phone out of my sweater pocket. It's ringing. It's him.

'Hi.'

'Hi.'

'Where are you?'

I look up at the sky and think of God. I wonder why I'm like this, why He made me like this. I don't answer.

'I can hear the noise on the street.'

I stare down at my shoes.

'Look outside,' I finally say. I honestly have no idea if God's happy with me.

'Huh?'

'Go out on your balcony and look outside.'

I hear his footsteps go shhr shhr shhr. I know exactly what he sees when he peers over the railing: a woman looking mildly unhinged in a sweater with the hood all the way up and drawn closed because it's glacial out here. In other words: a fool.

'Come up.'

'I don't want to.'

'Why? It's freezing cold.'

'I don't want to come up. If I come up we'll talk, and I don't want to talk to you.'

He has the decency to choke back his laughter.

'If you don't, then I'll have to come down to you, and I'm not as young as I used to be . . .'

My hood is still up when he opens the door, still up when I sit on the sofa and he sits next to me. He's watching the cooking channel. It's so . . . him that I might have laughed if I wasn't freaking out so hard. I grab the two drawstrings on my hood and pull them as tight as I can so that all he can see is my face. It's a little uncomfortable because the hood is pushing back on my glasses, but I feel safe this way.

'Nice sweater.'

'Thanks.'

'Is it the same one you wore to gym class in junior high?'

'And how old were you when I was in junior high? Twenty-four?' He takes a fake bullet to the chest.

'Did you have a boyfriend in school?'

'Of course not. The boys were all ugly, dumb, and smelly.'

He laughs. Sometimes it frustrates me that my only mode of communication is to dance around things instead of getting straight to the point. Especially if the thing in question is close to my heart. If you don't name something, then it doesn't exist. You need to be able to point to it and say: 'This. This bothers me.' If a thing doesn't exist, then you can pretend you're okay with it. I don't like change because I have a hard time adapting.

'The first time I saw you, you were wearing that black shirt with elephants on it,' he says after a while. 'You were in the cafeteria reading the label on a palmier . . . You were very focused.'

'You probably thought, *What a weirdo*.'

'No, not at all. I thought you were beautiful.'

I pretend not to hear that.

'Sometimes pastries have animal fat or gelatin in them,' I explain. 'And since the label doesn't say what *kind* of animal . . .'

'Yeah, I know that now. I'm a friend and ally of minorities. The point is you turned around . . . and saw me,' he goes on.

I remember none of this.

'And?'

'And you pushed up your glasses, put back the palmier, and left.'

'So charming of me.'

'I think you are.' He runs his hand along his jaw. 'Charming, I mean. You're fun. But whenever someone gives you a compliment or says something nice about you, you sort of go out of your way to change their mind.'

'I don't understand why you're acting like you don't get me. I like you a lot and we work together.'

'You think I don't like you?' He opens his mouth, closes it. I feel glued to the sofa, like if I move a fraction of an inch, the ground will swallow me whole. If only, I think. I wish a djinn would tear open a hole in his sofa and take me with it to the bowels of the earth, to the molten lava, and melt me away for good. 'You looked at me, turned around, and left. I wanted to talk to you. Instead I just stood there like an idiot.'

'I'm not . . . very outgoing. It's hard for me to . . .' I swish my hand around, I'm having trouble explaining myself. 'I like to keep some things to myself. What I mean is, I didn't leave because of . . . you. I left because of me, because I don't know how to, like . . . approach people, introduce myself, be friendly. I'm always saying stuff that's not as funny out loud as it is in my head, or putting my foot in things . . . It's embarrassing.'

'Then I thought maybe Yolanda would introduce you to everyone,' he goes on, 'but for some reason she didn't.'

'The reason she didn't is she hates me. I thought we'd established that.'

'Eventually, the first time we talked, you said, "I don't drink," all straight-faced. It makes me laugh every time I think about it.'

'I told you. I don't know how to talk to people. Sometimes I get the sense everyone projects these expectations on

251

me, that there's no room for me to just . . . be myself. No matter what I say, it's going to annoy someone. I don't have the bandwidth to deal with it, I can't be bothered to get into discussions or debates because most people I know don't argue for the sake of understanding the other person better, they argue to win. So I'd rather, like, just not say anything.'

'Is that why you walked out tonight?'

I stay quiet for a while.

'I was upset that you didn't tell me about the interview.'

I tell Omar everything. He's always asking me questions, wanting to know things about me. So it hurt to find out that he'd hid something from me, that he'd let me get all these ideas in my head about him and me, about us. The morning of our argument, he'd said to me, like it was no big deal: 'You know, the last time I went home, to Rota, I interviewed for another job . . . Just to see what it would be like, I don't know, I didn't think I'd get it, but I did. They made me an offer. I've thought it through, and I'm going to take it.' I'd opened my mouth over and over, speechless, then congratulated him. The difference between Omar and me is that I always choose my words very carefully when we talk about important stuff. I turn them over, weigh every single term. I ask myself, *If things were the other way around, would I be upset?* I take his feelings into account because they matter to me. But that morning, I understood it wasn't reciprocal. Omar said whatever popped into his head; he never considered how his words or actions might affect me. We weren't together, so neither of us had any rights over the other, but I thought of him as a friend, someone I cared about deeply.

All of a sudden, I feel ridiculous and lower my hood. I'm not a kid anymore.

'I didn't realize I'd be doing the interview. My sister knows someone at the company, so I just took it when I was home for the long weekend.'

'It's not that I'm not happy for you,' I begin, 'it's just that I wasn't expec—'

'I know, I know. Don't worry.' He covers my hand with his and gives it a gentle squeeze, then runs his thumb over my knuckles. *Help*, I think. I've totally forgotten why I was mad, why I decided to leave him hanging, to storm out of work without saying goodbye.

'I didn't come here to hook up with you,' I stammer. 'I have no intention of hooking up with you.'

The sofa vibrates with laughter.

'No?' he asks. 'You sure? I'd surrender willingly.'

'I'm sure. In fact, I think I'm going to head home. I'm hungry.'

'I can make you dinner,' he says, his shoulder touching mine. 'And we can watch the cooking channel for a bit. I know you're a woman of exquisite taste.'

I laugh.

'Listen, I like you a lot, I'm excited about you,' he says. He doesn't doubt himself, or hide anything. He just has a thought and voices it. I'm not like that at all. 'And you just said you're crazy about me. Sure, we won't be working together anymore, but I'm not in a rush. I can wait. I'll visit. You'll visit . . . How does that sound?'

I'm not under any obligation to act on my feelings for someone, regardless of how strong they are. I can choose to do nothing. We live in a world where we're endlessly trod on and pressured to act, to be in constant motion. Flow, get out of your comfort zone, rise to the challenge. Sink all your savings into a start-up, make an app, download Tinder. What if I don't want to? What if I'd rather take it slow?

'Fine, but could you make me a sandwich while you wait?' I ask.

59

June 2018

I learn through observation and turn into the kind of person who can weather whatever the universe throws at her. In my desk drawer I have: a pair of ballet flats, a pack of band-aids, a box of panty liners, a bar of deodorant, three hair ties, a stain-removal stick, a white shirt, and a navy blue blazer. Two toothbrushes and one tube of toothpaste. A toiletry bag with some makeup in it. One evening, I add a bottle of ibuprofen, some chamomile tea, and hand lotion. A box of tissue paper, colored pencils, and a coloring book for Matiqui's and our CFO Ernesto's daughters to play with. Matiqui steps out of his office one morning, comes up to my desk, and pensively strokes his chin.

'I need you to do something for me, but I've forgotten what.'

'You had a dentist appointment tomorrow at ten a.m., and you wanted it moved to after five. You're here to ask me if I've done it,' I say. 'I have. The confirmation's sitting in your inbox.'

Sometimes I wonder what it's like to live like that, with all the more tedious, grubby aspects of life sorted for you.

Mohamed Choukri once said that life is nothing but cold and heat until the coming of the plague and floods. It never floods here, so maybe for me life is nothing but heat and anxiety until the coming of my own death.

'Thanks, you're the best.'

He turns around and heads to his office. Halfway there, he stops and pivots back to me.

'One more thing. You wouldn't happen to have some ibuprofen, would you?'

'I do, but I can't give you any. It's against company policy.' I open my second desk drawer, take out a bottle of ibuprofen, and hold it out to him. 'In fact, I think you—'

'Yes, I wrote the handbook,' he smiles. 'Thanks. You should be in the clear, so long as no one finds out.'

He turns around again. It looks like he might just make it to his office when all of a sudden he lingers in the doorway. The right corner of my right eye twitches.

'Have you eaten yet?'

'It's only noon.'

'Do you mind calling Amaki and ordering lunch for me?'

'Sure thing. Bento box D, gyozas, and still water?'

I rub the eye with the twitch and wonder if I'm doing a good job of hiding it.

'Yes, that's exactly it. I don't know . . . I just don't know what I'd do without you.'

You'd call HR and get them to get RANDSTAD to get you another girl. In spite of myself, a feeling of competence settles over me like morning dew. Ten minutes later, he calls me on the phone.

'You know, I've been thinking,' he says. 'You need someone to help you with silly things like making photocopies. I'm going to talk to Alonso and Macarena, see if they can rustle you up an intern. How does that sound?'

255

A sticky substance forms at the back of my neck and slowly oozes down my spine.

'An intern.'

'You know, someone young who'd report to you and be under your charge. Someone you could send on errands while you focus on the important stuff.'

I am also someone young, and not only am I under his charge, I also 'report' to him. I open and close my left hand under the table. My right hand grips the phone so hard my fingers start curling into claws. Maybe I could focus on the important stuff if my middle-aged boss didn't need a babysitter.

'Sounds great.'

Though I can't see his face, I'm sure he's smiling, pleased as punch about his shitty idea.

'That's wonderful, Meryem, just wonderful. It'll be a great experience, you'll see. You're going to enjoy showing someone else the ropes.'

I've had approximately 537 experiences at this company to date, and they have all been a steaming pile of garbage.

60

June 2018

Alonso sends me thirty-four CVs for the thirty-four people who've applied to be my future intern. I print them, arrange them in alphabetical order, then shove them in a drawer.

61

June 2018

People grow apart slowly. I know something's the matter, but I don't want to accept it. First it's one day, two days, three days of not speaking, then it's a week, two weeks. I transform into the kind of woman who waits for her man to send her a text. It's pathetic. Even though I can see what's happening, I can't make myself bring it up with him. Nothing's going on, he's just tired, or he's got too much work on, or he forgot to call or text back or even remember I exist. I take his OKs and his two blue checkmarks and flush them down the toilet: by now, the toilet has swallowed hundreds of millions of the OKs and read receipts that stick to the sides of my intestines. Every time we talk, I feel worse, paralyzed, in a state of constant second-guessing. I go from *what's going on with him?* to *what have I done wrong?* to *I'm so stupid for feeling this way.* I get smaller and smaller, tiny, microscopic, and feed on the self-pity. I can't leave him because there's nothing to leave.

Carmen and Teresa's words haunt me: he's a loser and a fraud, a guy who's not like other guys right up until he is. One night when I can't sleep I text asking if he's awake, and he calls me beautiful and says he's awake but that he's nodding off on his new sofa in his new apartment, and my heart goes all weird and heavy in my chest. Another day I ask if he's busy, and he says he just got home, he'll call as soon as he's out of the shower. Obviously, he doesn't. I start resenting him for wasting my time and being careless with my feelings, when *he's* the one who chased me. It's so difficult to reconcile this detached side of him with the person I thought I knew that I start feeling a little crazy, like I'm an unreliable narrator, that I'm imagining things. Finally, one evening I can't take it anymore, and I text to say that I understand the situation, but I can't go on like this, that I'm tired, that I'm losing my mind, and he knows where to find me if he ever wants to see me. And he replies that of course he wants to see me, I'm one of the most important people in his life, that he cares for me, he's just going through a rough patch. But you said you were excited about me, that I was the best thing to happen to you in years. I say this to him like it's very important that he be reminded of this – just in case he forgot, in case he can't remember. He leaves me on read.

The next few days are a blur. I wake up, shower, get dressed, go to the office, come home, crawl into bed. I wake up again the next morning, shower, get dressed, go to the office. The Great Sadness smudges the line that divides time into seven distinct parts. It all mixes together. On weekends, I make an effort to appear normal to my family, not like I've spent the past few days breathing funny and gasping for air. One thing's for sure: I don't shed a single tear. Teresa texts: 'Come over for lunch.' Carmen texts: 'How're you doing, chicklet?' Some of my internet friends write to me. I delete Twitter and Instagram. I consider leaving social media for good. Forgetting the internet even exists. Becoming a regular person, reintegrating into society, like special agents do when they decide they've had enough of leading a double life. I can't read more than three lines of text without losing focus, or watch an episode to the end or listen to music without feeling like I'm drowning. I cancel my Spotify subscription. All the things I used to enjoy become static. I turn the same idea over and over in my head, every freaking day. Round and round it goes. My brain feels raw.

I wish I could just lie, say I forgot about him as quickly and easily as he forgot about me, but the truth is I carried a torch for him a long time, to the point that sometimes I couldn't even bear to think his name, because when I did, when I remembered it, I felt this sharp, throbbing pain at the base of my throat, in my collar bones, my chest, and I'd have to sit down and wait for the wave to crash over me and recede. Sometimes I'd be fine, then out of the blue I'd see or read something I know he would've loved, and a gloom would settle over my shoulders, leaving me speechless for the rest of the day. My old hideouts at work reminded me of him, so I tried to find new ones. The sadness pinned me down while I made photocopies and filled out our monthly estimated expenses, while I stood in line at La Garriga for a grilled-chicken sandwich with everything or in the gourmet section of the supermarket scanning the shelves for something to take to a party that I wouldn't end up going to because I couldn't be bothered.

It was days before I cried over him for the first time. Once I started I couldn't stop. I cried and cried and cried, sometimes with rage and others with this sadness that drained me and left me feeling like I'd just atoned for a lifetime of sins. I slept badly, then worse, stopped caring about food, and basically lost the ability to enjoy even the little things, like when Yolanda tripped on the stairs and flew down several steps, like the lobster-red bald spot Esteban came home with from Turkey, or like the no-confidence vote against Rajoy. Weeks passed and then months, and I survived the period known as The Great Sadness much like I've survived everything else: I let things pass and said nothing.

62

July 2018

In the summer, everything is yellow and blue. They're the only two colors I associate with the season. I see nothing but beach, ocean, and sun. Salty lips, wavy hair, warm skin – first red, then darker. I never get sunburnt on the beach. I'm always very careful. As a kid, before I'd learned to swim, I used to pretend I was drowning on the water's edge, and my parents would pretend to rescue me from the waves. They'd call out 'Where's our little fishy? Oh, no! She's dead!' And I'd hold in my laughter as long as I could, then shout 'Surprise!'

I catch a cold in late June and spend my two days of sick leave on the beach. I don't get in the water, I sit far away from it. The first time I saw a patero run aground I was seven years old, and when refugees started clambering over each other to get out of the boat and ran as fast as they could, I got so scared, I turned around and ran too. Eventually I became desensitized to the experience and no longer found it scary. I've watched several wars be waged – feminism, climate change, privacy – while feeling I'd let myself be defeated in one that seemed unimportant at the time but that I'm beginning to regret ignoring. Our words have lost all meaning. When I hear someone say that the rest of Europe should welcome more migrants, I wonder if the words *welcome* and *rescue* are synonyms, if a person drowning in the ocean can be welcomed, if talking heads should be debating this on *La Sexta Noche* while people die on the coast of my island, whether as a viewer I prefer the sound of *welcome* over *rescue*, though I guess you have to be rescued before you can be welcomed. Something that should weigh on my shoulders, crush me in its fist and stop me from breathing is instead just another drop I watch fall fall fall without sound. Reality only takes shape once we draw attention to it, but if the tools I use to do that lose meaning, then I am lost as well.

In the Canary Islands, everything looks blue and yellow from the beach. When the sun sets on Las Canteras, I get goosebumps all down my back as I lie on the sand. The sky turns purple and orange, and even though I'm sad, I feel like one of the luckiest people on earth. I walk all the way from Alfredo Kraus to Playa Dorada, then take the number two bus from Santa Catalina to Primero de Mayo, by the post office. There's this video going around social media of a young Black girl walking all over Wall Street with a microphone, stopping stockbrokers to ask them questions like 'Who did you exploit today?' and 'When the revolution comes, where will you hide?' Sometimes a patera capsizes and small children and pregnant women die. I haven't been able to get that image out of my head for a while.

63

July 2018

On the packet of dates, it says: PRODUCT OF TUNISIA. My dad points this out once, twice, three, four times. He jabs at the packet over and over with his finger. This is important. Very important.

'I refuse to participate in the extermination and exploitation of our Palestinian brothers.'

'Yes, Baba.'

'And don't buy it if it says, "Product of Jordan Valley," either.'

'Okay.'

He knows I know he's right. Even so, he says it again and again. Harvesting date palms is an exploitative industry. Many of its operations take place in illegal settlements where Palestinian workers are mistreated and underpaid. Since dates are really expensive, my dad buys them for me.

64

July 2018

A thought: when one of your relatives dies, say your favorite uncle or grandmother, you have to keep working. When you're in a deep depression, you have to keep working. When you're sick, you have to keep working. Our lives have been built in such a way that the only thing that *must* continue no matter what, despite everything and everyone, is work. It's insane.

65

July 2018

On my birthday, the team gives me a bottle of very expensive wine (I only find out how expensive later) and Matiqui lets me take the day off. I accept both things with a blank look on my face. Even though they've seen me turn down beer at lunch or after-work drinks, I don't think they've registered it. I add this to my theory about bosses: they pretend to want to get to know you just so they can tell themselves they're not exploitative assholes, but the truth is they couldn't list three facts about you if they tried. I give the bottle to Carmen and Teresa and spend the day running errands and meal prepping. I'm just as lost at twenty-seven as I was at twenty-six.

In the evening, the name OMAR flashes on my phone. I stare at it. When it finally stops buzzing, I slip it into my handbag, then put my handbag in the closet and spend the rest of the day hearing phantom vibrations, even though there's no way I could sense them from where I'm sitting. I think about something Emilio Prados wrote in a letter to Lorca: 'You didn't write, you didn't write . . . I tried to be dazed by the sounds of the wind.' I don't read his text until hours later, when I feel strong enough not to be affected. 'Thanks :)' I write back, then erase our text chain. Years vanish at the click of 'Delete chat.' I can't be tormented by something that doesn't exist. The next few days, I obsess over his message and my reply. Sometimes, I think I said the right thing; others, I'm convinced I was too curt. I'm periodically tempted to write to him and apologize for what a bitch I can be. Until one day I find myself drafting something like this:

'Sorry for the curt "Thanks :)" I sent the other day, the truth is I tried to tone it down with the emoticon but we hadn't talked in a while, and I don't know if I ever told you but I don't really like emojis, they feel really fake to me, and I realize no one gets that, no one gets me, I'm 16 all over again, listening to old Shakira songs on my bedroom floor while crying over you, a guy who legit came to work one day in jean shorts. Can you believe it? I used to be smart, now suddenly I'm not. See, the reason I added a period after the emoticon is that I'm the kind of person who ends her sentences, not a monster who leaves everything wide-open, hanging out, who doesn't know how to use periods or commas. Let's be honest now and admit that a thank you with a smile and a period is an appropriate reply, a civilized reply, you might even say a mature reply, given the circumstances. You always win, of course. Your message was perfect. I've thought about it every time I've wanted not to think. Every time I've tried to make my mind go blank, your words pop up, glowing against the back of my eyelids. I wonder about the meaning of that comma, those kisses, that joke, the way you're talking to me like you used to, back when you said you liked me. Remember? Though maybe, who knows, maybe it was all a lie, maybe I imagined it, made

267

it all up, maybe I saw something that wasn't there, I don't know, I don't know anything anymore, I'm just a girl thinking for the millionth time about a text sent to her by a dude who's a full decade older than her just to try and make sense of what happened. I wish I could hate you but I can't. I wish I could forget your nose, your crow's feet, your gray hair, your shirt collars, your preppy sweaters. I wish I could forget your face. That I could tear it off your skull with my bare hands and expose the red, throbbing flesh beneath, throbbing like the vein in my forehead when I cry myself to sleep and wake up with swollen eyes, face a complete mess, all because of you, you, throbbing like blood under my skin from how incensed you make me feel when you act like nothing's changed after all this time and call me "beautiful." *Happy birthday, beautiful. Whatever. Asshole.*' I save it in my notes. Even though I feel like something bad will happen if I don't hit send, I don't hit send. I don't do anything.

66

July 2018

A café called Slow Coffee opens up three blocks from Super-saurio. I come across it one day as I'm headed back to the office after notarizing some documents for Matiqui. I have breakfast there. It's not very big – the counter takes up about half the space, leaving room for only three tables – but the coffee's amazing, so I start going there a lot. It's new, some-where Omar has never set foot, somewhere I don't have to swallow his ghost one spoonful at a time. I tell myself every-body has feelings, that everybody's been sad at some point in their lives. I'm not the first woman nor the last to have felt and still feel the way I do now. It had to happen eventually. I go to Slow Coffee so much that the barista starts giving me the occasional freebie. *Try this filterless Rwanda*, he says to me one day, *then tell me what you think.* And I do: I let it chill in the jar and drink it after a bit. I can feel his eyes on me as I do this, but I pretend not to notice. I text Carmen: 'Movie tonight?' Received, read. 'Duh.' *Delicious*, I say before leaving, as I settle up. *It was super sweet. I got notes of, mmm, honey or something.* Another day, he says, *Try this Guatemala*, then makes Teresa and me two espressos, gently leaving them on our table. He has an unusual accent. Every so often, he lisps an ess instead of a zee, like he's not sure how a word is spelled or like he's trying to overcompensate. At another point in my life, I might've found this endearing. He says his name is Carlos. We tell him to call us Meryem and Teresa. *Beautiful names. Thank you, thank you so much.*

'He's nice, don't you think?' she says, excited.

'Yeah, he's very friendly.'

Another day, he brings me a plate of sweets along with the coffee. An unusually small donut, something that looks like a chocolate ball, and a white chocolate-chip cookie. *I want your honest opinion*, he says. *This is totally normal,* I think while taking small bites out of the cookie. It tastes like cinnamon. I put it back. I *hate* cinnamon. This is totally normal! My body and my chemistry are telling me it may be a good idea to spend some time at my parents' house because my apartment suddenly feels too big, and that's exactly what I do: I pack three T-shirts, a pair of jeans, and pajamas into a carry-on bag, then leave. I spend the next two weeks in Puerto Rico, where I take the 91 bus at 6:40 a.m., head resting on the window, so I can be at the office by eight. The sun always comes out when we roll past Monte Feliz. It's the same driver as always. He still plays *Es la mañana de Federico* (with Federico Jiménez Losantos) on the radio, still says goodbye to me when I get off outside the Teatro. I wonder: if he knew I was Muslim, would he still be this nice to me? Every now and then he nods along when Jiménez Losantos complains about the onslaught of Arabs, Islamists, and jihadists in Spain. Uncivilized terrorists, all of them. Every day without fail, I miss the 6:15 p.m. bus back to Puerto Rico and have to wait for the one that leaves at 7:15 p.m. I don't mind because I'm in the process of becoming a serene person, a calm sea. I no longer have a certain rage, only a certain exhaustion. Some evenings, I watch the sun set from the bus, the sky turning orange, pink, and blue the closer we get to Puerto Rico.

The next time I go to Slow Coffee, Carlos tests my decision to give in to a life of serenity when he steps in front of me as I'm walking through the door. *Well, well, look who decided to come back!* he says, grabbing my shoulders, to my annoyance. A couple at one of the tables turns to look at us. *Where'd you run off to?* he asks. I don't want to laugh. If I laugh, he'll think I'm amused by what he's doing, and I'm not, it actually bothers me, a lot. *I went on vacation,* I say. *Could I get an americano?* I gently shrug him off. This is totally normal, I tell myself again. He's just being nice. I'm being impossible, disrespectful, mean in fact. Chill out. I sit at my usual table, the one all the way on the left, and mess around on my phone, so uncomfortable I might just puke a little in my mouth. No free coffees or sweets today, thank God. I wonder if I've done anything to encourage so much familiarity. I wouldn't say so, but not only am I in my serene mindfulness period, I'm also spiraling with self-doubt and wondering if I'm imagining things (just like I imagined certain things, certain feelings that turned out not to be real, to never have existed, feelings that vanished poof! in the night, disappeared, big FOR SALE sign nailed to the front door). The coffee doesn't taste like anything. I knock it back, tongue severed from head severed from palate. I just want to go home.

This is what happens when I go up to the counter to pay: Carlos the Slow Coffee barista takes my hand, which is holding a five-Euro note, places it on his chest and says: 'Can you feel my heart? It's finally steady now that you're back.' Something inside me lurches, teeters, and disappears

271

out of sheer disgust, and I stand there staring at him like an idiot. He gives me my change, and I take it, avoiding his touch like I'm Lot's wife, a cursed pillar of salt. *I curse the day*, I whisper to myself on my way to work. *I curse the day I set foot in that place.*

Fandom: Supersaurio (Las Palmas – District 2)
Characters: Teresa
Tags: -
Category: General
Words: 442

Where I Answer Questions About Healthy Living

Teresa's parents were having a hard time understanding why their daughter would leave a stable job at a marketing agency to work full-time on her YouTube channel, even though she made a lot more money working for herself than she ever did working for someone else. She had 732,550 subscribers – every time she uploaded a new video, someone would comment, 'Not long until you hit a million!' Her most popular video had thirteen million views. It was called ASMR Massage with Gua Sha and natural oils. There was nothing all that special about the video. In the foreground, her friend Carmen sat in a chair while Teresa stood behind her and brushed her hair very slowly and carefully, then massaged her scalp, neck, and shoulders. In the background, a white wall and a dresser they'd covered with every candle they could find in the house. The atmosphere was warm, welcoming. Teresa barely spoke in her ASMR videos, and when she did, she used a very different voice. She also didn't show her face very often. There were too many crazies on the internet. The more she protected herself from some random guy coming up to her on the street the better. Most of her videos were in the same minimalist style. They were tagged as 'Aspirational' and 'Slow life.' She'd film herself buying groceries or running errands around the city, cooking, riding her bike, getting a drink with friends or un-boxing the gifts she got from the labels she partnered with. 'Join me as I get ready,' 'What I eat throughout the day,' 'My weekly routine.' When she reached more than half a million followers, two of the country's most important fashion magazines reached out to sign her. Her job would consist in creating content for them about anything she wanted, so long as it aligned with their respective philosophies. Every day, she got five, six, sometimes even seven packages with beauty, fashion, and home décor projects . . . Tired, she mostly gave these away to friends. Despite all this, her parents kept insisting that she should find a real job as soon as possible. 'What if you lose followers?' her mother would ask. What Teresa hadn't told them is that even if she lost every last follower she had, she'd made so much money in the past few years that she could afford to sit on her hands for a decade. They were a different generation. They didn't understand that what she did *was* a real job. She made sure that the camera was well positioned one last time, then tucked her hair behind her left ear and pressed record.

67

August 2018

The zillionth time I reactivate my Tinder profile, I match with Iván 28 fucking delusional man leaving the room Spanish flag emoji UK flag emoji pint of beer emoji running man emoji. His looks are the only reason I swipe right: he's hot enough that any validation from him is sure to boost my self-esteem, maybe even yank me out of my current state of emotional hibernation. Dark eyes, dark hair, dark complexion, not even a shadow of facial hair, the polar opposite of Om— I refuse to think his name, I will not think his name, I am not crying over him anymore, it doesn't hurt, the waterworks are off, what's done is done. Beyond that, though, I'm not the least bit interested in the guy, not in his personality, his past, or whether he's hiding eight dismembered bodies in a freezer somewhere, I don't give a damn. I am not a great person. Immediately after we match, we make plans to meet for a drink a couple days later.

I change in the office bathroom. Today's look: plum-colored high-waisted pants with topstitching in front and back, piped front pockets (false, too small to fit anything), extra-thin crew-neck sweater, flat leather boots with track soles. I smear myself in makeup, spritz so much perfume my eyes tear, and walk out of work like a penguin because the boots are new and not broken in yet. In the elevator, I bend over and shake out my hair. I study my reflection in the mirror: I look like I barely made it out of a car crash alive.

My resolve weakens the closer I get to the agreed meeting place, but I convince myself it's just nerves, I'm fine. I cross Triana, brain rattling in my skull. I try to negotiate with myself: you can't go on like this, you need to turn the page, heal. I am a strong, independent woman with a commanding presence and a steady job. My memories of Om——no, my memories of That Person – cannot keep hurting me, I will learn to forget him, I will purge him from my life no matter how miserable, sad, and tired I feel right now. I walk into Azotea de Benito like this, on the verge of tears. I sniffle quickly in the elevator up and carefully wipe my eyes with the back of my right hand, trying not to smudge my makeup. Iván 28 fucking delusional man leaving the room Spanish flag emoji UK flag emoji pint of beer emoji running man emoji looks just like his photos. He smiles when he sees me and immediately stands up.

'Meryem?'

'Yeah, hi. Sorry I'm late. I couldn't get out of work any sooner.' He shakes his head, like it doesn't matter at all, and leans in to give me two kisses. Something in my head goes 'whoa there, buddy' but forces me to accept them.

'Don't worry, I literally just sat down.' He's way too good-looking up close. I avoid his eyes as I put my handbag on the free chair to my right, then take a seat. 'I hadn't been to this side of town in years. It's one of my favorite areas.'

I nod.

'Yeah, it has its charms.'

'Do you live around here?' We look at each other.

'Yeah, sort of. In the neighborhood. What about you?'

'Nah, I live in Tafira.' He smiles again and gently shakes his head. 'You know, your pics don't do you justice.'

'Huh?'

He runs his hand down his left cheek.

'Nothing, I'm just shook is all.'

The *Kill Bill* siren starts going off, very quietly, in my right ear. I open and close my mouth. I don't really know what to say.

'Thanks.'

The siren gets louder by the second. It's not him. It's me.

'I promise I'm not just saying this so you'll like me.'

'Oh, um, thank you?' I grab my handbag. 'I need to go to the bathroom. Do you mind?'

'Go ahead. I'll take a look at the menu in the meantime.'

'Great, thanks!' I smile with my mouth closed so I won't accidentally puke all over him.

I move slowly, with intent. I take one step, then another, force myself to keep walking, to not turn around and look at him even once. There's no way he knows what I'm thinking, no way he can read my mind. I don't go to the bathroom. Instead, I turn right at the bar and walk out the door. I walk past the elevator, hang another right, and run downstairs. There's no way he's already realized I've walked out on our date. Even so, just in case, I run until I reach the street. Outside the Monopol hotel, I stare up at the sky and say, a little loudly: 'Why did you have to do me like that, God? Why?' I block Iván 28 fucking delusional man leaving the room Spanish flag emoji UK flag emoji pint of beer emoji running man emoji on WhatsApp. As I make my way home, I delete Tinder from my phone. I don't slow down until I'm outside my front door.

68

August 2018

Sanaa tells me:

'Last summer Khalti Amira touched my hair and said it was too long. It hasn't grown an inch since.'

I choke on my food. Btata whror and a Seven-Up, both of us sitting on the steps to my maternal grandma's attic. All of the cousins get together here in the summer. The harissa is so spicy, it makes my eyes water. I only see my family in the summer. I miss out on so much that when I'm actually here I feel like I physically need to see everything, hear everything, take part in everything. I'm scared they'll forget me one day, that the distance will turn me into a stranger, an occasional visitor, a tourist.

'What?' my voice is choked.

'Wallah,' she assures me. She sets her napkin on her right, gives me a serious look. She's acting weird. 'Haven't you noticed how she sizes you up when she hugs you? Touching you like this . . .' She imitates her, hands like a pair of tweezers, or rulers, I'm not actually sure what she's trying to get across, '. . . first on the shoulders, then the arms, then the waist . . . Oof. I'm not going down to say hi if she comes over.'

Khalti Amira is married to one of my uncles. She's a huge gossip with a barbed tongue, and no one comes out of a conversation with her unscathed. When we were little, she could even pry baby food from my cousins and me. Her interrogation tactics were subtle, extremely elaborate, and we'd find ourselves sharing information we thought was totally innocuous only to realize it was actually damning. *What did you girls get up to last week? We visited Khalti Kaltoum. Oh, but wasn't Khalti Kaltoum a bit poorly? No, she was fine. I'm so happy to hear that, I don't know why I thought she was under the weather . . .* Now we do what we can to avoid spending five minutes in the same space as her. She creeps us out.

'Well, now that you mention it . . .'

No matter how well a family gets along, there's always some iconic building that was raised over the ashes of an Indigenous burial site. None of my aunt-in-laws get along. Some – the ones who've been married into the family longer – see the new in-laws as intruders of a sort, external agents who are not to be trusted. They maneuver against each other like Russian chess players or KGB agents and seem inoffensive until they slide up to you as you're closing the trunk of your car, then immobilize you with a chokehold. The last thing you see before you die is their smile. With them, any word that is not the exact right word leads to a comment that leads to another comment that triggers a question that forces you into a lie.

'You're right, she totally does,' I eventually say. 'She feels you up to see if you've put on weight or something.'

'I'm being serious. Do not let her touch your hair. *Not one inch all year.*'

The first thing Khalti Amira does when she sees me a few hours later is plant her hands on my shoulders and squeeze.

Then she moves down to my elbows. She scans my body-work with impunity, and I let her because I learned in a documentary that when you step in quicksand you're supposed to relax and let yourself get swallowed up, easy does it, because the harder you struggle, the deeper you sink.

'Oh, Meryem, sweet pea! You don't know how much I've missed you.'

'Salam, Khalti! It's been so long!'

'You look beautiful!' She shakes my shoulders. She's coming on strong this afternoon. 'Tbarkallah w salat 'ala nabi!'

'You look lovely, too.'

'Oh, you know, I can't complain, alhamdulillah. You must be up to here with preparations for Hind, huh.'

'Mm-hmm.'

'Your aunt said it would be a small gathering.'

'Mm-hmm.'

'Tell me, how small exactly? How many guests are we talking?'

Sanaa walks into the living room. The way she looks when she sees us, it's like she's just sighted a djinn.

'Mmmm . . . Oh, Sanaa! I was looking for you,' I say. 'We've got to go get milk.'

'Milk,' she echoes, nodding. 'You're right. Mom said she wanted milk and butter.'

'And do you both have to go?'

I open my mouth. Close it.

'The thing is . . . Meryem's too embarrassed to go alone,' she lies. 'All the signs are in Arabic . . . she gets a bit confused.'

My Arabic is perfect. My accent is from the capital, like my mother's, and I curse like a native – I'm really proud of that last bit. Though I don't always get what's going on in Egyptian soaps, I think that's less to do with my Arabic than

280

with the vocabulary. Every dialect is its own world. Khalti Amira nods, sympathetic.

'You shouldn't feel bad. It's your parents' fault,' she sighs. *You hyena,* I think, but nod along. 'If only they'd taught you . . .'

A few minutes later, I'm imitating her as Sanaa and I walk downstairs.

'*You shouldn't feel bad. It's your parents' fault.*' We go *thwack thwack thwack* down the steps. 'Do you think she can hear herself when she talks?'

It's my first week off since starting at Supersaurio: I wake up at the same time as always, even though I don't set an alarm, and have the nagging feeling I should be doing something with my free time. What? you ask. No idea, *stuff,* anything, checking my email at the very least. It's like work has seeped into every corner of my life, even my sleeping patterns. I used to be able to sleep from eleven at night until ten in the morning. Now my eyes shoot open at quarter or half past six, even if I go to bed after midnight. As my cousins snooze, I read on the roof terrace while the sun rises, then pray. I wash, get dressed, and beg God to help me feel less sad, even just a little. After I finish praying, there's a mark on my forehead from pressing it against the rug. I pray for my parents and siblings, for my grandma, I pray for my aunt Hanana, and my whole family. I help my grandma make breakfast, then wake the kids by tickling or throwing cushions at them.

My maternal grandmother lives in a two-story house and yet somehow we still manage to squeeze everyone in there, all eleven of her children and the children of her eleven children, a big family, with after-dinner chatter that lasts close to four hours, and a ton of weddings and baptisms. At some of these events, one of my little cousins would always have

281

to be taken outside because they start giggling while pretending to be a professional wrestler and then they wind up getting rapped on the head and punched for real because one of them really hurt the other and so they hurt them back, and so on and so forth ad infinitum.

Every now and then, when I dream of Omar, I wake up crying. It's like the sadness can't leave my body all at once, like it needs a good chunk of time to ease out of me, little by little, slow but steady – it's a sensible, Canarian sadness. I dream he's washing my hair. I dream we're chatting on the Supersaurio roof terrace, like before, back when we used to be friends, back when I was naïve. I dream I'm sitting on the beach, and he goes in for a swim and I see him drifting further and further away until he disappears, and I don't do anything, say anything, I just sit there, unmoving. One morning, I stretch the full length of my body out on the sofa-bed and stare up at the ceiling. It's a one-hour difference between Casablanca and Las Palmas. I write to Teresa and Carmen: 'Do you think I'll ever stop being sad? It feels so endless.' One of my little cousins, Fati, startles awake and immediately sits up.

'Hey,' I whisper. 'Are you alright?'

'I had a weird dream.'

'Want to get in here with me?'

'Yes.'

* * *

I try on the takshita, careful not to tear it. First the kaftan, then the over-dress. It's tailor-made, a gift from my grandmother. The over-dress is handsewn with zagali from the shoulders to the waist, and also on the cuffs. My first thought is it must've been really expensive. I feel a kind of shame I can't put into words. I don't deserve this gift. My

282

grandmother gestures at me to fix the m'damma. It's hers, from when she was young, pure gold.

'All set,' she says.

I cinch the waist, and my grandmother takes a turn around me. The silk is so soft and light, I feel like a movie star. The skirt falls all the way down to my feet. I'll have to hitch up the tail, like a lady. My grandmother Zoubida is the second tallest woman in my family. I'm the tallest. I'd like to think that I take after her in this respect and in other respects too, things I haven't noticed in my parents: how I want to do everything on my own without asking for help or how we turn our backs on someone forever and say: 'I knew there was a reason I didn't like them, I knew there was something fishy going on there,' when time tells us we were right all along. We look at each other and smile.

'Ghzala.'

Even if my legs were flipped backward, my teeth were crooked and yellow, and I had a lazy eye, she'd still call me *ghzala*.

'How many camels would you trade me for, Mé?'

She laughs.

'I wouldn't trade you for any number of camels.' She fixes my hair, steps back to study her work. 'Maybe cows, though. Or chickens.'

'Jeda Fatma had cows and chickens,' I say after a while.

'Allah yrahma.'

'Allah yrahma. I have this image of her in my head. She's making baghrir in that outfit she always wore. You know the one? The apron . . .'

One of the biggest regrets I will carry with me forever is not making it to my grandmother's funeral.

'Ah, if Fatma could see you now . . .' She grabs my chin and hugs me. She's strong for her age. At first I think I'm the one holding her in my arms, but she's holding me. 'Sunna dial hayat, Meryem. We're born, grow up, have children, then our children have children, and in the end we die . . . It's the natural order of the world.'

'I know . . .'

'One day, I won't be here to tell you these things either.'

'Oh, Mé. Don't you start too, you're beginning to sound like Baba. "My only wish is to die before I become a burden . . ." Pffft. He drives me crazy. The other day he sat me down and explained how to repatriate him and Mom if they both die, who to call, the paperwork I'll need . . . Ugh.'

'Your dad can be a bit melodramatic. I don't know who you take after.'

'Beats me. I think I'm adopted.'

* * *

I scatter fistfuls of orange blossoms from the attic window. Three floors down, on the street, Hind walks toward a car in her bridal gown. The flowers tumble down, and when she feels their touch, she looks up and waves. Next to me, her sister is recording everything. My aunts and cousins are singing, taarijas, darbukas and bendirs in hand. Their sound is all you can hear on the street, in the whole neighborhood. Some of my grandmother's neighbors peer out their windows and join in, singing, clapping, and I think about how, even if I don't live here, even if I'm not from here, even if I only visit once a year, I still grew up here, in a way. I think about how when we were little, the three of us used to play on this street with other girls and boys in the neighborhood, even though Hind woke one morning and decided she was suddenly too grown-up to play with us, and it wasn't long before we were too grown-up as well. We didn't want to

284

hide, jump rope, play cards or shoot marbles anymore. Instead, we wanted to talk about makeup and boys, to do our hair, to watch Turkish and Mexican soaps dubbed into Moroccan Darija – and I was still this little kid in a Del Piero jersey doing tricks with the ball, because I was different, I was a girl who played soccer, I wasn't stupid or silly like the others. Some of the boys called me Pierita or gawrya and I hated when they called me gawrya because the way they said it sounded like an insult – foreigner, guiri, outsider.

These days, when I bump into these same people, some of them act like they don't know me because, as far as they're concerned, I'm still a gawrya, and they don't like that. Meanwhile, others show me pictures of their sons and their daughters and ask if I remember the time Fulanito called me a slut and I threw a rock at his face and shouted back, *Your mom's the slut*, and Fulanito dodged the rock, which hurtled through the air until it crashed through a shop window, and I went yellow, then white, and ran all the way to my grandma's, and by the time I got there I was already in tears, dribbling snot, and all I could think about was how God had seen me do that, how God had heard me say 'Your mom's the slut.'

This summer, I see Fulanito one morning and he looks the other way. He's wearing a white djellaba and a pointy beard, and Sanaa whispers 'what a freak,' under her breath, and the two of us laugh at him. My parents didn't get mad at me that day 300 years ago when I threw the rock at Fulanito for calling me a slut. My mother comforted me, my dad paid for a new window, and that was the day I learned I had a right to defend myself and also that I could tell my parents anything, anything at all.

Down on the street, everyone is celebrating. Some people are calling out *sla wslam ala rassoul allah*, and when Sanaa and I hear this, we join in *SLA WSLAM ALA RASSOUL ALLAH*. We get carried away and scatter more and more petals from way up high, until suddenly we remember we were supposed to be in that car, leaving with the bride.

'If I ever get married,' I say, racing downstairs, 'I want my wedding to last three whole days.'

Sanaa cracks up.

'Looks like someone thinks she's the future queen of Morocco!'

There are a ton of people downstairs.

'I mean it,' I shout over the music and voices. 'I'm going to throw a party that . . . Mmm. I'm not sure how to say that. Anyway, I'm going to throw an awesome party.'

'Then you'd better start saving up.'

'Saving up? Like I'd ever marry a deadbeat.'

The day before I head back to Las Palmas, I go to the market with my grandma. I borrow one of her white djella-bas – it's cool and comfortable. Ever since doing Hajj, she's only worn white clothes. She doesn't like any other colors. My cousins like to joke that taking me to the souk is kind of like getting a package from abroad: whether or not you get charged bogus customs fees is entirely up to the person reviewing the package. I speak like I'm from here, except I'm not. Maybe it's my gestures or syntax, but the people I talk to always figure it out, and whoever I'm with winds up having to pay a premium on everything they buy. But no one would dare do that to my grandmother. She's a Hajja. I wheel her market cart along the dirty, puddled floor while she buys fish, potatoes, and red bell peppers, spicy home-made olives, preserved lemons, cracked pepper, and butter. In the process, we interact with five million people, all of whom know my grandmother and can't wait to chat with her. I think about whether or not she'd enjoy doing her shopping at clean, spotless, alien Supersaurio. About how she would loathe the self-checkout machine and the muzak. There are plenty of supermarkets near her house – a Bim, a La Belle Vie, a Carrefour Express – and she hates going to them because nothing they sell seems good enough or fresh enough or worthy of being served at her table.

When we get home, we have tea and some pastries my aunt Kaltoum brought when she last visited. The tea is too hot. *Gümüş*, this Turkish soap my grandma's been hooked on for the past few months, is playing on TV. I try to catch up on the plot: Gümüş is a girl from a humble background who works as a fashion designer. Her millionaire uncle asks her to marry his grandson, Mehmet, so she can whip him into shape. Seeing as she's been in love with him her whole life, she accepts. Mehmet may be handsome and a millionaire, but he is also epically depressed because his girlfriend died in a car accident. But Gümüş doesn't care because true love conquers all. Eventually, they get married, and for several episodes she's sad because Mehmet, who is still mourning his dead girlfriend, refuses to touch her. I guess love only conquers all when it's mutual.

'Tell me,' my grandmother says after a while.

'Tell you what?'

'Whatever's going on with you.'

I take a sip of tea and burn my tongue, though I pretend it's nothing. The secret to good tea is rinsing it three times. My dad tells me this whenever he makes a pot, and I act like he's never shown me how to do this before, paying careful attention each and every time. You set the water to boil and wait. Then you rinse the tea leaves three times, this is important, swirl the teapot in circular motions – but careful not to burn yourself – then you set it back on the fire a few minutes. Finally, stuff some mint leaves in the cup and serve

287

the tea. Easy-peasy. Except it never tastes the same when I make it.

'It's silly,' I finally say. 'I hate that I need other people, though I guess it's kind of impossible not to, right? You need others and they need you. It's like that until the day you die. You fall in love, sometimes you're loved back, other times you're not, and you have to learn to . . . to . . . keep it from killing you. Except it does kill you a little! And then you have to go around like that, a little dead inside. I don't know. Though that doesn't make sense, does it? Because I'm here, I'm living. Except it's like someone else is living my life for me, and I'm just watching it all from the outside.'

My poor grandma looks at me, then leaves her tea on the table and switches off the TV. She seems smaller, with her white hair and wrinkled, almost-bony hands.

'Would you rather feel nothing?'

I shrug.

'Yeah, sometimes.'

'Honey,' she lays one hand over mine and gives it a gentle squeeze, 'you're still very young. When will you feel things, if not now? When you're an old woman like me, and you watch your grandchildren run around but can't run with them because you're on your last legs?'

'Come on, Mé, you're not on your last legs. Check out that grip. Any harder and they'd have to amputate my hand.'

She laughs.

'Listen to me. You have everything going for you. Time passes like this,' she snaps the fingers of her free hand, 'and next thing you know, you're asking yourself: "I was crying over *that guy*?" You won't even remember what you saw in him. It'll feel like it happened to you in another life.'

'Jeda, I didn't say anything about a guy.'

'You think your jeda doesn't see things, but I was young too, you know?'

'You're saying you weren't just born like this?'

She switches the TV back on, a smile lingering on her face.

'When you get cheeky like that, you remind me of your mother.'

69

September 2018

My first day back in the office after the summer holiday, I am still at my desk after eight p.m. My spirits are in the gutter and I feel like I've been socked repeatedly in the face by the time I get to my apartment building and find two twerps sucking face like animals against the door. I clear my throat one, two, three times, then have to clear my throat a fourth time to get them to realize that standing beside them is a human being who's been trapped in a small enclosure for upwards of ten hours, and that she is jumpy and absolutely not in her right mind. I don't yell at them or scream or make a scene, though maybe I throw them a death glare in the time it takes them to apologize, step aside, and let me pass, and maybe I, who am not well in this moment, clench my fists at the knowledge that both of them were expressly put on this earth to annoy the hell out of me.

'You think you're in love now. Give it a couple weeks and you'll have blocked each other on WhatsApp and Instagram,' I want to scream. I don't, as usual, and since I'm not really sure what to do with myself, I drop my stuff at home and head to the grocery store. There's something so comforting and familiar about supermarket aisles, about the different departments, the deal of the day (today, a kilo of nectarines is €0.98), their bland new products (green pea hummus! polvito uruguayo ice cream!), even the muzak. It always helps me clear my head. The routineness of walking in, grabbing a shopping cart, and stacking it with various items fills me with a false sense of control. I know what I have to do and how to do it. Plus, reading labels is basically therapy. By the time I walk out, I'm a new person – the distraction has helped me relax. I leave with a 1.5-liter bottle of store-brand milk and a packet of rolled oats. I hate rolled oats. Every time I make myself porridge for breakfast I feel like Oliver Twist. The only difference is that Oliver Twist had good reason to eat gruel – he was poor – and I don't. I don't think about how I have to be in bed in less than two hours so I can go back to work tomorrow, just another day. The price of taking two weeks' vacation to 'unwind' is the closest to a panic attack I've ever had in my life – eyes swimming in the screen, brain turned to mush after scrolling down an endless list of FYIs.

For the longest time, I wanted desperately to be one of those people who have everything figured out in life – especially in the supermarket. They come, they see, they conquer. They know exactly what kind of canned tomatoes to choose, the best mop for their floor, the exact percentage of minerals in the bottled water they consume, and whether it sits well with them or not. The deal of the day, of the week, of the month. I basically know fuck-all. I need to ask my parents about everything, from choosing the right melon or watermelon to the best brand of bleach. I wish I were the kind of person who buys everything she needs on her weekly trip to the supermarket, who can plan a menu and stick to it. The kind who organizes her life so that she gets in her eight hours – into bed at ten, out at six – who goes to the gym four times a week and doesn't buy anything that contains palm oil. I put a chocolate palmier in the shopping cart only to turn around and put it back on the shelf a few seconds later, replacing it with a box of sugar donuts, my favorite. Maybe my issue is that I'm an unhealthy eater, that I'm not totally sure how to sort my recycling, that my plants are always dying and I never meet my self-imposed reading goal of at least fifty books a year. I *always* buy way more than I need, and I let the little things drag me down until I end up at the supermarket just so I can come up, briefly, for air. I give in to the routineness of the process. The workday doesn't kill me it just makes me stronger, and tonight I will eat a bowl of spaghetti the size of my head. Because I deserve it. I am a strong, independent woman who is also totally unhinged.

70

October 2018

I buy one of those pink bracelets that counts steps from a
store in the Las Arenas shopping mall so I can keep track
of my runs and walks and follow my evolution. I throw
myself into the task: I create an Excel spreadsheet where I
record my times and progress. This quickly becomes one
of the few things that not only doesn't bore me but actually fills me with three milligrams of hope. The bracelet
pinches my wrist at first, but that doesn't stop me from
wearing it: I start competing against myself and try to do
more and more steps every day. I break 10,000 and move on
to 12,000, then reach 15,000. I start walking everywhere:
from San Telmo to Las Arenas, from Luis Doreste Silva
to La Laja beach. I'm pleasantly surprised to find that, by
night-time, I'm so tired I can't even think, I pass out with
the TV on. As soon as I see the effects of my new hobby,
I get hooked. I take 20,000 steps a day, walk up twenty
stories. I force myself to start cooking – easy things at first
– sign up for yoga on Saturday mornings, and enroll in a
gym, where I train on Mondays, Wednesdays, and Friday
evenings. I fill my days with activities that spill into each

other so that I won't have to sit still and think. In the beginning, not a single muscle is spared: everything hurts and I can barely walk. But I push through it. There's a morning when That Person isn't the first thing I think about when I open my eyes. I don't realize it in that moment – I'm in too much pain for it to register.

It's so hot in Las Palmas that I don't go out for walks in the afternoon anymore and instead swim at the beach. Swimming is the best full-body workout, Matiqui tells me one day over coffee. I don't laugh in his face, but I'm amused. I bob in and out of the waves. I let myself be pulled this way and that. I float on my back with my face angled to the sun and think of all the shades and variations of blue I have yet to see, that I don't even know about. I calmly wade through amateur surfers and teenagers on vacation. I try to locate the blue of his eyes, but I can't – they don't haunt me anymore. It's like it all happened in another life, to a different Meryem. I try to hold on to all the good things in my life, no matter how small. I learn discipline. My memories of That Person begin to fade, little by little. I swim less than an hour and burn 539 calories. So says the bracelet.

71

November 2018

Carmen and Mercedes go on vacation and leave Dana in my care for ten days. The dog and I look one another in the eyes as they wave us goodbye and walk out the door. Dana is a superlative dog: she barely ever barks, never hounds you, doesn't pee indoors. She has an air of melancholy about her, a sort of down-in-the-dumps aura that follows her around. She's been like this since I've known her. I feel the same about Dana as some parents do about their children: I'm convinced she's exceptionally gifted, a doggo with the highest of aptitudes. I say: 'Dana, sit,' and she sits. I say: 'Let's go, Dana,' and she gets up and follows me to the door. I say: 'Dana, foooooood,' and she comes to the kitchen. As she chows on her kibble, I arrive at the conclusion that dogs are a thousand times smarter than humans: she understands my orders while I would never understand hers, not in a million years.

I text Carmen and Mercedes daily updates about their dog. The photo album on my phone is cluttered with pictures and videos of Dana: our walk on Calle Tomás Morales where a little girl told her she was the cutest puppy ever, and another walk on Calle Luis Doreste Silva where a woman fed her half a sandwich without my consent while I ogled a window display. Going home after work is now my favorite time of day, not just because I get to leave behind the tedium of the office but because every time I walk through my front door, Dana greets me like I've been gone a million years. And I feel exactly the same: hours and hours and hours locked up at work running around making a million photocopies single-handedly decimating the Amazon taking notes in unpleasant meetings where a company employee is interrogated about whether he touched his work colleague without her consent or whether he hired a specific person as a favor for a coworker and not for their own merits, whether, whether, whether.

On day five, someone pounds on my apartment door. Dana, who is curled up in a corner of the sofa, instantly jumps down. It takes me a second to get to the entrance because I'm walking on my tiptoes, trying to make as little noise as possible. My landlord's nose is glued to the peephole. I hate him.

'Yes?'

'Mirian! Open the door.'

'Why?'

'Do you have a dog in there?!' he shouts. I stand frozen in place. Dana and I look at one another. The landlord's yelling is making her nervous.

'Why?' I ask again.

'BECAUSE DOGS AREN'T ALLOWED IN THE APARTMENT!'

'Where does it say that?'

I take two steps back. The dog stands still, her tail tense. I whisper, very quietly: 'Dana, come here,' but she doesn't move.

'OPEN THE DOOR RIGHT THIS MINUTE.' My land-lord furiously pounds the door. It's all so surreal, I bring my hand up to my mouth – I'm at a loss.

Dana barks a single time, then bares her teeth at the door.

'Don Francisco. If you don't leave *right this minute* I'm calling the police.'

Silence, then:

'THIS IS MY HOUSE. MY HOUSE! OPEN THE DOOR OR I'LL KICK IT DOWN!'

Dana goes ballistic. She throws herself at the door and starts scratching at it without mercy, like she wants me to open it so that she can chomp the man's head off in one bite. She is a feminist dog. If this had happened to me two months ago, I would've crumpled to the ground and sat in a corner somewhere shaking with fear, begging my parents to come rescue me. But I'm not the same person I was two months ago, someone who took one false step and wound up with her face smashed on the floor, teeth scattered every-where, no idea how she got there. No, I am the woman who dragged herself out of hell covered in soot and the chunks of all the djinns I shot point-blank on my way out. I fear nothing and no one, only God and tax returns.

I get as close to the door as I can.

'I swear to God that if you don't leave right this minute, I will call the police and report you not only for what you're doing now but for everything you've done over the past few months. I will report you for mail theft and suspicious activ-ity, like spying on me, I will get your ass thrown in jail so hard that you won't know if you're shitting your pants or dying. You choose!'

He chooses to breathe really hard on the other side of the door for another five minutes. I wonder how my parents would react if I told them about this and how

I really don't want them to worry or stress over me. I'd rather not call the cops. I grab my dog and the laptop and go to my bedroom. I've been religiously paying my €615 a month plus utilities for an apartment where the fridge doesn't get cold enough and the water heater half works and I barely get any light and the landlord's got me trapped like one of the victims in *Saw* all because I don't have the energy to look for a new apartment. Moving means forking out one month's rent, a security deposit, and a broker's fee – all in one go. It means handing over a copy of my last three pay checks, a bank statement, and a vial of my own blood – just in case the landlord needs to make sure his future tenant has regular blood, the blood of someone who wants to live in peace and quiet without some psycho pounding on her door or stealing her mail.

On day seven, Dana and I go on a walk along Avenida Marítima. I bring her to the office with me, and Matiqui is 'delighted.' She's the 'calmest dog he's ever seen in his life.' 'Relax, she doesn't bite,' I tell Otero when he eyes her from afar. 'I don't like dogs, they drool too much,' he answers. *You're one to talk*, I think, because who doesn't like dogs? Killjoys and psychos, that's who. That day on Avenida Marítima, Dana and I walk twenty kilometers, ten one way, ten back. We take a lot breaks, more for me than for her. I don't notice this at the time, but in the days when I'm dogsitting Dana, I don't think of That Person even once. Not when I decide to move apartments (without telling my landlord, without paying him for the last month, fuck him, let him take me to court), not when I make a list of places to see, and not when I curl my fingers around a set of keys to a two-bedroom unfurnished apartment with living room, kitchen, bathroom, balcony, big windows, natural light, and an oven. I move to Calle Benito Pérez Galdós where I pay

€700 a month plus utilities. I make over €30,000 a year now. I have savings. I can afford it. My landlady is a girl my age who's never on the island. 'Do whatever you want with the place. Just don't set it on fire.' I hate her, but not as much as I would've before.

One morning I wake up in my new apartment on my new street on a new mattress under a new window, and for the first time in eons, it's because the sun is touching my face. I reach for the ceiling and open my hand, like I want to catch the light. I philosophize that maybe happiness is not something we are but something we have. We can't always *be* happy. But we can have happiness sometimes. I fall back asleep.

72

November 2018

I look at my reflection in the tinted window of a car parked on the street and carefully wipe my lips with a napkin. It's my lunch break, I've got all the time in the world: I open my handbag, take out a matte lip color I've got kicking around called Dragon Girl, and paint my lips again, first the bottom, then the top. Man, I look good today. Before I get to finish, I hear a low whining sound as the car window slowly begins to descend. A woman I hadn't noticed earlier looks me up and down. 'Are you almost done?' she asks. 'You look great, mi niña. Go on, keep moving.' Standing there frozen, I whisper: 'Thanks.'

73

December 2018

On one of our insane walks, Carmen and I go past the building where That Person used to live. Right on the beach, I remember it perfectly. I went there so many times. I still have all the pics he sent me from his balcony saved in a hidden folder on my phone. Second floor, left. I can't bring myself to delete them because every now and then I'm seized by the thought that I'd made it all up, that none of it was real. But I'm not crazy. It all happened just as I remembered.

'What's-his-face used to live here,' I whisper.

'Where?'

I raise my arm just enough to point out his balcony. The fact that I don't want to burst into tears when he comes to mind makes me think I must be healing. All I feel is anger, grouchiness, an intense unease in my chest, blood pooling in my right temple and beating slow slow slow and then fastfastfast. She nods, eyes glued to where I'm pointing. I think about the day he told me he was leaving and about me standing down here with my hood up and my heart in my mouth. I wish he'd been honest with me then. It would've hurt anyway, but at least I wouldn't be stuck thinking it was all a sham. Not only had he undermined my self-esteem, he'd also robbed me of the only thing I'd taken for granted all my life: my instinct.

'Be right back. Wait here.'

I shove my hands in my windbreaker pockets.

'Okay.'

Carmen crosses the street and goes into the cheap supermarket next to his building. A few minutes later, she walks out with a carton of eggs. She approaches me with a faint smile.

'We're going to egg his stupid balcony.'

I laugh.

'What are you talking about?'

'That dude is like . . . Satan,' she says. 'We've got to exorcize him. You need closure, okay?'

I nod.

'Won't someone see us?'

'Don't worry, I'll keep a lookout.' She passes me the egg carton. 'Go.'

'Oof.'

My hands are tingling. It takes me a while to figure out where to stand so I have the highest probability of hitting the balcony. My first two shots are a failure: the first egg lands on the hood of the car, and the second doesn't make it much farther. The third egg hits the balcony railing.

'Yeaaaaaah!' I hear behind me.

The fourth egg hits the mark, smashing into the glass balcony door. The fifth egg smashes on the railing again. The sixth crosses the distance between both and hits the lamp beside the door. I decided to shuffle to the right and jump on my seventh try. The egg smashes on the door again. It's starting to look like a Jackson Pollock painting. Just as I'm about to throw the eighth egg (of a dozen), the balcony glows with light. I stay right where I am.

'Fuck.'

The balcony door opens.

'Run!'

'Fuckfuckfuckfuck.'

'Ruuuuuuuuun!'

I start running in the opposite direction of my house. I can't keep running with the egg carton, so I drop it on the ground. Carmen is right behind me. We sprint down most of Paseo de las Canteras. I don't turn around until we pass Old Peña's ice cream shop.

'Oh my God.'

If I wasn't dying, I'd laugh.

'We're idiots.'

'*You're* an idiot,' I correct.

'Have you seen your face? You're yellow.'

We lean back on the guardrail. I'm finding it hard to breathe.

'For a second there, I thought . . .'

'I know.'

'But it can't be.'

'No, it can't.'

I nod, grateful to her for not treating me like I'm crazy but like I'm doing something totally normal, like I have legitimate reasons to feel the way I do. The sun starts setting on the other end of the beach. We backtrack a little and treat ourselves to two ice creams – one polvito uruguayo, the other chocolate. We sit on a bench and eat them. For a long while, the only sound is the waves lapping at the sand below our feet. The sky is tinged in pink, orange, purple, and navy blue. The evening darkens over our heads, and it starts getting cold, but we don't move.

'Are you okay?'

'Yeah.' I take a deep breath. 'Yeah, I'm okay.'

For the first time in months, I feel something like hope.

74

December 2018

This time, I pretend to have a cold and skip the Christmas party.

75

January 2019

It's lunchtime, and I am slowly swiveling in my chair. Matiqui's office is empty. I touch my face with both hands and tuck my neck way down into my shoulders, wishing I could melt into a puddle and watch myself slowly dribble off my seat, until there's nothing left. I completed every assignment. I have nothing to do. I'm so bored, I flirt with the idea of photocopying my tits, just for kicks, just to see if I feel anything. I do another swivel in my chair, very slowly, I don't want to get dizzy, though maybe if I get dizzy, maybe if I spin so fast I make myself sick, I won't feel like this anymore, empty. I stare down at my hands a long time, sigh, and say:

'Enough. Stop. Astaghfirullah.'

I decide to do something I've been putting off for months. If my only friend at this company is gone and I've chosen to stick around only for the money that hits my bank account at the end of each month in return for the many hours I spend with my ass planted on this chair, then I will use whatever shred of power I possess to make sure the person who comes after me will not have as miserable a time

305

as I did. I pull the stack of intern CVs out of the drawer and set it in front of me. I rule out three guys and one girl because they're godos. Sorrynotsorry. Every Euro you spend at Supersaurio goes back to the Canary Islands. I'm not the one making the rules. From the rest of the pile, I pick out a girl called Guacimara Perdomo. Twenty-five years old, two prior six-month internships, zero work experience. Alonso doesn't raise any issues when I tell him my pick a few days later. He says: 'Consider it done.' We never talk about it again. For the next few days, I have this feeling I can't quite identify. I get that this is how things are done everywhere, at every level: one person points, the other provides. I hate it, and things shouldn't work this way, but at least this once, I'm the one doing the pointing. I could get used to this. And that's the worst part.

76

January 2019

A woman called Begoña asks me: 'What are your goals? What do you want to achieve?' I stare down at my hands for a minute, then say: 'I want to be able to lift a person up by the neck.' She laughs. 'Okay, anything less problematic?' I shrug. 'To do one pull-up without assistance.' I've got work goals and gym goals. To do a small box jump. Then a medium one. Then the biggest box jump. This last one is so hard, I cry from the frustration. Months later, I do my first pull-up at the bar right in front of the biggest mirror in the gym. As I watch my arm muscles flex, I am so obsessed and feel so powerful that I get distracted and nearly let go of the bar and plummet face-first onto the floor.

77

January 2019

I quickly cover my head with a shawl because I've left praying so late that I've nearly missed the window. My sister looks me up and down and she starts singing the first verses of 'There's a Party Here in Agrabah.' I try to ignore her. I throw on a kaftan I used to wear to baptisms and engagement parties but has gotten so ratty that I only wear it to pray now. 'Let's get you dressed 'cause you're the star.' I give in to the laughter. 'I hate you,' I say.

78

February 2019

I walk out of Supersaurio with two dying monsteras I got half-price. I drag them to the elevator (they're very big) and take them up to the eighth floor. Then I drag them back to the elevator and down again. I lift them into a shopping cart at the entrance and take a cab home. Past Meryem would've put the cart back, but Present Meryem leaves it right there at the taxi rank. I haul one of the monsteras upstairs first, then go back down for the other one. They cost ten Euros, and I didn't even have to pay because I swiped my Supersaurio loyalty card and saw I had a twelve-Euro credit on it. I refuse to leave either of them behind. I put one near the entrance to my new place and the other in the living room, then spend the next few weeks reading everything I can find online about monstera care. Bringing them back to life becomes a matter of priority. It's like my sanity depends on it. Like it could absolve me of all my sins. The taxi ride cost me more than those damned plants, but who cares. They make me happy. I tell Carmen and Mercedes. Mercedes laughs: 'Quite the savior complex.' She's a psychiatrist, but I take it on the chin.

79

February 2019

One morning I wake up without an alarm clock and or feeling like I've been beaten up in the night, then finish praying Fajr. Sometimes people ask me: 'But how can you believe in God? How can you believe in something you can't see?' That morning I eat breakfast on my balcony floor – because I still haven't gotten around to buying chairs – wrapped in a quilted blanket I got off Zara Home for seven hundred million petrodollars while sipping an Ethiopian brew with notes of orange blossom, honey, and saturn peach. I watch the sun slowly rise. My question to them is how could you watch the sun come up every day and *not* believe in God?

80

February 2019

The first few days, Guacimara becomes my shadow. She doesn't talk much, only observes me. When I get to work in the mornings, she's waiting, and she never leaves without saying goodbye. She reminds me of myself back when I was a douchebag. The vein on my temple is starting to show more than usual. It throbs at low-intermediate and then intermediate-low intensity. One day, Guacimara the intern points at my monitor and asks, 'You like Izal?' because my music player is open on my computer, and she smiles and has a friendly voice, and I decide right then and there that I do not like Guacimara the intern, and I never will, no matter what she says or does.

There are four parts to your life story, I'd like to tell her. You're born, you grow up, you work, work, work, work, then you die. The end.

'No,' I eventually say.

I turn off my computer monitor.

'Now chop chop. Follow me. I haven't got all day.'

She follows me, of course she does. What other choice is there?

Acknowledgments

On April 29, 2019, Jorge de Cascante asked me: 'Meryem, have you ever considered writing a book?' We'd never met. We just followed each other on Twitter. I read his DM over and over, left it on read, hid in the office bathroom, then sent my best friend a ten-minute voice note. I needed to tell her what had happened and for her to tell me I wasn't hallucinating, this wasn't a joke. There are times these days when I still doubt it, but everything seems to point to the fact that it wasn't a joke, it was real. *Supersaurio* exists, it's finished, I am holding a physical copy in my hands. I want to thank both of them. Violeta, for listening to that ten-minute voice note (and, let's be fair, all the others I've sent) and for having my back all fifteen years of our friendship. Life is less scary when you know that no matter how far you fall, there will be people at the bottom to cushion the blow. Jorge: A hundred million thank yous. Writing is hard, and it can be a really lonely process. You've always been there to guide me and give me advice and encouragement when I've needed it.

I want to thank my parents for always bringing boxes of fruit and veggies all the way from Puerto Rico, despite the fact that there are seven greengrocers on my block, and for educating me, even though there are still days when I wish

I didn't know how to read. Thanks to my siblings: I hope growing up with me as a sister wasn't torture. Thanks to Ángela, to the women in Señoras Ávidas de Emoción, to the members of Estercolero Multicultural, to Judith, and to Mercedes for being my friend and giving me the Spanish title of this book. Thanks to Jotagé and Antuán, there is such a thing as a good public servant. And thanks to Dana for being the best dog.

Thanks to Blackie for trusting me and taking a chance on someone who grew up like a wild thing in the darkest corner of the internet. Thanks also to anyone who's ever made fun of fanfiction. I've got a book. I don't know about you.

Lastly, to quote one of my favorite coaches, Snoop Dogg: 'I wanna thank ME for believing in ME, I wanna thank ME for doing all this hard work.'